Maria Gibbs
My World, My Word

Is this Love?

By

Maria Gibbs

Table of Contents

Copyright

I would like to thank everyone who has inspired or supported me in my writing throughout the years. I would also like to thank you the reader for purchasing a copy. I hope you enjoy reading it.

Dedication & Disclaimer

This book is dedicated to my fantastic family whose love and support of me throughout the years has been unwavering.

This book is set in England in the early noughties. There might be parts in this book that are not politically correct and may cause offence as my editor pointed out to me, although I hope not, as none is meant. The thoughts and words are not those of the author but of the characters and is in keeping with who they are and to a certain extent the time and place it is set in.
This book also contains some swear words which were used in keeping with the characters.

Also by Maria Gibbs

A Boy from the Streets

As Dreams are Made on (Novelette)

A Lifetime or a Season (Novelette)

The Storm Creature (Novelette)

Coming Soon:

Illicit Love (Book two in The English Love Series)

Sins of the Fathers

Part I–2003

Chapter 1

Gemma

"Two Bellinis." The barman's words broke through my thoughts. I averted my gaze from the green eyes holding me captive while fumbling in my handbag for money. When I glanced up, he had gone, and I was left with an inexplicable sense of despondency.

"Come on." Chris tugged at my arm. "Let's dance."

I allowed her to drag me onto the dance floor where the disco music pumped out at an ear-splitting

1

intensity. The floor vibrated as music pulsated through the room. The rhythm beat a tattoo inside my chest, as though my heart was pounding in time with it.

I scanned the room and saw him standing on the balcony looking at me with a warm smile that curled up his lips. My eyes travelled over his face, taking in his strong jaw line, full lips, fair hair and toned body. I returned a shy smile, cheeks burning under his gaze and heart fluttering in my throat. I glanced away to regain my composure as he sauntered over.

"Hey. I'm Theo. Do you mind if I come and talk to you?" His well-modulated voice lifted above the clamour.

He looked like he was expecting something. *Oh, I haven't told him my name.*

"I'm Gemma." I tried to sound casual.

"Nice to meet you, Gemma. I haven't seen you around here before." He extended his hand, holding it while maintaining eye contact.

A shiver ran through me at his touch. *I have to sort myself out. He's just a man. I meet guys all the time.* I took a deep breath and, smiling my most enigmatic smile, answered, "No, I'm from London. In Devon for the weekend. I came to visit my friend. We haven't seen each other in ages." *Like he needs your life story.* "And you? Are you a local?"

"Yeah, home's about a five-minute walk." He glanced down at my feet and added with a cheeky grin, "Ten with heels."

I kept my features deadpan as I pretended to misunderstand. "Whatever makes you think I'd lend you my shoes?"

"Touché." He grinned.

I introduced him to Chris.

"So where are you taking her after here?" Theo asked Chris.

Chris and Theo spent the next few minutes comparing the merits of the local nightspots. *What if he likes Chris? I might have been the icebreaker. How can I hope to compete with Chris?* I looked at my beautiful friend with her glorious curtain of red hair.

"Can I get you both a drink?" The smouldering

expression in Theo's eyes reassured me.

When he'd gone to the bar, I grabbed Chris' arm. "Oh God, Chris, I think I'm in love. He's gorgeous."

"I just hope his friends are as buff," she replied.

"My mates are sitting over there. Do you fancy joining us?" he asked handing us our drinks.

He led us to a table where a dark-haired hunk with a bad-boy expression sat with two others. Tom had lank brown hair and a face engulfed in acne. Stephen was fair-haired but washed out. The hunk's name was Jake, and from the outset, I knew he was trouble.

Chris took charge of Jake, Tom, and Stephen; enchanted, they hung off her every word.

"She handles them well." Theo sounded impressed.

"No one stands a chance when she turns on the charm."

"I'm sure you do okay yourself."

The corded muscles of Theo's hand tightened as he held mine. I smiled, nervous again. The others walked on ahead of us.

"Club's just around the corner," Theo said, a mischievous grin playing about his lips.

Tugging my hand, he pulled me to him and grasped me around the waist. A rush of heat swept over me. I blushed at the direction my thoughts were travelling.

Theo leaned in with a show of hesitation, tantalising me. I moved closer. His lips were soft as they brushed over mine. I longed to deepen the kiss, but he pulled back. *What the…?* I quashed the fleeting sense of disappointment. *We'll continue this later.*

Theo slung his arm over my shoulder with a casual air while I slipped mine around his waist. We walked along in companionable silence, grinning at each other with stupid expressions. We joined the others in the queue that snaked halfway around the club. It took half an hour to get into the venue. The night air was balmy, and my hair stuck to my neck.

"My feet are burning," the girl in front of us

complained. *I know how she feels.*

The club was overcrowded but we managed to squeeze into the red chenille booth. Theo and I squashed in together, thigh brushing thigh.

We stumbled over who spoke first.

"I was just going to ask about your taste in music."

"I enjoy an eclectic range of music, but jazz is my thing. And you?"

"Pfft. Jazz? I can't listen to it for too long or I'd get bored." I flashed him a cheeky grin. "I lurve Robbie Williams."

Theo rolled his eyes.

"Hey, there's nothing wrong with Robbie."

"Depends on whose perspective you're coming from," he teased, "serious music lovers or females who go weak at the knees over a pair of trousers."

I gave his arm a playful slap and fixed him with an I'm-not-impressed glare. His lips twitched, and we ended up breaking into easy laughter. We discussed our respective families. Theo talked about his sister Cass, whom he was close to. I experienced a fleeting sadness as I contemplated the detached relationship I had with my siblings. We did the whole 'What's your favourite thing' and discovered that we both loved *E.T.* I coaxed him onto the dance floor just as "Crazy in Love," by Beyoncé and Jay-Z, exploded around the room. At first we moved together with the uncertainness of two strangers but soon we merged into a sensual rhythm.

"Let's get a drink." Theo's hand moved to the small of my back as he guided me back to our table.

The smell of smoke and sweat assaulted my senses as we threaded our way through the throng of writhing bodies. We fell onto the couch, where Chris and Jake sat talking. When we straightened up, our lips brushed. I moved in closer until our mouths clung together, soft and caressing. The kiss deepened, lips and tongues came together, exploring and tasting. His hand splayed against mine, fingers entwined, palms cleaving together.

The night was over too soon. We stood outside in the warm night air. People drifted out in varying stages of inebriation. In the doorway of a shop, a man fell to his knees and spewed out a stream of liquid and undigested food. Eager taxi drivers stood around touting for business. The occasional police car crawled along keeping a watchful eye on the revellers, alert for the slightest sign of an altercation.

A catfight broke out between two girls who'd had too much to drink. Two policemen separated them as clumps of peroxide hair came away in the taller girl's hands. Skirts the size of belts hung askew and beer-stained tops rode high up their flabby midriffs. Hair coiffed to within an inch of perfection at the beginning of the night was now lank, while makeup ran down their faces, and they screamed abuse at each other.

"Come back with me?" Theo whispered.

Every inch of my body screamed to go. *I've come here to spend the weekend with Chris. I can't just leave her. She'll understand. No, I can't.* I tried to explain to Theo, and saw his fleeting look of disappointment. We gazed at each other until he pulled me closer. I nestled against his chest.

"Can I see you again?" he murmured against my

ear.

Phew. We exchanged mobile numbers and then kissed again before Tom and Stephen dragged a reluctant Theo away.

"Was Theo a good kisser? I want all the details," Chris asked as we lay in bed ready to dissect the night.

"Mmm." I grinned.

"Are you going to meet him again this weekend?"

"No, he's busy." I fought back the overwhelming urge to sleep.

"I got the impression that Theo's the only one who's comfortable with himself... like he wasn't putting on an act."

"Stephen struck me as being gay and not ready to admit it, not that I spoke to him much."

"You were too busy playing tonsil hockey with Theo," she teased, "but your gaydar is spot-on; Stephen is sooo in the closet. Jake played hard at acting 'the lad', but I sensed a deeper side of him. Tom appeared to have no real opinions, a carbon copy of

Jake without conviction."

"And without his dark and mysterious good looks," I added.

"He is gorgeous."

I caught a faint trace of wistfulness, but my mind was clouding as sleep descended on me. I snuggled into the duvet mumbling goodnight. My head spun as I drifted into blissful oblivion.

Theo

The drumbeats rolled signalling the end of another episode of *Eastenders*. The doorbell shrilled just as I brought the can of Fosters to my lips. *Who's that?* With reluctance, I peeled myself from the sofa. *Jehovah's Witnesses?* I hesitated.

The bell rang again. It would be easier just to send them away with a polite but firm refusal. A third chime sounded as I entered the hallway. *Pushy bastards.* I flung the door open ready to hurl abuse only to find my girlfriend, Claudine, standing there. She had the air of a forlorn and frightened animal as tears rolled down her cheeks.

"What's wrong?" It wasn't often that Claudine displayed any kind of emotion.

"Oh, Theo," she sobbed and flung herself into my arms.

"Honey, what's happened?" I sought to console her while I held her close stroking her short brown bob. *I wish she'd left it long.* This thought was followed by guilt.

"Come in." I closed the door behind her and led her into the front room.

"What is it?" I asked. "Has someone done something to you?"

She withdrew and paced over to the window, staring out before turning to face me. She gnawed at her nails, which were her pride and joy.

"I don't want to see you anymore," she blurted out.

She's finishing with me. I didn't see that coming. We didn't have an exciting relationship, but it had been easier than being alone.

"Well, say something." Claudine stamped her foot.

"What do you want me to say?" I was being deliberately obtuse.

Her face turned puce as she looked at me through narrowed eyes. At that moment, I wondered what I'd seen in her. Once I'd had that thought, the floodgates opened. Instead of being upset, I was relieved. *I'm free.* Exhilaration bubbled up inside me.

She waffled something about not being compatible. I studied the battered red sofa. The curry stain caused by Tom's clumsiness after a night of drinking had resulted in a quarrel with my female housemates. I stared at the dull and dirty beige walls. *The landlord needs to redecorate.*

"Aren't you upset?" Her lips trembled. I had some fast thinking to do.

"Of course I am but I realise that you're right. We can always stay friends."

Friday night I celebrated my freedom in The Crypt with three of my workmates.

"It's good to have you back. Friday nights haven't been the same without you." Jake toasted with a pint.

"Yeah, never did understand what you saw in her," Stephen said.

You wouldn't.

A tall blonde sashayed towards the bar with her redheaded friend. Her hair hung to the middle of her back. She had graceful features and legs that went on forever. Her simple dress fell to just above the knee, modest at the front, but the back was scooped out and fell to the small of her back. She was exquisite. I became aroused just thinking about her.

She perused the cocktail menu, then, with confidence, caught the attention of the barman. As she scanned the bar, her face was alight with pleasure. Her gaze intercepted mine. Green and blue eyes merged with an intensity that I found disturbing. As we stared across the space that separated us, I felt a connection. I laughed a self-conscious tinkle, almost girly in sound. I was beginning to sound profound; the truth was she was stunning, and I wanted her.

The barman came back, and her friend dragged her away. I ordered our drinks and then stood chatting to the boys for a few minutes. *What are you waiting for? If you don't do something now, someone else will.* I hesitated then told the lads that I was going after the gorgeous blonde.

"Give her one from me," Jake said.

I laughed, shaking my head as I walked away. Life was never dull with Jake around.

I stood on the balcony, looking out onto the crowd. Some of the diehard jazz fans had gone since the band had left, and the DJ had taken over. The Crypt had achieved the dubious acclaim of becoming the *in place*, and the dance floor throbbed with people gyrating to the music. I spotted her. She seemed to be looking for someone, and when our eyes met, I realised it was me. *I'm in there tonight.* Her eyes slid down my body and up again while mine took the same route over hers. That was an invitation, and I didn't need asking twice. I was halfway across the room when I found my palms sweating, my mouth was dry, and I hadn't thought about what I was going to say.

"Hey. I'm Theo. Do you mind if I come and talk to you?" *God, how lame was that?* A surreptitious slide of my hands down the back of my trousers removed all traces of sweat.

"I'd like that."

Her name was Gemma; it suited her. It was then that I said *it*. I didn't think I could say anything so feeble but, in my defence, I was talking to a virtual goddess, and I hadn't seen her around before. I was pleased she was only here for the weekend. It didn't matter how beautiful she was, I wasn't looking for another relationship. She introduced me to her friend, Chris, a stunning willowy redhead. I offered to buy them both drinks and headed back to my mates, who seemed to have taken up permanent residence at the bar.

"She blew you out, then?" Stephen chortled.

"No. I'm buying drinks for the two hottest women here tonight. Is anybody up for checking O2 out tonight?" I asked.

"We're going to The Cube; it's meant to be heaving with hot chicks," Tom protested.

"Come on, lads, I think I'm in with a chance with this one. She's hot."

"Bit of a slag, is she?" Jake drawled. "What about her mate? Is she up for it, too?"

Tom and Stephen brayed like a couple of hyenas.

I frowned. "No, I don't think she is. Neither is her mate. They're both stunning and good company. But hey, it's no big deal. If you believe we can get better at The Cube, then we'll go there." I tried to sound nonchalant.

"Is she anything like Claudine?" Jake asked.

"Hell no," I laughed.

Jake and I had worked together for over five years and became friends in that time. I sensed a more vulnerable side to him, which he kept hidden. I often wondered if something had happened to make him behave in his callous manner, but I didn't probe.

A group of drunken women staggered to their feet, relinquishing their table. Jake made a crude remark to them that earned him a tongue-lashing as we took their seats. I wondered whether it was a good idea, after all, to introduce Gemma and her mate to my unruly bunch.

My mates were enthralled by the girls, and behaved themselves.

I found Gemma easy to talk to, and her sense of humour matched my own. We talked about London, and I found myself thinking that maybe when I went there on business it might be possible to meet up. There was no reason we couldn't have 'just sex' on more than one occasion.

I wondered how someone so gorgeous was single; I asked her.

"Oh, you know," she dismissed, her tone airy, "just haven't met my millionaire yet."

"So he has to be rich. Any other criteria?" I questioned, getting into the spirit of things as her eyes twinkled with latent mischief.

"I don't mind as long as he has the money to give me a lifetime of indulgence."

"Dark or fair?"

"He could be ninety-eight and getting ready to push up daisies so long as he leaves me his money," she teased.

"Cold-hearted adventuress."

"Absolutely, darling," she affected a falsetto accent before becoming serious again. "I've just never found the right person."

I placed my hand on Gemma's bare back ostensibly to guide her out as we left The Crypt. Her back was like silk against my fingertips. I felt the same euphoria you experience when you hit the jackpot on a one-armed bandit and the coins pour out.

Jake led the others in front and flashed me a conspiratorial grin. I took Gemma's hand, as delicate as a butterfly's wing. Her eyes shone as she looked at me, making me feel godlike. I contemplated lifting her caveman-style and carrying her back to my house to ravage her. Those red lips pouted in a way that cried out to be kissed so I pulled her into my arms. I kept the kiss light, just a mere meeting of lips coming sensually together. I longed to deepen the kiss, but the familiar stirring in my trousers precluded any such manoeuvre.

I held her to me as we walked along, aware of the envious glances thrown at me by both men and women alike. The streets were a hive of activity as Devon came to life and the young set partied. Laughter rang out around us.

We struggled through conversations in the club. Music from Christina Aguilera and The Black Eyed Peas bounced from wall to wall in an ear-splitting cacophony.

I allowed Gemma to drag me onto the dance floor. I'm not sure that what we did was dancing. My hands encircled her tiny waist, skimming over her back. One hand held the base of her spine while the other travelled up, caressing between her shoulder blades.

She clasped her hands around my neck while her body pressed against mine. Her breasts strained against the flimsy material of her dress, and likewise, my disloyal cock showed arousal, betraying me to the outside world.

After a few songs, I couldn't endure any more of this exquisite torture, so I led her through the crowds. Back at our booth, we tripped onto the sofa. I used this opportunity to kiss her again.

Thousands of stars lit up the warm night sky while all around us was floodlit by harsh street lighting. The club's doors were flung wide open, spewing forth a stream of people no longer allowed the relative security of its environs, thrust onto the streets.

I turned to Gemma. "Will you come back with me?"

Had she been leading me on all night? Those eyes didn't seem deceitful. My disappointment subsided. *I'll have her even if it isn't tonight. There's always my trip to London.*

We exchanged numbers. I kissed her again. Slowly

at first, building the crescendo. Our mouths and tongues merged, tasting, teasing and provocative until the silent music we were making demanded an increase in tempo that we were unable to fulfil.

"So she didn't put out," Tom's crude words reached me as we walked away.

"Shut up."

I hit the sack at six a.m., after a further drinking session with the lads. Struggling to sleep while the light filtered through the chinks in the curtains and the birds chirped, I lay thinking about Gemma's body and wasn't surprised when I found myself aroused. *I'll have to see her again*, I thought as I sought release. Contented and drowsy now, I slipped into a comfortable slumber.

Chapter 2

Gemma

Chris pulled the chintz curtains open with a dramatic flourish. The morning light streamed through the windows, flooding the little room with light. Screwing my eyes up, I groaned when the pain hit me. It felt like a herd of elephants was doing the River Dance on top of my head.

"Go away," I moaned, throwing a pillow at Chris, hitting her straight in the face.

"I'll make you coffee and get you something for the

pain." She chucked the pillow in my direction.

I gave up attempting to sleep as Chris pulled back the covers and thrust a glass of water and a couple of tablets at me. "I'll treat you to a cooked breakfast in the local greasy spoon," Chris coaxed, offering my preferred hangover cure.

After breakfast, Chris manoeuvred us to the old part of the town, where all the antique shops were. I followed her into a minuscule curio shop crammed full of junk. *At least she can't stay long in a shop this size.* I meandered around, trying to take an interest in the old vases, grandfather clocks and furniture.

"Can I help you?" The old man in a battered cardigan and brown cord trousers peered at me, pushing his spectacles lower down his nose while he glared over the top. *He knows I have no interest in anything in his shop and has written me off. How dare he?* I traced my hand over a shiny walnut table.

"A fine example of Regency craftsmanship."

I'd shocked him. I savoured every bit of my

shallow victory. He moved onto Chris and greeted her as one lover of all things old to another. My triumph was short-lived as I trudged past him a dozen times in the forty-five minutes that it took Chris to finish her browsing. Each time, he shot me a knowing look. My eyes and nose became irritated by the dust and the musty smell permeating every inch of the claustrophobic shop.

"Your mum has the same table in her hallway," Chris said, unaware of my silent sparring with the old guy. The lifting of the corners of his mouth alerted me to his conquest; I'd won the initial skirmish, but he won the war.

"Are you buying anything?"

"Not today. I may come back another day; there's a couple of things I like."

Sunday mid-day saw us sitting on the quayside, having lunch. The temperature soared into the thirties, and the sun beat down on us without mercy. I longed to be lying on a beach now, topping up my tan. Chris, however, wasn't a sun lover. She preferred the salon spray tan and was keen to be out of direct sunlight. *Probably wishes herself in some musty old shop with an equally old relic serving her.*

"I bet those apartments across the water are the last word in luxury." I caught a glimmer of excitement in Chris' eyes. "Spill."

"I wasn't going to say anything yet..."

"Uh-huh. Yeah. Out with it."

"Well... okay, okay." She held her hands up in surrender as I glowered at her. "I've got an appointment on Wednesday for a viewing."

"Oh, Chris." I jumped up and hugged her.

Her dark green eyes glowed with excitement.

"They'd be so proud of you," I choked the words out.

Chris grasped my hand across the table and squeezed it.

"Do you remember that night, a few months before my sixteenth, when they caught me trying to sneak out of the house as we were going to attempt to get into that club?"

"I remember. We didn't get in." I smiled at the memory.

"I was furious with them at the time, but they just hugged me and packed me off to bed. They weren't even angry. I heard them laughing about it later when they thought I was asleep."

"I can still taste your mum's scones."

"And Dad's homemade lemonade. They loved having all my friends around. It made up for them not having any more children."

"They doted on you."

She gave a sad smile.

"We used to love your mum's hugs, and your dad gave us such good advice." Tears welled up in my eyes, and my throat constricted.

"I miss them so much," Chris whispered letting out a ragged breath. A solitary tear fell from her red-rimmed eyes and slid down her cheek.

"I'm sorry, I shouldn't have..."

"No, it's all right, I'm glad you did. Everyone

avoids talking about them for fear of upsetting me. I can't believe that it's almost five years."

I stroked her hand in a feeble gesture of comfort, knowing how the death of her parents still haunted her.

"We were so worried when you left London and moved to Devon. You knew no one, had no-one to support you."

"I needed that. Every nook and cranny in the house held memories. I couldn't live indefinitely on antidepressants, and talking to councillors didn't even begin to make it right. I needed to start over, to be anonymous. I hated the pity I saw in people's eyes."

I squeezed her hand. "You can't go cluttering a modern apartment up with ancient relics."

Chris spluttered a hoarse laugh. "Just you try stopping me."

After lunch, we went for a walk, stopping to browse at some of the jewellery stalls.

"Come on, I'll treat you to a crêpe," I offered.

Chris linked her arm through mine as we ambled along the waterfront. The sun bounced across the surface, providing a magical appearance, while the willows dipped their boughs into the water. We sat down, dangling our legs over the side, to eat our crêpes.

Theo

My head pounded; little shards of pain slicing my brain at regular intervals. The incessant ringing took a while to break through my subconscious. I stumbled out of bed, tripping on the sheet that had curled around my foot, sprawling face down on the floor, arms akimbo, my head just missing the computer workstation. With a groan, I unfurled the sheet and crawled towards the door. My fingers gripped the landline phone just as the ringing came to an abrupt halt.

Slumping onto the battered sofa, I dialled 1471,

listening as the automated voice recited Claudine's number. *What does she want? Probably wants to see if I'm miserable without her. What did I ever see in her?* Gemma had elicited more excitement with one kiss than Claudine had in the two years we'd been together.

As I stood up, the room spun on its axis. A brass band struck up a loud symphony in my head; I hoped that the cymbal player's piece would be short. With the help of the wall, I made my way to my stockpile of hangover cures.

The Royal Chester Hotel was a pretentious five-star affair: a fourteenth century castle set amongst acres of land. Generations of dissolute aristocrats who'd understood nothing about estate management had fallen on hard times after years of profligate living. The final nail in the coffin came in the guise of World War One. The eldest son, an officer who hadn't strayed too close to the front line, was struck down and killed. Hailed as a hero. His younger brother, the last in the line, sold the estate to an American who solved his increasing debt problem. He drank and gambled the rest of his money, and within two years was laid to rest beside his brother.

Swathes of land surrounded the extensive drive. Horses grazed. A few pricked up their ears at the sound of the car disturbing their tranquil environment. As the car drew near, the fields were replaced by formal gardens enclosed by four-foot symmetrical hedges. Arched entrances led from one garden into another, with stone statues and water-feature centrepieces adorning them.

The wheels crunched across the gravel on the driveway. Before me stood the imposing edifice crafted in medieval stone that had been sympathetically restored. The Keep housed the main foyer, where the functions were held. The castle had four other towers set in a rectangle, with the Keep at the front, central to the whole structure. Parapets linked the buildings to each other. Glass domes had been added later, fusing old and new. The other side of the castle housed an enviable stable of horses, which were available to the clientele.

I paid the taxi driver and walked through the massive oak studded doors, my shoes tapping a staccato on the stone floor. Ahead was a reception desk, behind which a spiral staircase led to two bridal suites taking up the whole of the upper floor. Two reception rooms led off the foyer either side, with a large board outside bearing the names of the wedding party. A guard in the guise of a green liveried footman held a list of all guests.

Gourmet finger food graced the tables. The band was poised to play. Along the walls were huge oak tables and throne-like chairs. I spotted my parents chatting to friends. Cass was at the edge of the dance floor, wearing a pained expression while pretending to listen to our cousin Giles. He was in all probability pontificating about how well he'd done in life. My sister needed rescuing.

"Where were you? You were supposed to be here an hour ago."

"I was just telling Cassandra here how I..."

"Yes, quite, Giles," I interjected. "I would love to hear it; perhaps some other time, though. I must steal Cass away."

Giles' face reddened, echoing the colour of his hair as his jaw dropped open causing his jowls to wobble.

Cass tugged on my arm. "So, what kept you?"

"Had a heavy night. Could've stayed in bed."

"Whose bed, though?" Cass enquired waspishly, but then softened it with an affectionate smile.

"You've heard," I laughed. "I was going to save it for you till tonight as a special treat. So, the gossips got in first. So who was it?"

"I got it from the horse's mouth." Cass' strident tone held a sting. "She said the relationship was too boring for words."

I refused to rise to her bait. "Your words, but true nonetheless."

"You don't appear distraught."

"Should I be?"

Cass grinned. "Come on, let's see 'The Parents'."

We reached the table where our parents sat with

Jeremy and Kate Rose, their friends, part of the narrow, almost incestuous social set to which everyone here belonged. I kissed Mother's cool cheek and shook Father's hand while greeting the Roses with a smile and a nod. I'd just decided that this would be a tedious evening when Cass winked, an air of barely suppressed mischief shining from her eyes.

"How was the ceremony?" I asked with no real interest.

"It was lovely."

"It will definitely be in the society pages," Kate gushed.

"Sandra looked divine and carried herself well. She did your uncle Geoffrey proud, but then that is no more than one would expect from her." The inference was that Cass and I failed to live up to her expectations. "You have spoken to her, haven't you?"

"Er... well..."

"Out with it, Theodore. I can't tolerate stuttering; it plays havoc with my nerves." The last, she confided to Kate, who nodded in sympathy.

"I haven't seen her yet." Cass glared, her crimson painted lips puckered. The skin between her lips and nose reminded me of a concertina. Her eyes, the same unusual shade of green as mine, a Perkins family trait, flashed in resentment. My eyes locked with hers. As the silent understanding passed between us, she deflated, and her jawline jutted out as she sought to regain her composure.

"Theodore. Well, really, how terribly ill-mannered of you. It isn't how I brought you up," Mother hissed. Her colour heightened as she contemplated what her best friend would think of me and whom she'd tell.

"What would you know?" Cass' voice trembled, barely coherent.

"What was that, Cassandra?" Mother demanded, puffing up her bosom as she fixed her with a penetrating gaze.

"I said I'm sure he didn't know." Cass smiled, a picture of innocence.

Mother swung back to face me, missing the fleeting and rebellious smirk that crossed her friend's face.

"I take it you deposited your present in the reception safe?"

Shit! I was supposed to buy it today. Mother will have me hung, drawn and quartered for this. My chaotic thoughts were mirrored on my face, because Mother turned an interesting shade of puce. As she opened her mouth to rain abuse down on me, Cass interrupted, grinning like the cat who'd not only had the cream but who'd savoured every lick.

"We bought the present together," she lied. "That hideous crystal vase on the gift list."

Mother nodded, rising to circulate. She'd wasted enough time on us. Kate followed in her wake.

"Make sure you congratulate your cousin," she threw over her shoulder as she departed. I relaxed back into the chair, letting out a sigh of relief.

"Bitch," Cass hissed.

"You saved my life. I could see the gibbet being erected."

"Right to the noose tightening around your neck," Cass finished.

"How did you guess I'd forget?"

"I bumped into Claudine while I was picking a present. I figured you'd be out celebrating; ergo, with a rotten, stinking hangover, you'd forget the present." Her smile held a strong suggestion of self-satisfaction. "Soooo, I bought that horrific vase, forged that scrawl you call a signature on the card, et voilà."

She reached over and gave me a quick hug; it was a symbol of our solidarity, gaining strength from each other. "All this affection is giving me a headache." She affected a theatrical leading lady's voice. "I'm going to powder my nose, darling." She flounced off and left me laughing at that unlikely prospect.

I headed across the grandiose hall, searching out my cousin. Yards of white silk and lace gave her away; there was no hiding in that getup.

"Theo, glad you made it," Sandra prattled as I greeted her with a kiss on the cheek. "You've met Garfield, haven't you?"

"Yes. Congratulations to you both." With reluctance, I gave him my hand, which he shook as though he was trying to draw water from an old-fashioned water pump.

Someone else claimed their attention, and I was able to escape. Grudgingly, I made polite conversation with anyone I couldn't avoid on my route back to the table. I was scrutinised and reminded that I should attend their functions more often. My smile never wavered, neither did it reach my eyes.

"How much longer are we expected to stay?" I asked as I flopped down beside Cass.

"You've only been here an hour. Another couple at the least. Your drink's there."

"Did you see the meringue that Sandra was wearing?"

We sat back for a good bitching session, which was a pleasure Cass had introduced me to at an early age.

"You act like a King and Queen sitting holding court," one cousin complained after trying to socialise with us. "You could circulate. It's not the done thing, you know. One feels one must come to you."

"No one asked you to come," I snapped, fed up

with this farce and feeling delicate from my excesses of the night before.

Cass laughed, adding to her humiliation.

"Yes, well..." She scraped the heavy chair back. "You have always been weird. Too cliquey by half. It makes one wonder – you being brother and sister and all..." She left the rest unsaid, but her intent was all too apparent.

Cass chortled, unwilling to let her have the parting shot. "Let's go before all hell breaks loose. We'll go to yours and get slaughtered."

"So what's new?"

"There's a cute new editor at work." She grinned, belying the casual tone of her voice.

"Go on."

Her fingers played absentmindedly with the thick black curls of her hair that hung to mid-neck. I smiled; she always twisted her hair when she lied.

"There's nothing more to say yet. Tell me about Claudine." She reached into her bag and pulled out her cigarettes and lighter. She placed the cigarette between her lips, lit it and took a drag. The smoke rose upwards, to dance above our heads before forming a cloudy mass. She leant forward and refilled our drained glasses.

I told her about Gemma, but I wasn't sure why.

The grass on the pitch crunched underfoot. Taut as a bow due to the lack of rain, it snapped as we trod on it.

"Are you ready and raring to go?" Jason laughed as he saw my face.

"Only in the direction of my bed," I parried.

"The delectable Claudine keeping it warm, is she?" Toby joined the verbal affray.

"I'll tell you later over a pint."

"Come on, lads, this is pathetic," Coach screamed. "You're never going to beat The Crown's side on Tuesday. You're a bunch of useless bastards. I don't know why I get out of bed on a Sunday morning."

"He doesn't get out of bed. His wife kicks him

out," Jono guffawed

"What was that, Jono?" Coach shouted.

"Nothing, Coach."

"We haven't got a chance against The Crown even if we play our best," Toby murmured.

"You're not wrong there," Jason agreed. "We're going to be shown up as a bunch of amateurs."

The thought of the match on Tuesday and the conditions of the pitch left our usually enthusiastic team feeling low, which was reflected in our performance.

Toby stooped, to avoid hitting his head on the black Tudor beams adorning the low ceiling. The wooden floorboards resounded with the tramp of weary feet. Everyone was in need of that after-match pint.

"Did you see how the ball sailed through the air, finding the back of the net?" The blue specks in Toby's grey eyes flashed with pride after scoring the only goal of the match.

"Yeah. I hate to rain on your parade but our

goalie's shite; he's worse than the rest of us."

"I 'eard that," Peter called across the pub.

"You were meant to," I shouted back in good humour.

"I didn't see you doing any better," Toby joshed.

"I was awake until two a.m. drinking with Cass."

"How is the hedgehog?" Jason's pet name referred to her sometimes prickly nature.

"We escaped the reception of a family wedding." I pulled a face, which produced a chuckle from Toby and a perplexed look from Jason when I added, "I left her sleeping it off in my bed."

"So if Cass' got your bed, Claudine isn't in it." He raised an eyebrow, his face taking on a quizzical expression. "I worry about you sometimes. Why are you in a rush to return to your bed?"

I waited while the two of them stopped chuckling.

"You're the second person to allude to an unnatural alliance between my sis and me."

"So where is Claudine, then?"

"Claudine put me on the transfer list on Thursday."

I grinned at their shocked expressions

"Shit."

"I thought you'd end up married, with kids, like us." Toby's dazed expression made it hard for me to keep a straight face.

"We never had anything exciting."

"The excitement wears off."

"I'm not sure we ever had it." I was glad when Toby changed the subject.

As if on cue, after our second pint, Toby and Jason both stood up in unison, saying they had to get home to their families.

Jason's head tilted sideways, blond hair flopping over his face.

"Come back to mine for dinner? Cathy always cooks extra, and the kids love seeing you."

Cathy walked through the archway that led from the kitchen, wiping her hands down the blue striped apron as she came to greet me.

"Jack, Katie, Daddy's home. And he's brought

Uncle Theo with him."

The scurrying noise grew louder until it became a dull thud. Five-year-old Jack flung himself at my knees, demanding I join him for a game of footie in the garden. Three-year-old Katie hung back, bashful, smiling under her lashes.

"Have you got a hug for me?" I tickled her, bending down to her level.

She wrinkled her nose, the feathery dusting of freckles on it shifting with the movement.

"Come on." Jack tugged at my arm.

"Jack," Cathy admonished.

"Uncle Theo will play later. Let him sit awhile," Jason broke the sternness of his wife's rebuke.

"It's fine. I'll go and play now, or else he'll be bouncing off the wall until I do." I ruffled his tousled blond hair as we walked together to the garden, stopping to plant a kiss on Cathy's cheek.

"Watch my flowers." Cathy adopted a harsh tone to detract from the grin that lit up her face.

"Charmer. She holds you up as the shining example

of how to be a gentleman."

I shrugged my shoulders and held my hands up, "What can I say?"

"You and me 'gainst Dad and Katie."

"Against, Jack. Don't drop your A's."

Jason swung Katie up onto his shoulders. She squealed with delight as he ran after the ball with her bouncing on top, blond ringlets bobbing.

"Jay, be careful with her up there." Cathy stood in the doorway, smiling. "Shall I ring Claudine? She can join us for dinner, too."

Both Jason and I halted, turning to stare at her, while Jack took advantage of the situation and commandeered the ball.

"Shit."

"Jason!" Cathy admonished.

"You didn't hear that, kids," Jason ordered.

Jack stood there with a cherubic expression, a hint of devilment playing about his brown eyes as he wondered whether to repeat it. His mother's stern face made him change his mind. He kicked the ball and screamed.

"Goaaaaaal."

Cathy placed her hand on her hips.

"Okay, boys, what gives?" Her American drawl was evident when she was serious, angry or flustered, even after so many years of living here.

"Claudine dumped him," Jason said.

Cathy's face dropped. "When? How? What?"

She crossed the vast expanse of grass like a whirling dervish and grabbed me by the shirt.

"Game over. I want information; every detail."

Katie, now consigned onto the carpet of grass, tottered after us. My expression pleaded for them to rescue me. Father and son shook their heads in sync, throwing their palms skyward.

Cathy directed me to a chair, stopping to turn off the radio. She opened the fridge, drew out a can, pulled the ring and poured the beer, setting it down in front of me. She waited until I'd taken a mouthful and then said, "Now talk."

I took a deep breath. Her attention to detail was

painful, and the pain would be all mine. Something soft touched my legs. Katie's soulful eyes burned into me. Placing a hand on my knee, she pulled herself up onto my lap.

Once I'd fulfilled Cathy's need for detail, she hugged me and allowed me to re-join the lads. I experienced a yearning for the love and comfort of a family of my own. I'd never pictured Claudine in that role, but Gemma's face sprung to mind. I pushed that thought aside as fanciful. I didn't want a relationship with her but I did want to see her again so I texted her, asking her to meet me in a couple of weeks when I was in London. She replied in the affirmative. I stood grinning for a moment.

Chapter 3

Gemma

The car keys lay discarded on the glass-topped dining table as I fumbled in my bag for my mobile. My flatmates, Carla and Joanne, watched, amused, as I lost my normally calm demeanour. I encountered and pushed aside a comb, lipstick and purse before wrapping my fingers around the phone.

Hey, Gemma, I njoyed meetn u. B in Lndn in 2wks. Wud luv 2 meet. Theo x

I bit down on my lower lip in an attempt to mask

my excitement.

"Gemma's met someone," Carla cooed, her timbre gently teasing.

"I'll get a bottle of wine from the fridge," Joanne said, pulling Carla along with her.

I laughed as they walked past me in the direction of the kitchen; the cool, self-assured blonde being dragged in the wake of the ditzy strawberry blonde whose heart was as wide as her smile. I contemplated my reply while perching on the dining chair.

I decided to keep it simple. ***Gr8, look 4ward to it. C u soon. Gemma x***

"So there you have it," I concluded, downing the dregs of my glass before reaching for a refill.

"He sounds lovely," Joanne sighed.

"Mm, a real dreamboat," Carla enthused. "Why didn't you shag him? I would have."

"Never mind, you," Joanne said. "I think it's romantic. He'll respect her for that. I wish I had your self-control, Gem. You know me, after a couple of drinks I don't even realise I have the word 'no' in my vocabulary."

"I don't need a drink. Sex is a liberating experience for women. We're as entitled to have sex in the abandoned way men do and not be made to feel guilty. Guilt is men's way of placing us into roles they cast for us, it's a wasted emotion. I say..."

"Yeah, okay, Carla, we know what you have to say," Joanne interrupted, breaking up the monologue and the evening simultaneously.

Kerry and Tracy bounced into the salon just before ten a.m., talking about their weekend. I pointed at the clock, arching an eyebrow.

"Sorry, boss." Kerry laughed as she hugged me. "How was Devon? Meet anyone?" she asked as Tracy prepared for the first client.

My cheeks stained red.

"You did. Tell me all," she gushed in her inimitable way.

"I'll fill you in at lunch if you squeeze me in for a firming treatment."

"Mm, I've got no plans. You're on, boss."

"What about me?" Tracy asked.

"I'll fill you in over a pint tonight," Kerry promised.

Kerry and Tracy were a breath of fresh air in the workplace.

I headed back into my office after my lunchtime treatment. Monday was our quietest day, and it gave me a chance to catch up on the mounds of paperwork that appeared whenever my back was turned. The phone on my desk shrilled, breaking the silence and shattering the illusion that I was going to have an easy afternoon.

"Hello?" I tried to think which of the girls was manning the phones.

"Your friend Susie for you."

"Thank you, Kerry. Please put her through."

"Gemma." A distressed sob came down the line.

"Sus? What's wrong?"

"Can you come over tonight?"

"Of course. What's wrong?"

"I can't talk now. See you tonight." The phone went dead.

Susie was the happy, positive one in our group of friends. She never held a grudge, and could always be relied upon to understand everyone's problems even though she'd sailed gaily through her own life. Ted had been her childhood sweetheart, and they'd married five years ago. I smiled at the memory of her wedding; we'd all been bridesmaids, Jackie, Chris, Amanda and I. We'd worn the most unfortunate pink outfits. Actually, not everything had been plain sailing; Susie had suffered in life but she never let it show.

The sterile stench permeated through the cobalt-blue walls. The supercilious consultant peered over the rim of his thick glasses at us before perusing Susie's notes, as though he were reading them for the first time. We received a brusque grunt, no hand-shaking, no greeting. He didn't even tell us to take a seat; we did so with trepidation. Why is it that doctors and headmasters can reduce even the most confident adult to a shell of their childhood self?

Is This Love?

There's no good way of telling a couple that they wouldn't have children, but the unfeeling jumble of facts he threw at Susie was the wrong way. He didn't give her time to process the words or discuss options with her. He eyed the old-fashioned timepiece that had probably belonged to his great, great-grandfather with barely concealed impatience.

Susie held herself up straight, back ram-rod, head tilted up. The only sign of her distress was in the darkening of her eyes as she tried to digest the news. She hesitated as she reached the door. Her trembling hand gripped the handle and then she turned to thank the consultant, only to find that he'd dialled a number on his telephone and was unaware of our continued presence.

In the corridor, she stood for a moment, staring at me as she tried to feed off my strength. Turning to her husband, she wrapped her arms around him and held him close, giving and receiving comfort in that enormous gesture.

"At least we can adopt now."

My heart contracted as she attempted to find the positive. She even made it sound as though that was her preferred option. I knew, though, that deep inside she'd buried the pain and would only take it out and scrutinise it when she was alone.

Whatever it was had to be bad. I flicked my screen from the accounts to the internet connection, going straight to my personal e-mail account.

TO: jackie_dolan@yahoo.com;
amanda_Giles@hotmail.com

SUBJECT: Susie

Have you spoken to Susie? Something's wrong. She's crying and asked me to come over tonight. Do either of you know anything?

Gem

A response pinged back within minutes.

FROM: Amanda Giles

DATE: 19 May 2003, 15.25

TO: gemma@stephens95.fsnet.co.uk;
jackie_dolan@yahoo.com

SUBJECT: Susie

No idea. Up to my eyeballs but keep me posted.

I leaned back into my chair, chewing the end of my pen. I grabbed the phone on the first ring. "Hello?"

"Another one of your friends."

"Gem, what's up?" Jackie asked.

"Not sure but she sounds in a bad way."

"That's not like her." Jackie couldn't hide her worry. *"Keep me posted. Let's meet tomorrow for lunch. I'll e-mail Amanda. But if it's bad, ring me tonight, no matter how late."*

The door was flung open by a hysterical creature that resembled my friend. Strands of her intractable shoulder-length fair hair clung to her wet face. The rest sat starkly on her head like a mad professor's. Her brown eyes, reminiscent of a puppy's, were clouded by a mist of tears. Black splodges accentuated the lines the tears had created. Holding her in my arms, I stroked her matted hair. When the sobbing lessened, I led her into the living room.

Magazines, books and CDs lay discarded in a messy heap on the floor. A cup sat on the marble-inlaid coffee table, a brown stain marking its surface, the coasters sitting idle. The white fluffy cushions held the imprint of the head that had lain there, black sooty mascara smudges evidence of whom the head belonged to.

I led Susie to the sofa and sat her down, holding her hand and waiting for her to talk.

"What's wrong, Sus?"

She stayed mute.

I poured out two glasses of wine and handed one to Susie, who grasped it between shaking hands. She drained it in a single gulp and handed it back to be refilled.

"What's happened?" I settled down beside her.

"Ted!" The violence reverberated in the stillness, like a meteorite exploding in the night sky and raining debris down on the world below.

"Where is he? Do you want me to get him?"

Susie's wild mane tossed from side to side, her eyes dilated, mad with an unnamed emotion.

"Tell me," I urged.

"He's having an affair." The simple words tore

through her lips like a bullet ripping from a gun. She slumped back. I sat frozen, trying to inject the words into my consciousness. It hit me with a sickening clarity. I reached over and took her still form into my arms, trying to induce comfort where there was none.

"Bastard," I hissed, expelling the breath from my body. "Fucking bastard."

"Six months..." Little sobs punctuated the gaps between the words. "It's been going on... for... six months and I didn't know. He said... he said... his workload had increased... I believed him. How could... I have been... so... stupid?"

She drained the rest of her glass and tipped the last dregs of wine from the bottle.

"I'll get some more." I made to rise.

"No, I'll go."

I watched her shuffling dejected out of the room. Ted had idolised Susie, placed her on a pedestal. What had changed? With a jolt, I realised the significance of six months. It was around that time that Susie had been told she was infertile.

"How did you find out? Did he tell you?"

"Yesterday evening I came home early from my parents' house."

She hesitated. I saw her face as it must have been then, shocked and vulnerable, as she relived the moment when she had caught them in her bed. "They were in my bed, writhing around, sweat-soaked bodies entangled. I cried out and startled them. Ted's face drained of colour. Desperate to get to me, he threw aside the whore that sat astride him."

She told me how she'd stumbled from the room. How he'd followed her.

"I screamed at him to get out."

Her voice had risen in pitch. I yearned to reach out to reassure her, but she wasn't with me here and now. She was reliving the scene.

"He begged me to listen to him but I said 'Leave and take that dirty whore with you.'" The gutter language so alien to Susie's personality dripped like burning acid from her tongue.

"'I'll get her to go,' he said, but I shouted at him to

go, too. 'I'll be back later, when you've calmed down.'"

I hissed at the cruelness of his words. She turned in my direction then, as though just noticing I was here.

"I hit him." The energy drained from her, the shadowy presence of her husband fading like a ghostly apparition. "I hit him hard; his nose bled... a lot."

She lapsed into silence.

"He came back later. He said she meant nothing... a mistake. A mistake would be forgetting to put the black bags out on bin day or dark clothing in a light wash, not sleeping with a whore in my bed." She hurled the last words at me and then broke down crying.

The houseboat was full when I arrived. Sweat poured from my brow from the sun beating down on me as I rushed from work. Jackie and Amanda were already seated, overlooking the river, on the upper deck. My sandals flopped against the decking. They were engrossed in conversation, brown and black shocks of hair pressed together until they were almost touching as they spoke with an intimacy that few would want to disturb.

"What are you two hatching?"

Two heads looked up at once. Amanda's ebony skin was aglow, her full lips parted, giving her a pouting look that men found irresistible. The dent on her regal nose was the only thing that marred the perfection of her face.

"Hey." Her dulcet tones stroked the air.

"You're late." Jackie was never one to mince her words.

Her long curly hair was pulled back and tied by an elaborate clip with a fake white lily attached in an incongruous statement that symbolised Jackie's personality to a tee. The light dusting of freckles on her retroussé nose wrinkled up as she parted her small lips – her least favourite part of her body – in a smile.

"We ordered a bottle of wine," Amanda said as I sat down.

The water sparkled, clear and beautiful. Beer cans and bottles were strewn amongst the rushes bobbing in the mossy scum. A faint damp smell floated somewhere on the breeze. By unspoken agreement, we left the serious topics until we'd been served. I savoured the first sip of wine after the waiter had poured us a glass and placed the bottle in a holder on the table.

"Ted's having an affair."

The words acted like a slap in the face. Two pairs of eyes stared back at me, dilating, shaped brows lifting. Jackie was the first to respond.

"Shit!"

"This is too bizarre." Amanda breathed at last.

They made me re-tell sections until they were satisfied that I had imparted everything I knew.

We moved to Jackie's life. Rory had come into her life a year ago and had broken through all the barriers she'd erected. "He's taking me away to the Lake District this weekend." Her eyes shone. "To celebrate our first anniversary."

"What's new with you?" I asked Amanda.

Amanda had worked in the advertising industry as an executive planner since leaving school, and an opportunity had come up for promotion, which she unfolded to us over lunch.

"I'm up against Tara and a couple of unknowns; word out is that there are some real hotshots amongst the outsiders so competition is fierce. My interview is tomorrow; keep your fingers crossed." We automatically overlapped our first and index fingers in the age-old symbol for luck.

I managed to squeeze in the news of my weekend in Devon and briefed them on Chris' quays apartment.

Theo

It was Sunday night when Claudine caught up with me. I was feeling relaxed after a day spent with Jason and his family. I answered the phone, beating my flatmate

Katherine by the slimmest margin. If she'd picked it up, would things have worked out differently? Would I have been able to prepare myself for the coming conversation?

"Hello, Theo?" Her voice sounded unsure.

"Claudine."

What the hell does she want?

"How are you?" I managed to keep my voice neutral.

"I've missed you, Theo." She paused for a second. *"Can I come over?"*

I hesitated, which she took as an affirmative.

"I'll be around in ten minutes."

My facial expression said it all.

"Like that, is it?" Katherine asked, adopting her earth-mother tone of voice.

"Like what?" Linda looked at Katherine, to me, and back again.

"Claudine's coming around." My words were chosen with care. They'd pick over them later, when they were alone, like a scavenger over a carcass.

"I thought you and Claudine had split up." Linda's cloying concern grated on my jangled nerves. Her cow-like eyes fixed on me with an intense stare I found disconcerting.

Katherine and Linda were the original flat-share friends, having lived here half their lifetime; hippies from another time and place where free love and joints reigned supreme.

"If you want to talk…" Katherine said.

If I do, it won't be to you two old crones. "Thanks."

When Claudine arrived, I took her straight to my room to guard my privacy. That was my second mistake of the night, and as I was about to discover, mistakes, like everything else, come in threes. Claudine greeted me with a hug.

"I've missed you," she crooned into my ear in a crude attempt at seductiveness.

I pulled back. "It's only been a weekend."

"Enough time for you to hook up with someone else," Claudine bit out.

"I fail to see what business it is of yours."

"I'm sorry; I'm just jealous."

What's going on here? My head felt like it was

spinning.

"Theo, I've made the biggest mistake of my life."

I regarded this woman with whom I'd spent the last two years. A soupçon of affection remained for her. She threw herself into my arms, clinging to me with tears in her eyes, looking vulnerable as she whispered, "I love you, Theo." I still had no intention of changing my mind. Her lips pressed against a sensitive area on my neck, which never failed to elicit a response. She rubbed her warm, soft body against me, and God help me, but I'm a man, and my body responded.

My third mistake was only recognised as such when two sated, sweat-soaked bodies pulled apart to lie back. It was then that my brain kicked in, pissed off at the malfunction created when my cock had pressed the override button, which could have averted this disaster.

She clung to me like an octopus, arms thrown over my naked chest, legs wound around mine, anchoring me in place.

"Thank you for giving me another chance," she purred and gave me a dazzling smile.

Tell her! the voices screamed inside my head. *How can he? How about this? Claudine, the sex was okay but it doesn't mean we're back on. See how easy that was?*

I couldn't be that callous. No doubt Jake and Cass would despair of me. Sometimes I despaired of myself. I had no choice. I had to forget about sex with the gorgeous blonde with legs that went on forever and just get on with things as they were. Thus began my fourth mistake, and as they go in threes, it was reasonable to expect two more.

"Heavy night?" Jake enquired as I rushed into work, unkempt after waking up late. I'd been forced to remember my lapses of judgement as the evidence was still wrapped around me.

"Claudine came around last night," I said as I switched the computer screen on.

"No wonder you look bad. One for the road, was it?"

I stayed silent, putting off the inevitable while I typed in my password.

"You didn't? You did." He shook his head and turned his attention back to his own screen.

Our boss, Martin, was headed in my direction, a man on a mission. "What's with the appearance, Perkins?" He addressed everyone by their surname. I think he had a control fetish.

"You look like you've been dragged through a bush backwards."

"He has. Claudine's," Jake interrupted, his crass words eliciting a titter from our colleagues.

Martin's craggy face reddened as he sought to control his anger. He always came off worse from Jake's razor-sharp wit.

"Sort yourself out, Perkins," he blustered. He turned to get away from the mocking laughter.

"Give me ten minutes," Cass said.

I poured myself a glass of wine from an opened bottle in the fridge. Cass tapped away on her laptop, emotions flickering across her face. She glanced up as she finished her article.

"What's this one about?"

Cass wrote for a popular magazine, doing the human-interest stories that tore at the heartstrings of its readers. Cass managed to convey the horror of the people she wrote about as though she'd experienced it herself. Cass, despite her prickly nature, had a wonderful ability to empathise.

"Okay, brother dear, you didn't come here to get the low down on my latest article. To what do I owe this pleasure?"

"I'm back with Claudine," I blurted out.

"Why?"

I poured out the whole sorry story that was no credit to me, but Cass was the one person I didn't need to hide anything from.

"You still should have said no."

"After using her that way?"

"She tricked you into bed, you fool. Okay, you want to believe the best in people. Where do you get that from? You don't want her so you're only setting her up for a bigger fall later on?"

"We might make it work." She wasn't convinced, but I did manage to half-convince myself.

"What about the girl from Friday?" Cass tried one last tack.

"What about her? Come on, Cass, you of all people should be able to see that for what it was."

"I've never seen you that animated over Claudine." She was pulling out all the stops.

"How's the new editor at work?" I parried.

"I asked him out."

"So when are you going out?" She wouldn't be telling me now if his answer had been negative.

"Tonight at eight."

"Shouldn't you be getting ready?"

She gave me her 'Don't-you-know-me-better-than-that' look. I laughed and, getting up from my chair, said, "I'll let you get on anyway."

Chapter 4

Gemma

The bar was heaving. Kingston groaned under the collective weight of so many people clustered together enjoying the warm, indolent evening. This was the second weekend since I'd been back from Devon, and the silence from Theo, after the initial text, spoke volumes. *How can I feel like this for someone I've only met once?* I tried to push the image of him aside.

"What are you having?" Carla asked.

"I'll have a bottle of Smirnoff Ice."

Is This Love?

"Come on, you," Carla cajoled. "We'll find you someone better tonight, and who knows, he may be making you breakfast tomorrow morning."

Amanda choked on her drink, laughing. "You're outrageous."

"Oh, come on. Sex is good therapy. It releases endorphins, which, in turn, make you happy. Men and women can only be happy when there's not the unnatural pressure of a relationship. So, the equation reads Woman + Sex with gorgeous stranger = happiness. I defy anyone who says otherwise. Take that friend of yours, Susie. She was screwed over by a man. If she'd done her sums correctly, she wouldn't be hurting now."

"Yes, but what about love? You need someone to cuddle up to in bed, to hold you tight and make you feel secure." Kerry's tone was wistful.

"How secure does Susie feel now? Get with it, ladies. You don't need a man to make you whole – just to fill one, if you get my drift." Screams of hilarious outrage erupted.

"What about him?" Kerry pointed at a wimpy man in tweed and corduroy.

"Don't be so obvious." I slapped her hand down.

"Oops. He'd be so utterly grateful for your attention he'd treat you like a princess."

"I don't want to be treated like a princess, just as a woman."

"I love this song." Christina Aguilera's dulcet tones warmed the air. "Come on." Amanda grabbed me and Carla and dragged us onto the dance floor, which was pulsating from the tread of so many feet.

Joanne and Kerry joined us. We danced and laughed with abandonment. Heads turned, and we became the object of much male speculation. Five gorgeous women enjoying ourselves without restraint.

The bar was crowded. People jostled for a coveted space. I managed to squeeze in. A rotund middle-aged man with a florid face grinned at me with a suggestive leer. One glare left him in no doubt as to the state of his chances should he be foolish enough to try. The man to my right was more pleasing on the eye. He was in his mid-to-late twenties. His brown hair was a little too long, but the style suited his chiselled features. His eyes twinkled as he beamed at me, and I found myself reacting to his charms. *He's rather cute.*

"Robin," he stated, extracting his hand from his jeans pocket, and extended it in my direction.

"Gemma."

"Humph," the man to my left snorted. He was pressed impossibly close to me.

I rolled my eyes, which made Robin laugh.

"Mate, could you give the lady a bit of space?" His words were calm, with no aggressive overtones. With another unimpressed snort, the man stepped back, the vile cigarette and whiskey breath no longer blowing its nauseating stench against my neck.

After a while, Robin's mates and mine merged into one large group. Robin was good company, yet a voice in my head kept taunting me. *He's not Theo.* I tried to drown it out, but the pesky voice resounded until it reached an ear-splitting intensity. I wanted to block my ears with my hands but it would make no difference;

the voice was internal.

"Are you all right?" Robin enquired.

"Too much alcohol."

"I was going to offer to buy you another, but if you've had too much already…"

"I'll take a rain check on that."

"That would suggest we'll see each other again," he laughed. "How about tomorrow night?"

My inner voice taunted me again and, to silence it, I beamed my most radiant smile and said I'd love to. As soon as I'd said it, I knew it was stupid. I mean, I'd just agreed to a date to shut up a voice in my own head. *He probably won't ring*, I told myself as I gave him my number. He planted a wet kiss on my lips that left me cold.

Heaving myself out of bed, I peered into the mirror as I pulled on my robe. It wasn't a pleasant sight. The pain attacking the right side of my brain needed serious attention, so I padded towards the kitchen in search of an Alka-Seltzer fix.

Is This Love?

My eyes dilated, eyebrows shooting towards my hairline. Six feet of bronzed and toned naked male flesh sped past me to the bathroom. Carla had hit the jackpot with Robin's mate Tony last night. His baggy clothes hadn't given any indication of the body underneath. There should have been a health warning on someone like him, and that's not even taking into account the weapon of mass destruction that swung freely as he ran. I set off once again in search of my holy grail.

My mobile phone rang, disturbing my peace. "Hello," I answered, all the while pleading, *don't let this be the guy from last night.*

"Gemma?"

You gonna turn every bloke down cause some idiot you met doesn't wantcha?

"Hey, Robin, how are you after last night?"

He laughed. *"To be honest, I've only just got up."*

"Ditto." I found myself smiling. *He really is a nice guy.*

"Do you still want to go out tonight?" I heard the slight

break in his voice and realised that he was nervous.

He's probably plucked up the courage to ring after hours of deliberating. Can you really say no?

I walked into The Chariot in Uxbridge and spotted Robin straight away. He looked handsome in jeans and a crumpled shirt. He checked his watch with what seemed like impatience but I realised was apprehension. His features relaxed, and he broke into a wide grin when he saw me making my way through the light fog of cigarette smoke towards him. He stood as I approached and planted a kiss on my cheek.

"I'm glad you could make it."

As the night progressed, I was surprised by how easy I found Robin's company and how funny he was. I told him about my encounter in the hallway with his mate.

"He's learnt to hide his body under unflattering clothes. The attention he was getting was too much. He was mobbed whenever we went out, like a celebrity. At first, we thought it was really cool – like the rest of us would do well by association. Get the crumbs, so to speak, but it never happened." He pulled an anguished expression that made me laugh.

At the end of the night, Robin waved me off in a cab. He kissed me again, better than the last one but still minus any real connection. He said he'd call me the next day as he closed the door and stood looking forlorn on the pavement until the taxi was out of sight.

Over the next week, I spent a lot of time with Susie, whose mood varied from day to day. Anger replaced tears, only to give way to despair. We tried to make sure that someone was always with her during the evenings. Susie had sunk into a deep depression. She needed reminding to wash, and we virtually force-fed her, slaving over a hot stove only to watch her pushing the food around her plate.

The bags delineated under her eyes betrayed not only the tears but also the lack of sleep. We despaired of reaching her, of breaking through her blank expression. The house was dirty; it smelled of body odour, damp and the rubbish she'd allowed to accumulate. Windows were never opened. We tried to help but sometimes she'd get angry and throw us out so we were careful not to upset things too much.

With a sigh, I settled into the leather office chair and waited as the computer booted to life with a demon-like groan. *We really need a new one.* The first item on my agenda, each morning, was checking my e-mails, both professional and personal.

FROM: Chris Butler

DATE: 15 June 2003, 12.25

TO: gemma@stephens95.fs.net.co.uk

SUBJECT: Greetings!

Hi, Gem. Been meaning to e-mail you for the last few days but have been really busy. Anyway, it's Sunday mid-day and I've got half an hour before I go to the quays for my second viewing. When I saw it for the first time, I fell in love with it, but I've been told that

Is This Love?

the second viewing is about the head, not heart. Can you imagine that for a moment?

Jackie rang on Wednesday. She said Sus is still bad; I'll have to come to see her. I've tried ringing, but she doesn't answer. Tell her I'm thinking about her.

Heard that you had a hot date last weekend. I want all the gory details. Robin – I do like that name. Very manly. Reminds me of that cute guy in science. You remember the one I used to sit next to?

I bumped into Jake, the guy we met when you came to see me – Theo's mate; the gorgeous one. He's got quite an edge to him. He said Theo got back with his ex; apparently they'd only split up the day before you met.

I'll try to come down soon and you can entertain me with some more anecdotes on your customers.

Speak soon.

Love, Chris

X

Theo

I slumped into a chair at The Dog and Duck. Cass and Keith, sitting opposite, were also exhausted, although Cass had that awestruck look that signalled her enjoyment.

"Never again," Keith, Cass' editor-cum-new boyfriend complained.

"Note to self: no staying power," Cass chided him with noticeable ease.

This was the second time I'd met Keith; he was a calm yet firm man who held his own against the big personality that was my sister. They made an unusual couple; the small, wild-haired, green-eyed Little-Miss-Independent and the towering six-foot-five, rangy man with placid hazel eyes.

"How was paintballing?" Jake asked as he flopped into the chair next to mine.

Keith had been warned about Jake but asserted that, if he could handle Cass' outrageous comments, then Jake's wouldn't faze him. Cass and Jake were well into their familiar banter when Claudine and her friend Caroline turned up sporting disgruntled miens. In the last couple of weeks, I'd put a lot of effort into rebuilding my relationship with Claudine. Is it right to have to try so hard?

I used to worry that Jake would crack onto my sister, but she seemed to be one of the few females he actually respected. Keith found himself sucked into a conversation with the mousy-nondescript Caroline, who glowered at Jake. Caroline was one of his casualties, and she hadn't been able to tolerate him since. If she'd been any other female, I might've had some sympathy towards her, but she was a dour, colourless human being. I'd never seen the attraction myself, but then Jake often wasn't choosy. He was indiscriminate in whom he picked up and hurt.

I wondered sometimes if he set out to charm the ugly ones to see if he could transform them. Sometimes I found it hard to reconcile my beliefs with those of the friend whose behaviour trashed them utterly. But Jake was a complex character, he wasn't your average run-of-the-mill bastard, and the glimpses of a different, more humane person made me like him.

"Hey, Theo, do you remember that Gemma chick?" Jake grinned at my discomfort.

"Who's that?" Claudine's ears had pricked up; she watched me for a reaction.

"Some bird I know," Jake answered with a smug grin.

"So why are you asking Theo?"

"That's the bit you fail to understand," Jake snarled. "I was talking to Theo, not you."

"Jake, lay off." Despite the quiet timbre of my voice, he recognised the warning. Their active dislike of each other was one thing but being downright rude, I couldn't tolerate.

Claudine's cheeks stained crimson, her eyes blazed, but she wasn't stupid enough to continue when Jake made her look insignificant without trying.

"What about her?"

Cass watched from the other side of the table with a protective expression on her face. She reminded me of an eagle with talons primed, viewing its prey and waiting to swoop in for the kill.

"I've heard that she's found herself a new boyfriend." Mischief oozed from Jake's tongue.

"How do you know?" Cass asked.

Claudine was alerted to the fact that the usually blasé Cass was taking an interest in someone who'd been dismissed as one of Jake's playthings. I'd get the third degree later.

"Saw her friend. You remember the stunning redhead, don't you?"

I shook my head in wonder. Jake had a real talent for stirring. He must be really bored if he'd turned his attention on me. I knew he was trying to give me a get-out-of-jail-free card but I was adamant that I didn't need it.

Keith seemed to be stifling a smile under the bushy brown beard. A diplomat, he steered the conversation in another direction.

"I'm going to London middle of this week," I answered, grateful to him.

That conjured up an evocative image of the long legs that graced that exquisite body. Her hair hung like an elegant blond curtain, invoking an image of it teasing my chest…

"Theo!" Claudine's shrill voice pierced my daydream.

"Sorry, what?" I shifted in my chair trying not to draw attention to my embarrassment.

"Keith was speaking to you."

"Sorry, mate." I turned to Keith. "I was miles away. What were you saying?"

"Mm, in London," Jake mumbled.

Keith spoke at the same time as Jake. I hoped that Claudine hadn't picked up on Jake's words. At first I thought my luck was in, but Caroline whispered something in her ear.

"Have you given up swimming?" Cass inquired of Claudine. I recognised the dangerous tone as she sought recompense for the way Claudine had spoken to me.

I wanted to just get up and go, stuck between the trouble-making Jake, over-protective Cass and the – I didn't even want to put an adjective to Claudine at this moment.

"No, why?" she walked straight into it.

Cass gave her a slow, disdainful perusal. "Oh, my mistake." The creamy texture of her tone was perverted by the hostility of the look.

I decided to take Claudine to her favourite Mexican restaurant, wearing the tight black trousers she liked and a white shirt that accentuated my physique, in an attempt to sweeten her mood.

"So Caroline and I decided that the fitted blouse was more flattering on me than the red one, which was rather shapeless," she waffled.

Is This Love?

I hunched over the steering wheel as I awaited the bitter recriminations. For whatever reason, Claudine was choosing to ignore this afternoon. My shoulders sagged with relief. I shifted my head from side to side to release the tension.

The waiter, kitted out in traditional attire, led us to a table. The dim room was lit by flickering candles, dipping and swaying as a breeze wafted past them. He held out a chair for Claudine while I pulled back my own without the fanfare that she enjoyed.

We shared a starter of tortilla and dips while indulging in general chat. Everyone was wrong. We were right to give it another go. I watched Claudine dabbing at the side of her lips after taking a bite of her enchiladas. I placed strips of chicken and onion onto the fajitas wrap and rolled them with practised ease. Biting into the overstuffed wrap, I was blithely unaware of anything other than a sense of well-being and the guacamole that had dripped onto my chin.

"So?" Claudine drawled the words.

I chewed furiously, but no response was needed.

The 'so' was a moment stopper.

"Was it Gemma or the stunning redhead?"

My cheeks burned. She'd lulled me into a false sense of security, my guard was down, and this time I was the one who'd walked into a cleverly laid trap.

"Please don't insult my intelligence by denying it. I know that one of them was the tart you hooked up with when we split. My guess would be Gemma." Her clipped words demanded a reply.

My anger, typically slow to rise, blasted to boiling point. The coldness of her approach and the vitriol that spilled from her tongue were unacceptable. The harmony created by her false calm was shattered, the whole thing an illusion.

"It really is none of your business. Now if you wish to pursue this conversation any further, you can do so on your own, as I will get up and leave you sitting here. Don't underestimate me on this, Claudine. If you push me, I won't hesitate to leave you stranded."

A dense, choking atmosphere descended on the evening as she clearly decided not to test my resolve.

Any attempt at conversation was stilted at best. I was forced to reconsider my previous thoughts about our relationship. *I'll think about it while I'm in London.*

"Hello, stranger," Jon greeted me when I walked into the intimate office. "You back again? Like the proverbial bad penny." His thin face, dotted liberally with freckles, broke into a grin.

"You bet. Come to give you hell, my friend."

"Does that mean I've got you again as an unwanted houseguest?"

Our familiar banter produced a smile from the others who worked in the office. The layout of this diminutive room had desks crammed together; the scene, cosy due to the close relationship of the dozen or so staff who worked here, could so easily have been claustrophobic. I would be spending the next few days here auditing their accounts.

"You'd better go and see the big chief," Jon drawled. "He's been waiting for you. Oh, and I got us some tickets for the Chelsea pre-season friendly at

Selhurst."

Friday night loomed ahead of me like a frightening spectre. We headed to the pub straight from work just as we had every night that week. Jon's capacity for alcohol belied his weedy frame. We arrived at the large Georgian house with a crate. The décor was a tribute to bad taste. *How can anyone think fluorescent pink is a decorating statement?*

Jon's friends opened the door and ushered us in with affectionate hugs and kisses on the cheek. It is somewhat overpowering to be kissed by two men you've just met – in fact, by any man, but more so when they're gay. It doesn't matter how liberal you think you are, you can't help wondering, *Is my arse safe?* George and Ray had just bought the house and decided to throw a party to end all parties before they undertook the task of modernising and redecorating.

We had arrived too early. The quiet, rather tired quality of the half dozen stoned other early comers did nothing to enliven me. By eleven thirty, I was dreaming of my bed. As I disappeared into the kitchen to procure more cans for Jon and myself, the front door opened, letting in the cold breeze and a stream of people. The music cranked up, loud voices mingled with laughter, and cigarette smoke wreathed its way toward the ceiling. I found myself in a crowd of women courting my attention. I enjoyed the pleasant flirtatious company. Dissatisfied as I was with Claudine, I would never commit the cardinal sin of infidelity. That went against the grain and my every principle. A young couple disappeared up the stairs, their pace frantic, unconcerned with anyone else's opinion.

Another couple slobbered over each other on the sofa, hands roaming as though the audience were invisible. A dark-haired beauty pouted at me, seduction written all over her.

"Do you want to go upstairs with me?" Her red lips were parted, and eyes glazed.

I declined.

Jon and I staggered home in the early hours,

accompanied by the clinking bottles as the milkman delivered his goods to the doorsteps of the quiet neighbourhood. A black cat shot by at speed. Close on its heels, another cat followed, larger and more menacing. Somewhere ahead of us they must have met up, as we heard a cacophony of squeals and shrieks.

Jon, now very drunk, told me about a girl he liked, averring that she was out of his league.

"Nonthense," my words slurred. "You've gotta go f'rit."

"I will," he promised.

Alcohol has a habit of loosening the tongue and inviting confidences. I found myself talking about Claudine, and somewhere, somehow, Gemma popped into the conversation.

"Fnish wiv her." It was Jon's turn to encourage me. I lapped it up. "Ring her – blonde wiv legs, ring er."

"Yeah, I will," I vowed. In my inebriated state, I knew what to do.

With a pounding head and a tremor that attacked my stability and sense of gravity, I somehow got up the next day. I faced Jon in the kitchen where, in silence, we downed thick black coffees. Neither of us mentioned the conversation of the early hours. It had merely been the ramblings of two drunken men. Jon's mates, a crowd of about ten whose names became a blur after the third introduction, met us in the pub. After a swiftly downed pint, we headed for the train station, walking along the road as the blistering sun singed the surrounding air.

The train was mobbed by football fans. Each stop produced more burgundy and blue shirts, the Chelsea blue strip amongst the minority in our carriage. An elderly couple opposite looked uncomfortable. The only other non-supporter in our carriage was a tall, lanky youth with green spiked hair and piercings sticking out of every visible orifice. He sat in seeming ignorance of the vibes, engrossed in the music blaring from his iPod despite his headphones.

Every time I thought it wasn't possible to fit another person on, in squeezed a few more. A writhing mass of human bodies. The smell of body odour was offensive. Supporters of both teams jostled shoulder to shoulder, friendly rivalry stood side by side with outright antagonism. I prayed that violence wouldn't explode.

We exited the train at Selhurst and turned left out of the station into Clifton Road. Against my better judgement, we went into the Clifton Arms for a pint first. The place was full of Palace supporters. Tensions in the pub were rife, even more so than on the packed train. All it would take was one stupid remark from either side and a full-scale brawl would erupt.

Turning into Holmesdale Road, we were greeted with the sight of a sea of bodies merging like a mythological beast, joined, yet separate entities. We headed towards the Arthur Wait Stand where the away supporters were situated. Everyone shuffled along converging on the turnstiles to go through in single file.

"We love you, Chelsea, we do." The crowd took up the chant. "Come on, you Blues." The pre-match atmosphere was electric.

Colourful language flew from one side of the stadium to the other as the fans' enthusiasm ignited. The Mexican Waves felt as though they were choreographed except for the dim few who stood up and raised their arms after the wave had passed them by.

The game kicked off, and four minutes in, Mikael Forssell scored a goal.

"Ye…ah. We love you, Chelsea, we do." Our side of the stadium erupted.

"What a blinder," Jon shouted.

"Did you see how he curled it in? Pure bloody genius," said a thuggish-looking guy with glasses, whose name I couldn't recall.

Palace equalised to curses and derogatory chants from our side. A few minutes were given for injury time just before the half-time whistle blew. Geremi was fouled thirty yards out. *Come on, Geremi, you can do it. Come on, son.*

Silence filled the stadium as Geremi took the free kick. The ball flew through the air as though in slow motion. We held our breaths, expelling it only when the ball sailed into the top left corner; a spectacular goal. The noise was deafening.

We celebrated our two-one lead at half time with a swift pint and a burger behind the stand.

"Did you see the way that ball cut through the air? The way it curled into the back of that net; pure bloody genius."

I tucked into my second burger. I had no intention of being inebriated again tonight. This wasn't going to be my last pint of the day. I could have said no if I wanted to but the escape was just what the doctor ordered, even if he wouldn't approve of the sheer quantity.

Ambrosio was swapped for Cudicini, Huth for Desailly, and Duff came off. The second half started. The first quarter of an hour was uneventful, but the last twenty minutes saw Palace taking control as they broke free. I held my breath in fearful anticipation as Tommy Black then Freedman both shot wide of the post. Chelsea romped home to a two-one win. Time for another beer.

We surged past the Clifton Arms on our way back to the station singing, celebrating the result of some truly beautiful football. Someone suggested we go in for a pint, but I wasn't the only one who thought it a bad idea.

Chapter 5

Gemma

I spent two days brooding. Although Theo hadn't contacted me, a small shred of hope had clung with surprising tenacity. Confirmation of a definite nature blew away any lingering expectation. Those little excuses we like to make to ourselves: he lost my number, my text never arrived, or he had an accident. A non-serious accident, enough to keep him unavailable for a few weeks, or a very short burst of amnesia – anything non-life threatening or temporary that would explain the lack of contact. Maybe, though, the cold, stark facts were better; it gave you the chance to move on without the shroud of a metaphorical question mark hanging over your head.

I considered where Robin was in all this. The truth was I didn't view him romantically. Would things have been different if I hadn't met Theo first? That was something I would never know, and I'd spent enough time ruminating the what ifs tonight. I decided Theo must be banished from my head and Robin from my life.

As I lay there, locked in my bubble of thoughts, it came to me, straight out of the stratosphere, an involuntary notion. A holiday. There was nothing like a holiday to escape reality for a while and put things back into perspective. My brain was awake. Excitement coursed through me as I focused on possible destinations.

I looked at the illuminated figures on my alarm clock and groaned. *When am I going to get to sleep?* I tried to focus my mind on a blank canvas, but splashes of colour appeared. *What will I say to Robin?* I tried counting sheep but the fuzzy shapes refused to form. One more attempt and then I'd try reading. I pictured myself lying in a boat under a starless black sky, the sea surrounding me as far as the eye could see, inky blackness enfolding me. Laying back in the boat, I closed my eyes feeling the gentle lap of the waves against the vessel, lulling, rocking as I tumbled into blissful oblivion.

The following evening I had a date with Robin, and after my decision last night, I knew it would be my last. Applying a splash of colour to my eyes and lips, I stood back to survey my appearance. Nervous now, I smoothed out a crease in the fabric of my dress. I slipped into a pair of low-heeled sandals, grabbed my bag and stuffed in my mobile. I rechecked that the hair straighteners were turned off and took a last glance around the room. As I passed a mirror, I glanced at my appearance and then hurried down the stairs to answer the door. Robin let out a wolf-whistle as I opened it.

"You look lovely."

"Thanks."

There was an awkward silence for the first five minutes as Robin drove us to Richmond. Talking was much easier on the phone. I wracked my brains staring down at my hands, searching for the words that would break this stifling silence.

"Did you have a nice time with your family?"

"Oh yeah. Everyone's a bit mad, but it was nice seeing them." He laughed. My mobile rang, interrupting him. I grimaced when I recognised Mum's number. It was either her or my sister Kelly. Either way, it wasn't a conversation I wanted to have right now.

"Gemma."

"Mum. How are you?"

"So you do remember who I am."

I rolled my eyes heavenward; I wasn't in for an easy time. I sometimes wondered why Mum bothered to keep in touch with me, because all she did was give me a hard time.

Is This Love?

It had been okay once upon a time, but it had gone awry on the 1st of June 1978, Mum's birthday, when I was five years old.

A pillow brought down with force woke me from my sleep, making me jump, startled and scared. I made as though to scream, my eyes blinking in rapid succession.

"Shush," Andy, my eight-year-old brother whispered.

I looked trustingly up at him. "What's wrong?"

"It's Mum's birthday. I thought we'd make her breakfast in bed."

I was proud that Andy had included me in his plans when he so often left me out.

We crept into the kitchen and made Mum a cup of tea. Well, Andy did. He put the toast under the grill; I got the cutlery, milk and marmalade out.

"Shush," he urged as the fridge door slammed.

"Surprise!" we shouted from the doorway.

Mum and Dad sat up, shocked, in bed. Mum's face was wreathed in smiles.

"You did that for me?" she cooed. "Come here, my darlings, and give me a birthday kiss."

Andy placed the tray on the bedside cabinet and climbed with care onto the bed, feigning disinterest, as would any boy of his age. I bounded up to claim my kisses and cuddles.

"Be careful of the baby," Dad admonished gently.

Mum's belly was big. She said there was a baby in there. I couldn't see how, but Andy said I'd been there once, too. He was older and knew about these things so I had to believe him.

I remember that cuddle well because it was the last one I got from Mum.

Mum's pains started soon after, and she was rushed to the hospital. Andy and I were bundled into clothes and taken next door to Mrs. Kellett. I remember being frightened, not knowing what was happening. Andy didn't say it, but he was, too, because he was quiet and didn't tease me.

Kelly was born on Mum's birthday, and when they came home a few days later, Mum couldn't take her eyes off her, although Andy and I thought her ugly. She still called Andy her special boy, but I must have done something wrong because it felt as though she'd stopped loving me.

"What do you want, Mum?" My exasperated tone pushed aside the memories that had risen spectrally from their shallow grave. I felt Robin's speculative gaze on me.

"Is that any way to speak to your mother, Gemma? After all the sacrifices I made for you."

That's a joke.

"...at home first. Joanne answered — what a lovely girl; so polite. You could learn from her, you know..." I zoned out again. *"...holiday, she says. I'm the last to know..."* Her voice rose to an unbearable pitch.

"I only booked the holiday this morning. I was going to call you tomorrow. I'm out now; I can't really talk."

"No time even to speak to your own mother." She sniffed, and I pictured her pained expression.

I can't win.

"Your sister's going through a hard time with her boyfriend."

Boyfriend, my arse. Kelly has one-night stands, not boyfriends.

"You didn't think that she might like to go away on holiday, too? You might ask her."

"Mum... you're breaking up…" I faked. "...can't hear you." I ended the call and then slumped back into my seat.

"You're going on holiday?"

I groaned in silence.

The cinema was packed with teenagers. Popcorn sailing through the air, high-pitched laughter and a rumble of conversation interrupted the film. Robin had insisted I choose the movie, and the most promising one was *Charlie's Angels: Full Throttle*. Robin's arm crept around my shoulder feeling like a lump of wood weighing me down. I wanted to have tonight over with, to be tucked up at home in bed.

"We've got time to go for a quick drink."

"Actually, Robin, I just want to go home."

"You tired, babe?" His brows wrinkled.

"Mm, yeah. Robin, I need to talk to you." Butterflies fluttered beneath my ribs.

"Are you okay?"

Why does he have to be so nice? It would be a lot easier if only... but he's not, and I knew I had to just come out and say it.

"You don't want to see me anymore?" His words were flat but the darkening of his eyes showed traces of hurt. I felt guilty. "You don't have to say anything. I can see it in your eyes."

"I'm sorry, Robin. This sounds trite, but it truly isn't you. You're a lovely man but..." I faltered.

"Come on, I'll take you home."

The short ride home seemed interminable, the goodbye stilted.

With reluctance, I picked up the phone and tapped in the familiar number.

"Hello, 4219, Esther Stephens speaking." Her false telephone voice made me smile. It didn't matter how many times we told her not to give her name out over the phone, she still insisted, saying that it was telephone etiquette.

"Mum, sorry about last night. The phone cut out."

She sniffed. *"Convenient, if you ask me. Your sister Kelly,"* her voice softened, *"needs a holiday. Try to please me this once, Gemma."*

"No, sorry."

"Why do you always go out of your way to upset me? Why can't you be more like your sister?"

"And why can't you accept me as I am and stop comparing me to your favourite?" Tears welled up in my eyes. I can't believe I still let her affect me.

"Oh, Gemma, how can you say that? I've never had a..." she trailed off.

"I've got to get back to work." My voice shook.

"Gemma..." Her voice sounded tremulous.

I sighed, "Yes, Mum?"

"Have a good holiday."

I sat dazed for a few moments after I'd replaced the receiver. It wasn't like her to back down, and never had she been so magnanimous in defeat. I wondered whether she'd never admitted it to herself. *Had I shocked her?*

I need an early night, I thought as I drove to Susie's. I was drained, and my emotions were all over the place.

"Hello, honey," Susie said when she opened the door.

"Sus, you look great. How are you?"

"Come on in. There's a nip in the air tonight."

I walked into the living room and smiled. The room was back to its normal spotless state. The wine glass sat on a coaster on the coffee table, any evidence that a stain had once marred the surface now eradicated.

"I'll just get you a glass," Susie said.

I sunk into the black leather sofa, kicking my shoes off.

"I thought we'd get us a takeaway on me – no, don't argue," her voice rose above my protests, "– after all you've done for me."

"What have I done?"

"You were there for me again when I needed you most."

"I'm your friend. That's part of the job description."

"Then, as a friend, humour me this once."

I threw my hands up in defeat.

"Before we get bogged down in the next instalment of my story..." she paused for effect and smiled, "...I want to hear all about you. What have I missed out on?"

I skimmed over my dates with Robin, my trip to Devon and the whole Theo thing, and slipped in about my holiday.

"You really connected with him, didn't you?" Her perception was not startling, as she knew me almost as well as I knew myself. Her eyes searched my face for clues. I gave her a sad smile and then changed the subject.

"So, come on, what's occurred to bring the old Susie back?"

"Was I really that bad?"

"No worse than any of the rest of us would be in the circumstances."

"Ted's been around every day begging me to forgive him and take him back." She paused for a moment, a frown burrowing between her eyebrows. "I can't get that picture out of my mind." She stopped again, choosing her words with care, "And, you know... oh..." She seemed flustered.

"It's okay, Sus; you know you can tell me anything."

I suspected she wanted to talk about sex, and surprisingly, for a married woman, she was quite shy about discussing it.

"We-ell the position... I mean... the way I found them... you know, with her..." Her cheeks stained red, spreading to the corners of her fair hair.

"Yes, I know what you mean." The picture she'd painted was still vivid in my head.

"I wanted to, once."

She wanted to what? Have an affair?

"You know," she looked at me, willing me to understand.

It dawned on me, my eyes dilated, and a grin tugged at the corners of my lips.

"You wanted to ride him."

She looked ashamed.

"What's wrong with that?"

"Ted said only sluts do that, or people having casual sex. It has no place in a loving relationship, that he wouldn't get pleasure from seeing me degrade myself like that."

I was rendered speechless. *Oh, poor Susie. If I get my hands on that bastard…*

"I shouldn't have told you." A shroud of shame permeated her.

"I'm not shocked at you. That fool of a husband of yours has a lot to answer for. There's nothing wrong or dirty in what you wanted to do; it's normal. If you don't believe me, then ask the girls; they'll tell you. It's so normal, everyone does it." I tried to lighten the mood. "Well, not our parents. Ooh no, I don't even want to contemplate that."

The doorbell pealed through the house, interrupting our laughter. We jumped, confused.

"Chinese," we chorused.

Susie rushed out to collect our food while I poured out some more wine.

"So what else has been happening?"

The darkening of her eyes, the way her lids flipped down to conceal them, told me that I'd been right to be worried.

"She came to see me." I had to strain to listen to her words. "Jane."

"What did she want?" I tried to keep my righteous indignation to an acceptable level.

"She asked me to talk to Ted, to tell him that it was over and that she... was right for him."

"She did what? What did you do?"

"I told her to leave. She said it was no wonder Ted had left, given the state of the house and me. I taunted her that he still wanted me, though. *'But you can't give him what he really wants, can you?'* I thought she was talking about sex, so I said to her that he didn't want a wife who acted like a whore. *'I mean a baby.'* With a self-satisfied smile, she rubbed her stomach, a small round lump evident. *'I'm having his baby, something that you can't do.'*"

Theo

When I arrived back from London, I found a red rose in the middle of my bed with a note underneath on fancy notepaper sprayed with her favourite perfume. *I'm sorry. C x.*

The smell of the perfume clung to my room and made me uncomfortable. A relaxed weekend without Claudine had given me back a sense of tranquillity, and now I didn't know what to do. Okay, so maybe I did, but I wasn't ready to make that decision.

Over the next few weeks, I drank too much, even though I'd vowed to cut back. Claudine continued to display a tolerant attitude. She even accepted my decision to go on holiday with Jake for two weeks without complaint. That night in the restaurant had flipped a switch for me, and I found myself wondering when she'd revert to type. This whole niceness felt like a charade.

My mobile rang, and Claudine stirred in bed beside me.

"Jake, what are you doing up this early?" I blinked, wiping sleep from my eyes, trying to focus on the red digits on the clock: eight a.m.

"I haven't been to bed yet. Well, not to sleep, anyway. I've just got home. Get your arse out of bed and get over here. We can go to the travel agents and then I can hit the sack."

"Who is it?" Claudine demanded.

"It's Jake. He wants me to meet him now so we can book our holiday."

"This early? Tell him you'll meet him later." She turned her back on me.

I'd intended to do just that, but a spark of stubbornness asserted itself at Claudine's imperious manner.

"I'll see you soon, mate," I said, and hung up.

Claudine turned around as I swung my legs out of

the bed. "You did that to spite me. Oh, just go. See if I care," she snarled.

The door was opened by a bleary-eyed, grinning Jake.

"All right, Theo, you managed to escape the scorpion," he drawled.

"Go and put the kettle on and make me coffee."

"Let's just go."

I sauntered past him. "It doesn't open until ten."

His flat was immaculate, as always. Wooden flooring ran throughout, accompanied by clean white lines, chrome and a splash of colour, which gave the flat character and charm.

"You do the coffees. I'm going to take a shower, see if I can wake up a bit, seeing as how I'll be up for a while."

Half an hour later, Jake emerged in a cloud of Burberry, clean-shaven and looking sharp in his white, fitted Ted Baker shirt and tight jeans.

"Are you going out on the prowl?"

"Never know what cute bird might want to take

down my particulars."

"Hoping to work the famous Sutherland charm?"

"Always. You should try it. Where's my coffee?"

There was no mistaking that women found Jake irresistible. I didn't know if it was his dark good looks or his roguish air. Yet, for all of that, there was a vulnerability that shrouded him at times, and maybe this was where the attraction to the opposite sex lay. He was never short of offers; his conquests would have filled more than one bedpost.

The incorrigible Jake winked at the travel agent across the desk from us, and her cheeks broke out in a furious red hue. The poor woman was middle-aged, with thick NHS glasses that perched on her nose. Greasy black hair hung down her back. Her left hand was conspicuous by the lack of a ring, and I felt sure that she'd never been with a man in her life.

I aimed a sharp kick at his shins.

"What?"

"Stop," I hissed, glaring at him to make my point.

She fumbled for control, hiding behind her computer.

"Erm… we've got two weeks, all-inclusive…"

"No," Jake stopped her and, chewing lazily on a piece of gum, he fixed her with an intense gaze.

"We're not interested in all-inclusive," I added, coming to the aid of this poor harassed woman.

"Ayia Napa, self-catering, for two weeks?"

"We've been there."

"Remind me why we didn't do this online, Theo," Jake asked.

"Maybe the fact that you didn't want to had something to do with it – just a thought."

She ran through a dozen or more options. Jake slumped back in his chair, arms folded over his chest, legs spread akimbo in front of him. He'd grown bored with baiting her.

"Crete?" she entreated.

"I've got nothing against that one. You?"

"Let's hear it." He launched forward in his seat, resting his elbows on the desk, interest revived.

One more week, I thought, struggling with a balance sheet as I spied Martin weaving his way over.

"Your head or mine?" Jake joked.

I stifled a grin as he loomed over us, and tried to appear engrossed in my work.

"Perkins, have you finished the accounts for XL Ltd?"

"Not yet. I can't seem to get the balance sheet to tally. The accounts department at XL are rubbish. Their purchase and sales ledgers are almost illegible. The profit and loss accounts are nearly done but... oh, there it is; this debtor figure was wrong. Give me ten minutes."

"Well, make sure it isn't any longer. You're not on holiday yet, you know."

Miserable bastard.

"I'd better get this account finished," I said, masking my amusement. Jake needed no encouragement.

"Have you seen that hot new PA?" Jake enquired

with seeming innocence.

Without looking up from the balance sheet, I answered, "Mm, she's not bad."

"Not bad? Mate, she's hot. And she's gagging for it. You should have seen the way she looked at me this morning."

I leaned back in the chair; he had my full attention now. I nodded, indicating for him to go on.

"She'll be in the bag before we go away." He chewed on his pencil with a self-satisfied smile.

"That long?"

The rest of the day fared no better, none of the accounts tallied, and I spent most of the day chasing figures. After my rough day, I decided to have a pint before heading to Claudine's.

Knocking on the heavy oak front door to her apartment, I pondered again how she afforded it. I stepped over the threshold and reached across to kiss her. Her cinched lips and ice-glazed eyes told their own story.

"What's wrong?"

"You reek of booze and cigarette smoke." Her nose wrinkled in distaste.

"I went for a pint after work. I've had a hard day."

"You knew I was cooking for you," she accused. "Dinner is ruined."

You can't blame me for that. "You never eat before eight. It's a quarter to now."

"So you think it's all right to turn up just before dinner. I suppose you see nothing wrong with leaving straight after." Venom poured like molten lava from her lips.

I inhaled, then emitted a sharp sigh. "I told you, I've had a bad day." *I don't want a bad night, too.*

"So you needed a drink. I do have alcohol here. You could have told me about your day."

Why can't she see I just needed some time to myself to let off steam? I don't want to talk. Can't she just be happy that I'm here now?

"There's not a lot you don't have in this apartment."

"Well, you're here now. Give me a kiss and then you can open that bottle of red on the side."

She never engaged in conversations about how she'd acquired this luxurious apartment with all the top-of-the-range gadgets and gizmos. Her position in the bank hadn't risen from clerk in the sixteen years she'd been there; a mystery for someone who was such a climber. She'd hinted a few years back at money left in her mother's will, but she never spoke of her. I wondered if I would ever really know her.

The night was full of undertones of things left unsaid. Neither of us elicited pleasure in the other's company. I made an excuse to leave early. Hesitating at the door, I clasped the handle.

Finish with her now.

I half-turned to action my thoughts, but hesitated. Now wasn't the time. I was too tired and couldn't contemplate the ensuing scene.

"Gooaal." A cheer went up as Toby sank the ball into the back of the net.

Is This Love?

I stood back, laughing, as he did the famous Brewster wiggle celebrating his goal, which seemed incongruous in this giant of a man. The whistle blew, and Coach indicated for us to gather around.

"You played better tonight, everyone, but if we're to stand a chance against The New Inn's team on Sunday, I need to see more commitment. Theo, your mind's not on the game. I don't give a fuck what's going on in your private life. You need to give a hundred and one percent." A snigger accompanied his words. "He wasn't the only one, though, was he, Jimmy? You may as well have not been here at all. Nice goal, Toby. I want to see a few of them on Sunday. All right, lads, go and shower. You stink."

We walked off in the direction of the showers, laughing.

"So how are things with Claudine?" Toby asked.

"Not good. She always blows hot and cold. I never seem to know where I am with her."

Jason thumped me on the shoulder. "The joys of women, mate."

The spotlight flashed on, illuminating the pink-rendered walls of the sprawling bungalow where Toby and Lisa lived. The night air was clement, with only the merest whisper of wind ruffling the leaves. The aromatic scent of flowers rose above that of our food as we stood outside, waiting, while Toby rootled inside his jacket pocket for his keys.

Toby threw his dirty bag down onto the immaculate carpet in the hallway that now held traces of the football pitch. Jason and I didn't bat an eyelid; this was Toby's way. Jason's wife, Cathy, would have beaten him black and blue for that offence. Lisa rolled her eyes heavenward and set about cleaning it up and taking the kit out to the utility room.

Toby flung himself down onto the sofa, resting his legs on top of the coffee table. The pizza box lay sprawled beside him on the couch. With a lack of finesse, he peeled off a slice and ate with gusto. Lisa re-emerged with three cans of cold beer and warm welcomes. She carefully lifted the pizza box, sat down and placed it on her lap, selecting a slice for herself.

"How's things with you, Lisa?" Jason asked.

"Not bad, Jay. Bit tired. The twins have me run ragged all day."

"What'd they do now?" The chunk of pizza he was busy chewing muffled Toby's words.

Lisa leant over and wiped tomato sauce from his chin.

"Just the usual squabbles. They warn you about the terrible twos and threes, but ours don't seem to realise at four things should be calmer," she laughed. "Don't have any, Theo."

"You don't mean that, Lis."

"Don't I?" She smiled. "So what's new with you and Claudine?"

"Don't ask." I rolled my eyes.

"That bad, is it?" She smiled and left it at that. Cathy wouldn't have let me; Lisa was a much gentler person, but no less loving.

"Have you heard from Cass?" Lisa asked.

"She seems totally smitten with Keith."

"I did wonder if Cass would ever let her barriers down. Do you remember that shiner she gave that lad in year seven who tried to kiss her?"

"Do I? She told the headmaster she was sticking up for herself as a result of sexual harassment."

Jason and Toby guffawed.

"That's right. I wonder what he's doing now. What was his name... Darren, was it?" Lisa asked.

"Dillon. He works in the bank with Claudine. I think he still bears a grudge."

"Go away. Are you serious?"

"Well, he works there. The grudge is an exaggeration." I chuckled.

"I'll leave you lads to it. I'm off to bed." She rolled her eyes. "You always did manage to fool me."

"You were ever the gullible one. We'll shoot off." I made as though to stand.

"No, no, stay," she insisted. "We'll arrange a barbie soon, Tobe. We haven't all had a proper get-together in a while."

"I hear the Inn's new goalie lets nothing in," Jason

grumbled.

"Didn't he have prospects of becoming a premiership goalie? Apparently, he couldn't handle the pressure." I shrugged.

"I heard that, too. Whether it's true..." Jason trailed off.

"So how did Claudine take your news of a holiday with Jake?" Toby asked, moving away from the subject of our forthcoming match.

"Surprisingly well, but she did have a major strop last night." I winced at the thought.

"You can't have it all," Jason replied. "What you should appreciate is that, after telling her, you're lucky to still be alive."

"You've agreed to do what? You're about to go away for two weeks with that male slag, and instead of spending your last days here, with me, you've got a football match."

The sounds washed over me; I longed for peace. The shrill pitch rose higher, words blurred into notes a tenor would be hard pressed to reach. Her voice soared higher until it crashed through my subconscious, forcing me to attend to her words once more.

"...and you think that's acceptable? Are you trying to put our relationship in jeopardy? Is that what you want?"

Finish it now. "For God's sake, Claud', I asked you to come and support me. Toby and Lisa are having a barbeque after; we'll be together then. What more do you want from me? I can't let the team down."

"But you don't mind letting me down."

"I'm sick of being the bad guy, Claudine. If I can't do anything right, why did you want to give our relationship another chance?"

A fleeting expression of fear flashed in her brown eyes, which surprised me. Her lids fluttered shut, masking her expression. When she opened them again, she gave me her most winning smile.

"Don't let's fight, darling," she purred.

I shook my head. A mixture of wonder and disgust surged through me. With a withering glare, I walked away.

"I have to talk to you, Theo."

"I need to get away. I'll see you on Sunday."

Chicken. Yet again, I found myself outside her apartment, wondering why I hadn't dumped her.

The sun warmed my limbs as I emerged onto the pitch with Toby and Jason on either side. We were buoyed up, our adrenaline was pumping, and our steps were light. The parched brown grass looked sorrowful, dried crisp blades giving the impression of a field of straw. I noted with relief Claudine and Caroline in animated conversation with Lisa and Cathy.

The Inn won the toss and shot the ball to the right where a midfielder received and passed it, only for it to be intercepted by Jason. He dribbled the ball around full circle, slipping past The Inn's defence, transferring it from one foot to the other before arching it up into the air. It sailed over the defenders' heads, slowly descending to the waiting head of Ben, who just missed scoring as the ball floated an inch wide of the far post.

Is This Love?

The first half continued to challenge us as the superiority of The Inn's side became more apparent. Luckily, their ability to pass was hampered by our own fierce defending. The halftime nil-nil score was quite a feat and something to be proud of.

I spotted Jake heading in the direction of the girls and groaned. I hadn't known he was coming. He was sure to sour Claudine's mood, and today was going to be a long one.

Five minutes into the second half, Ben was given another opportunity, and this time one of his famous headers hit true and sweet into the back of the net. The team and supporters alike went wild. The Inn's despondent faces boosted our self-esteem further. With confidence surging through us, we charged down the pitch like conquering heroes. Toby set up a pass to Ralphie, and I moved into the five-yard box as the ball soared towards me. I shot it with precision between the legs of the goalie and into the back of the net. Cass' screams rose above the rest, while Lisa and Cathy jumped around with excitement. Jack bounced and cheered, pulling at the bemused four-year-old twins, Tim and Joe.

"Come on, Uncle Theo," he screamed, with Katie copying, "Unca Feo."

Claudine looked on with a disdainful air. A few minutes later I took a fall as I tried to gain possession of the ball again. I limped around the pitch, unwilling to leave the game, but Coach substituted me. Five-year-old Jack flung himself at me as I hobbled off the pitch.

"Careful, Jack, Uncle Theo's been hurt," Cathy's gentle tone warned.

The other kids crowded around for the usual hugs. Cathy, Cass and Lisa smothered me in female arms. Disentangling myself, I walked towards Claudine, who hung back. She always put a bit of space between herself and Cass. A fleeting wave of sympathy washed over me as I knew my sister to be a formidable foe. The sentiment dissipated the instant she spoke.

"You didn't tell me *he* was coming." She looked pointedly at Jake.

No congratulations for the goal or concern over my fall. "I didn't know," I said, and swung back to the warmth of my friends, intercepting a look passing between Cathy, Cass and Lisa.

"Where's Keith?" I asked to divert Cass.

"He's finishing an article for the publication. Deadline's tomorrow. He'll try to join us later."

"Go on, Toby," I shouted as Toby roared down the pitch, weaving in and out of the opposition.

"Go on, Dad," chorused the tousled-haired twins who gripped my hands.

Toby lost the ball, and The Inn's star player thundered down the pitch with grim determination etched on his hirsute features. Twenty minutes to go. My chest tightened. The ball slipped past our goalie to uproarious cheers from the other side.

"Shit," I cursed.

"Shit." All four children looked up at me with angelic expressions on their faces as they echoed my expletive.

"Sorry," I chirped, turning my famed boyish charm

on the none-too-impressed mothers.

Jake watched me with amusement. His hard, pebble-like eyes glittered, danger stalking them like a prowling tiger.

"At least you know he'll make a good dad, Claud', even if you do need to curb his tendency to curse when excited." He stopped and smirked; I waited for the rest. "You haven't noticed?" I knew where this was going. "He obviously doesn't get excited in your presence."

Claudine reddened.

The last minutes were excruciating, crawling by. Our team were flagging, exhaustion written over their faces. *Don't let them equalise.* With ninety seconds left to go, Toby scored our third goal. The twins let go of my hands and cheered, jumping on top of Jack in a parody of what was happening on the pitch. I swung Katie up in my arms, out of the way of the boisterous celebrations.

"Unca Feo," Katie whispered into my ear.

"Yes, honey," I replied, distracted.

"That's your girlfriend, isn't it?"

"Yes." I gave her my full attention.

"I don't like her," she stated, her chin jutting out with determination.

"Katie!" Cathy exclaimed, her cheeks turning to pink.

"I'll let you into a secret, Katie." Her little face lit up. "I don't think I do, either."

The laughter dancing in Cathy's eyes was mirrored in my own. I hugged Katie to me.

"Unca Feo, you're squishing me," Katie announced.

"What's so funny?" Claudine demanded.

Katie squirmed in my arms. I stroked the golden spirals, watching fascinated as they bounced back up like a spring. I smiled at her and winked conspiratorially. She grinned,

delighted that I wasn't going to betray her little secret.

"Nothing."

"Well, it's obviously something." Caroline's vitriolic tone slashed the happy atmosphere.

"Theo, I hope you're going to help Toby and Jason with the barbie," Lisa interjected.

"Not like that," Jake exclaimed at Toby and Jason's unsuccessful attempts to light the coals.

The sausages and burgers were squeezed on. Toby and I manned the first watch, trying to side-step the smoke that blew when the wind picked up. The girls prepared salad, dips and snacks. Lightly grilling rolls, onions and peppers alongside the meat, we served up the first batch.

Jake and Jason took over while Toby and I stood, eating and drinking, laughing at their attempts to be better than us. Keith and Cass took over the last shift.

"Look at the result. You can't say it's not beautiful," Lisa said to a disgruntled Claudine.

"Oh, I don't deny that, but what I'm saying is that I'd hire a gardener to do it. I see no pleasure in backache and dirty, chipped nails." Claudine's eyes flicked with contempt to Lisa's short nails.

"Hey, you." Cass sidled up to me, and took the can

I'd just opened and drank from it.

Reaching behind, I took another can, giving her a playful nudge. She perched beside me on the table.

"You okay?" I asked.

"Do you think our combined weights are going to tip the balance of this table completely? It's already on its last legs."

"We can ease the burden and get a few more down our necks," I teased, "if you're up for it."

"I hope you're not drinking too much." Claudine and Caroline materialised in front of us.

"I'm up for getting wasted if you are, Theo," Cass challenged.

Claudine backed down and retreated with Caroline a step behind.

"What are you still doing with her?" Almond-shaped eyes identical to mine stared back at me.

"I've been thinking that myself recently."

"So why haven't you done anything?"

A hazy picture of someone I'd long thought forgotten popped into my mind. I shook my head to remove her.

"Just..." I shrugged. "I never seem to find the right time. I will do it, but when I get back."

"What's wrong with before you go?" Cass persisted.

The idea formed and took shape, dancing around in my head. *Finish with her.* There really wasn't a good reason to stay with her. Once I'd made that decision, it seemed as though a weight had been lifted from my shoulders.

"Decided to hijack the alcohol, have you? What a marvellous idea. Think I'll join you." Keith's wide-lipped smile took us both in.

"Don't sit." Our simultaneous warning rang out causing both of us to laugh.

After a few minutes, I said, "I'd better circulate."

"Sorry, was I interrupting..."

I cut Keith off with a hasty reassurance.

Claudine started dropping unsubtle hints that she'd had enough and was ready to go. I, on the other hand, was having a good time and wasn't eager to leave. As I continued to ignore her attempts to draw me away, she increased the volume.

"Well, you do wonder when your own boyfriend would rather spend two weeks in the company of another man. Any hot-blooded man would surely want to spend some time with his girlfriend before he goes away."

Silence descended on the gathering, her vicious barb embarrassing everyone.

"Maybe he won't go without," Jake's voice broke the deadlock, and a chortle passed around the group at Claudine's expense.

"Are you okay?" Toby's hand settled on my shoulder.

"We should just go, then everyone else can enjoy themselves," I retorted, and then, noting his stricken expression, added, "Sorry, Tobe, I didn't mean to snap at you."

"Hey, that's all right. The stuff you were trying to say the other night, Jase and I didn't understand. Is she like it a lot?"

Is This Love?

I shrugged.

I shifted from one foot to the other, wondering how I should say it. I'm not sure who we thought we were fooling if we claimed to love each other. I'm not sure that we even liked each other.

"Claudine, we need to talk..." My words were cut short.

"Theo, I need to tell you something."

My initial thought was that she was going to beat me to it, but my relief was replaced by a sensation so intense that I stood paralysed and mute.

"I'm pregnant... We're going to have a baby."

My eyes dilated, mouth dropped open, slack with shock, while the blood pounded in my ears.

"How?"

"Even you aren't that dense."

"We never... we always... we used protection."

"They do split, you know."

"I can't do this now. I have to get out of here."

"Theo, you can't go. We need to discuss this."

"I need time to think. We'll talk when I get back."

Chapter 6

Gemma

"Thanks for letting me use your car while you're away." Susie glanced across from the driver's seat. "I wish I was going, too."

"I should have asked you."

"You need some time alone. I get that. It doesn't stop me from being a touch envious."

"Why don't you go away on your own?"

"I'm not that brave."

"I think you underestimate yourself."

"I'm thinking of changing careers – a nursery or

crèche. In the future, I'd like to foster a child."

"What's brought this on?"

"After everything, I think I need a rapid overhaul."

"A new hairstyle or a complete new wardrobe I get, but a new career?"

"I'm never going to be able to have a child of my own, but I've got so much love to give."

"And you think you're not that brave? I think it's a lovely idea."

"You do?"

The heat hit me as soon as I stepped onto the brilliant white pavement. Turning left out of the hotel, I walked the few hundred yards to the supermarket. The street was lined with every kind of shop, although most of them were as yet not open. Only the supermarkets were coming to life, and a few establishments that advertised the 'Full English'.

The air conditioning in the supermarket whirred overhead emitting a pleasant breeze. The rep on the coach the night before had informed us that Crete was experiencing a heat wave, which was evident already at this early hour. I picked up some hard bread, bottled water and a few other essentials.

"Kalimera," the dark-haired assistant smiled showing gaps in her teeth.

"Kalimera," I replied smiling back, while my tongue struggled to get around the word.

"Ti kaneis?"

"Sorry. English. I don't understand."

"Eeh Eenglish. Parakalo, welcome." Undeterred by my ignorance, she kept her smile warm.

She showed me the amount on the till "Exi Euro. Seex Euro."

"Efharisto." I mumbled.

After a lazy morning by the pool and a leisurely lunch, I went for a stroll along the beach. The cotton sundress I'd thrown on top of my bikini clung to me like a second skin as the sun soared overhead. A gentle breeze blew in from the sea, brushing my skin as my toes curled into the wet sand. Children splashed around enjoying the freedom and the cool water on such a hot day. Balls whizzed past, hitting the water and splashing me. A Frisbee sailed by, hissing past my face with a resonant whirr.

Two mischievous children were burying their father, who'd fallen asleep, leaving himself to their mercy. Playful little giggles escaped their lips when he woke up disorientated and unable to move. I left the beach front and walked along the main strip. After a while, I came to Star Beach, which was an eighteen-thirties heaven. Tons of bodies crammed onto the manmade surfaces, water sports jammed the sea, while music and foam pumped out.

"Hi. Are you here alone?" I glanced up from my book.

Two women of about my age sat on the neighbouring loungers.

"I'm Lucy. She's Jen," one of them said, flicking her dark red hair from her face.

They'd arrived in the early hours of the morning and were dying to check out the nightspots.

"Come with us," Jen insisted after we'd talked half of the afternoon away.

"Oh..." I hesitated.

"Come on, don't be such an old woman." Lucy's green eyes flashed a challenge.

"Okay," I laughed.

The coach deposited me at the entrance to the national park of Samaria, in the White Mountains. We were all herded together by our guide, who proceeded to give us a short pep talk about the terrain we would be traversing, the conditions and the need for safety.

"We'll meet up in six hours' time at Agia Roumeli, by the exit of the National Park. There are guards all along the route, who will provide any information or assistance you need. Drink plenty, enjoy the walk and please, be careful. Observe the rules. Enjoy the splendour of the gorge and mountains. For all those who are interested, Samaria Gorge was carved by mountain torrents making their way from the Libyan Sea. Although Greek mythology tells a different story."

He paused. "One of the Titans living in Crete slashed the land with his knife to create the gorge..."

"Must have been one helluva knife," a loud American woman interrupted.

The guide wore a tight smile as he continued, "It is said that Zeus, the god of the heavens, placed his throne on top of Mt. Gygilos and raced his chariot on the plain of Angathoti."

We began our descent. A stream of people traversed the gorge, snaking in and out at varying stages of their journey. The view of the rock face was indescribable. To say it was incredible didn't do it justice or conjure up the majesty of the craggy surface soaring into the sky. I tried to capture the view from every angle with my camera. We walked slowly down a well-built zigzag path. Our guide informed us that it was called 'The Wooden Stairs'. My guidebook called them by their Greek name, 'Xyloskalo'.

The path dropped a thousand feet in half a mile, and even at such an early stage I could feel the strain on my knees. The air was fresh with the smell of cypress and pine from the trees surrounding us, while wild herbs grew in nooks and crannies. I knocked back my water, stopping a number of times to refill the bottle from the fresh, clean springs we passed.

When we reached the streambed at the bottom of the valley, the way levelled out, but walking became tougher as there were now only loose rocks to walk on. The small pebbles were slippery. I had to tread with care.

I gazed up in wonder at the cliffs that towered aloft making me seem insignificant. Birds circled and scaled the overhangs, plunging down and rising again, with wings outstretched, to glide overhead. I explored the church of Aghios Nikolaos that was said to house the Sanctuary and Oracle of Apollo, and the church dedicated to Saint Maria of Egypt after whom the gorge was named.

Extracting plasters from my little rucksack, I applied them to the blisters dotting my feet as sweat raced down from my brow. I groaned, bemoaning the loss of sexy holiday feet, which had been replaced by scabby old-crone's ones.

After a pleasant fifteen-minute break, I continued my journey. My feet burned. I could feel the sharp little stones through the sturdy soles of my boots. Arriving at the gates, I looked around in stupefaction, trying to capture the dramatic fall of the cliff-side with my camera. The high rock walls of the gorge were narrow, about fifteen feet across. A stream of water cascaded through the gorge, the silvery flow bounding over the stones. Weary limbs and sore feet were forgotten as I gasped at the outstanding beauty.

Theo

The phone trilled, and in my mind I heard Claudine's irritating ringtone. She sounded wary as she answered the phone.

"Theo. So you've decided to speak to me."

"Yeah. I'm sorry for running out like that. I just... well, I can't take it in."

"You're not the only one."

"How long have you known? In fact, how many months pregnant are you?"

"We can't talk over the phone. Can you meet me?"

"I can't; Jake's on his way over right now."

"You mean you're still going?"

"I need to get my head around this. We'll talk when I get back. How many months did you say you were?"

I heard the hesitation in the silence that greeted my question, so I repeated it for a third time.

"Three months."

The horn sounded outside. I spied Jake's cherry red Porsche from the big bay windows.

"Jake's here. I've got to go. I'll call you." I hung up with relief, attempting to blank out the unwelcome news.

Jake sat waiting in the driver's seat, Gucci sunglasses pushed up to the top of his head, while I struggled to squeeze my old battered case in beside his Louis Vuitton.

"You ready?" he enquired.

"Get me away from here."

Jake thundered away from the curb. With the soft-top down, a breeze filled the car. He reached forward and flicked a Nickelback CD on. The volume cranked up, the music blasted with deafening resonance. I sat back, savouring the glimpse of freedom. I could go away and not come back, never have to face the stark reality that beckoned me.

After checking in, we headed in the direction of the bar, where Jake ordered a couple of pints. A group of blondes caught his eye. He switched on his charm mode. The three women, all caked in make-up and hidden under litres of peroxide, were perfect Jake material.

"Come on, let's go and join them," Jake said,

nodding in their direction, handing me a pint.

"What have I let myself in for?" I groaned in mock horror.

"You sound like your dappy bitch of a girlfriend. It's not too late to claim your freedom before you go. I'll even let you use my mobile." He reached into his trouser pocket and, with a dramatic flourish, proffered his phone to me.

If only I could make that call, claim my freedom. I pushed those thoughts aside.

"Hello, girls," Jake drawled. "Thought we'd come over and give you the pleasure of our company."

Two of the girls giggled and moved over to make room for Jake between them, but the other one stared at him with disdain. "Are you staying there all night or are you gonna give us the dubious pleasure of your company, too?"

I felt myself reddening, and muttered something as I took a seat next to her. I knew that I'd just met the female equivalent of Jake.

"So where are you girls off to?" Jake asked.

"Crete. I'm Candy. Bernie," she said, indicating the girl next to her, "and Mandy."

"We're going to Crete, too," he said with a knowing smile.

"Are you on the six o'clock flight, the same as us?" Bernie asked in amazement.

An amused smile passed between Jake and me.

Mandy's sensual lips pouted. She looked as though she wanted to devour me. I shifted in my chair. She appeared to be a very confident woman, very much in control and used to getting what she wanted.

"What resort are you staying in?" she asked.

"Malia," I answered.

"We're staying there, too. We should hook up. Or better still, we can check out the membership for the mile-high club." Her tone dropped to a fondling purr.

I spluttered on a mouthful of beer and proceeded to have an embarrassing coughing fit. Jake watched with evident amusement.

"I was thinking 'bout taking out membership myself. We should hook up," Jake drawled, his eyes sweeping down to the display of cleavage and large firm breasts threatening to spill out.

"The offer isn't open to you," she retorted. "What do you say?" She placed her hand on my inner thigh and rubbed in an upwards motion.

"I have a girlfriend." I removed her hand and placed it back on her lap, silencing the little voice that added, *and a baby on the way.*

"I don't want to be your girlfriend. I just wanna sit on your cock."

My eyes met Jake's in amusement. This was one cheap tart.

"No."

"What she doesn't know won't hurt her," she crooned.

"No." I moved her hand more firmly this time.

"Then why don't you just fuck off! You're unnatural," she growled, her face turning red.

I stood up quickly; the chair fell backwards with a resounding crash. The other girls fluttered around in an attempt to detain Jake.

"What part of you is natural?"

"Nothing worse than a pushy slag," Jake snarled at her.

"You weren't that fussy a minute ago."

"I'm not; I'll sleep with any old dog. My mate here is choosier."

I leant against the bar as Jake sauntered over. For a moment, I considered confiding in Jake, but the moment passed with his next words.

"I told you that you should have finished with Claudine first."

"My choosing not to sleep around shouldn't affect you in the least," I ground out between gritted teeth.

"Yeah, well, I could have had the ditzy twins."

"They aren't twins."

"Both as thick as pig shit and ripe for some action." He winked and tilted his head in a sardonic attempt at an apology.

I laughed.

The bar was crowded. Smoke wreathed in thick spirals

above our heads. Loud laughter and babble bounced from one end of the room to another. Scantily dressed women paraded around in various states of intoxication. Jake's eyes roamed over bare legs and cleavages, a grin playing about his lips.

"Like being in a sweet shop," Jake drawled as I passed him his bottle of beer.

"Don't tell me – pic 'n' mix, and you're going to try one of each?"

Brilliant white teeth grinned back at me.

"I'm going to do my best."

"Watch out that you don't get sick."

"Don't worry, I've always been able to handle my sweets."

A long-legged, black-haired woman flashed him a come-and-get-me look. She managed to achieve the dubious acclaim of being the first in his long line of conquests in Crete. Although abstaining, I didn't lack opportunity, and enjoyed the attention. Relaxing as the drinks flowed, I felt the worries and stresses drop from me as I enjoyed the risqué banter. I allowed myself to be dragged onto the dance floor by a small group of women who were trying to work out who could coax me into their bed. Needless to say, none of them did. At some ridiculous hour in the morning, my head thumping and the music echoing, I crawled fully clothed into my bed at the hotel while Jake headed in the opposite direction with the luscious Sonya.

I awoke to a resounding banging on the door. My eyes flew open, but the pull of gravity tried to press my lids back down.

"Theo, open up," Jake shouted.

I tumbled from the bed.

A sharp pain attacked my frontal lobes making me wince as I lurched to the door. Jake stood leaning against the doorjamb, grinning.

"You look worse than I do."

"Good night?"

"I'll tell you about it over breakfast."

I glanced at my watch.

"Late brunch, then." Jake shrugged.

"I'm going for a shower first," I said, heading for the slightly dingy, damp-mottled bathroom. *We could have done better than this place.*

Jake winked at the dusky waitress who took our order down on her notepad. Her solemn face lit up as she smiled back.

"Is there anyone you don't hit on?"

"No." Jake laughed as I shook my head.

"Are you seeing whatsername from last night again?" I asked.

"Doubtful. What was her name anyway?"

"Do you ever plan on settling down?" I asked.

"Not sure that I've found anyone worth settling with," Jake replied.

"Not sure?"

"What's so special 'bout settling down to a nagging wife and squawking kids? Anyway, I've got too many skirts left to chase."

The words 'squawking kids' reverberated in my brain. I shook my head to clear the unwelcome thoughts; there was time enough to consider the implications without ruining my holiday. The waitress turned up carrying two plates groaning under the weight of a Full English.

The restaurant was a typical Brits-abroad hangout. The walls were draped with St. George's cross bunting, football paraphernalia and pewter tankards hung from the bar. As I polished off the last sausage on the plate, I began to feel a bit more human.

We spent the rest of the day relaxing by the pool. Jake made his way back from the bar carrying the two pints, weaving in and out of the sunbeds, taking a more circuitous route than was needed as he checked out the scantily clad bodies stretched out, shimmering with lotion.

"Do you need a hand?" he asked a woman who was bent over, rubbing oil into her legs.

"You're the one who needs a hand," she answered in kind, and then turned back to her legs while Jake walked on.

I sat on the sunbed, pint in hand, relaxed and

enjoying the occasional fresh play of wind in the searing heat. Afternoon shadows encroached on the other side of the pool. The sun sparkled on the water while a swimmer caused tiny ripples to arch outwards, disturbing the otherwise serene, still pool.

The next morning, I left Jake sleeping off the excesses of the night before while I went to explore the area. I spotted a sign that drew my attention as I wandered down the quiet streets with the sun blazing down on me. On impulse, I headed towards the red-painted sign and enquired about the price. After settling on a 110cc scooter, I headed towards the impressive mountain range that towered above us. Coasting along the potted road, I took in the exquisite view. Tranquillity settled onto my shoulders, and for the first time in ages, I felt free. The cool breeze brushed my arms as the scooter ascended the mountain pass. I stopped at a clearing and pushed the bike onto the grass verge. Leaning against an outcrop of the mountain, I watched a gecko delve in and out of the clefts in the rock.

I'm going to be a dad. The thought of spending the rest of my life with Claudine horrified me. *She's three months pregnant. How long has she known? She's been strange since our short-lived split. She couldn't have known then, could she?* There was something nagging at the back of my mind. *Just because you're having a child together doesn't mean you have to be a couple. Do you really want your child brought up in a broken home?* Thoughts tumbled around inside my head.

Taking a deep breath, I filled my lungs with air before expelling it with a mournful sigh. A bird took flight, startled by my unexpected noise. I watched its journey until it was out of sight. I wasn't going to be able to make a decision now. I needed more time to consider everything. *I have to talk to her, too. Does she even want to keep the baby?* For a heart-stopping moment, I realised that, while I didn't want Claudine, I couldn't contemplate the thought of her aborting my baby.

The path wound around the mountains and led to a quaint village in the foothills. I parked the scooter, in desperate need to stretch my legs. The old-world charm of this village appealed to me; the buff-coloured stone buildings with flowers creeping up the walls and door frames made me feel that I'd stepped back in time.

A toothless crone sat outside on a timber chair, a faded blue cushion perched between her and the structure. Knitting needles clattered away, a brown length of wool hanging between her knees over the black shapeless dress that shrouded her ageing form. Her keen eyes pierced through me. She smiled a wordless response to a middle-aged man who called out a greeting as he ambled past. A scrawny albino cat arched its back and rubbed against my legs. I moved away. It looked disease-ridden, with patches of fur missing.

As I meandered down the streets, a rustic Taverna caught my eye, precipitating a growl from my stomach. I'll go there for lunch, I thought just as a full-bodied laugh grabbed my attention; it was almost like a caress. *The Cretan sun must have gone to my head.*

Her hair was tied back, with bits tumbling around

her face, framing her long, delicate features. Her long legs – legs that I'd imagined in my fantasies – were there before me. My breath caught in my throat as warmth spread through my loins. I tried to convince myself that I was suffering from the onset of heatstroke at the slight trembling that shook my body.

I closed my eyes in an attempt to blot her out. *When I open them, she'll be gone, a figment of my imagination.* She spun around, the red dress flapping around her thighs. My eyes travelled up her lean torso, over her full breasts and elegant neck. Our eyes locked, engaging in a fierce interplay. She shook her head as though, like me, she couldn't believe it. Standing about six feet away from me, she blinked, breaking the spell, and spun on her heels. As she turned, she stumbled on the uneven paving. Galvanised into action, I caught her before she fell. One hand grabbed her elbow, and the other reached around her waist. A shudder swept through me when my hands encountered the silky softness of her skin. She turned back. We stood inches apart, her eyes misty. A longing so intense buffeted me that I almost reached across to kiss those full pouting lips.

Grasping her arm, I stopped her from leaving again. My hands itched to trace the lines of her face. I felt shaken by the sensations that reverberated through me from the merest touch.

"Theo," she rasped, "let go. Let me go."

I shook my head. "Come to lunch with me?" I indicated the Taverna.

Her eyes dilated like those of an animal caught in a snare. *Do I pose that much of a threat?*

"Please."

I knew then, like she did, that what I asked was madness. I couldn't spend time alone with her; I desired her too much. My God, if Claudine hadn't dropped that bombshell on me. She tilted her head to the left in acceptance. Too late. *I can't back out now.*

We walked the few yards in silence. The restaurant was fronted by a large gnarled tree, with flower pots stretching along one wall and bougainvillea creeping up the cool whitewashed walls. A thatched umbrella sat in the corner, providing shade over the small cluster of tables. I studied her profile as I sat across from her. Silence descended. The waiter came over to take our order. It annoyed me, as he eyed Gemma with evident interest. She smiled at him as she handed back her menu.

"How are you?" I asked, a lame attempt to start a conversation. "You're looking great."

"Thanks. Yes, erm... I'm fine," she breathed, then almost as an afterthought added, "And you?"

"I'm well. I still can't believe I've bumped into you here. Are you here with your boyfriend?"

"I don't have a boyfriend."

"I... I thought you were seeing someone…"

"It was only a couple of dates." She shrugged.

Silence enveloped us. The flickering flame on the candle, sitting in the jar on the table, danced a lonely beat. I tried thinking of something to say. Gemma stared at a point somewhere over my left shoulder. *She isn't making this easy. Damn her. It's not as though I've done anything wrong.*

"I heard you got back with your ex." She smiled doe-like at me.

I acknowledged her words with a slight inclination of my head.

"Is she here in Crete with you?"

"No, I came with Jake."

I had an urge to tell her the shocking news that Claudine had dumped on me before I left for Greece, news that I hadn't shared with anyone else, but I stayed silent. Selections of Greek dishes were placed before us. The mood between us changed as we relaxed. A comfortable silence accompanied the meal. I watched as she used her long tapering fingers to pick off a piece of meat. She placed it in her mouth, then sucked the juices from her fingers in an unselfconscious manner. I found this innocent gesture disturbingly erotic and had to turn away so she wouldn't see my eyes glazing.

"I've hired a scooter for the day. Do you want to join me for a ride around the island?"

I'm not sure what prompted me to ask, but I knew it was wrong. I should be distancing myself from her.

She nodded as a warm smile lit up her face.

We ambled along, marvelling at the ancient stonework and the quaint atmosphere of the whitewashed hamlet.

Gemma stopped to take photographs. "I'm a keen photographer," she confided.

"Any good?"

She wrinkled her nose and shrugged.

I grabbed the sleek silver camera from her.

"You've not gone digital?"

"I nearly bought one in Duty-Free but thought I needed to do some more research rather than my usual impulse-buy."

"Go on," I urged, framing her in front of a house with flowers creeping all over the outside. "I'll take you."

Before I had a chance to take the picture, an old lady approached and grinned widely, showing a couple of teeth and pink gums. She insisted that she take a picture of Gemma and me. I knew it was a mistake as soon as I put my arm around Gemma's shoulder.

Afterwards, we moved apart as though we'd been burnt. The crone told us we were a lovely couple, and we didn't correct her.

We rode through the mountains, through similar villages and back along the seafront. The vista that spread around us was breathtaking. I couldn't help comparing her refreshing attitude to Claudine's materialistic one.

Gemma's long legs rested against the back of mine while her arms encircled my waist and her breasts pressed into my back. It took all my willpower not to reach out to touch her, to respond to the urgent sensations surging through me. Instead, I focused on steering the scooter along the winding roads.

I dropped her off at her apartment block in Hersonissos. She swung her legs off the bike, allowing me a fleeting glimpse of red lace knickers, eliciting a groan. *Stupid fool, she must've heard that.* I ached to follow the path my eyes had taken.

"Do you want to meet later for a drink?" she asked.

"I don't think we should. It wouldn't be right."

Is This Love?

I watched her walk away fighting the desire to follow, to stop her, hold her in my arms and make love to her. Instead, I turned the keys and eased open the throttle. I rode away with the realisation that I'd let another opportunity for happiness slip through my fingers.

Chapter 7

Gemma

The taxi driver laughed and teased me about my pronunciation of Koutoulafari. He was a real comic of a man with a round florid face, a beaming smile and booming laugh. He amused me with his well-stocked library of anecdotes and descriptions of the people he'd driven in his taxi. When we reached the village, he dropped me at the black well in the middle of the road, which doubled as a roundabout.

"Koutulafari is to the left and Piskopiano to the right." He indicated with his hands.

I thanked him, dropping in a generous tip.

"However many people I drive in my taxi through the years, you sure are the preetiest."

I laughed at his outrageous compliment and cheeky wink. When I spun around, I saw Theo. All the illusions I'd had that I was over him were shattered in that moment. My heart began pounding, and my legs turned to jelly. He looked equally shocked. *I have to get away.*

The taxi pulled away, and in my haste I stumbled on a loose brick on the floor, pitching forward. The ground came up to meet me but I didn't hit it. Strong arms gripped me from behind, pulling me close.

His touch burnt me with little frissons of desire. I ached to turn around and touch him, to trace the outline of his face, fleshy red lips, and the muscles rippling on his masculine torso. Uncomfortable with these thoughts, I twisted away from his arms and turned to face him. I fought back tears. *How the hell can I be feeling like this?*

"Thank you," I mumbled.

Theo whispered my name making it sound like a caress. He grabbed me for a second time, to stop me leaving. For a moment, I thought I read a trace of the same emotions in his eyes, but I rejected the thought as fanciful. *I'm not his beloved girlfriend. I'm the... ex-potential-one-night-stand.* I cringed, but I had to be honest with myself. This hearts-and-flowers thing, so unlike my usual self, was all in my imagination.

"Theo," I managed to say, "let go. Let me go."

Instead, I allowed him to talk me into accompanying him to a Taverna. The setting was more romantic than any other I'd ever been in before, the mountains as a backdrop on one side and a glimpse of the sea on the other. When Theo asked me if I was in Crete with my boyfriend, it took a while until the penny dropped, as I remembered Chris' e-mail.

"I don't have a boyfriend."

I'm sure it wasn't my imagination when I saw the leap of something in his eyes and the way he stumbled over his explanation. We sat through another uncomfortable silence. "Chris told me you were back with your girlfriend."

He acknowledged the truth of this statement by a slight inclination of his head. It was probably my imagination, but I thought he looked sad. Why was he on holiday with Jake and not his girlfriend? Something niggled away at me. He seemed a decent sort, so what was he doing there with me? Or maybe I'd just become lousy at evaluating people.

When he asked me to go for a ride on his scooter, I accepted with alacrity, but my inner voice wouldn't be silenced. *He's got a girlfriend. What are you doing? You think I don't know that? Where's the harm in going for a ride? Are you stupid?* The internal battle raged.

That night I drowned my sorrows alone at the bar until Lucy came over.

"Mind if I join you?" she asked. Without waiting for a response, she sat down in the chair next to me.

"I won't be good company," I warned.

"I'll take my chances." She ordered some drinks.

"Jen's got a tummy bug – something she ate earlier,

she thinks."

I made the appropriate sympathetic noises.

"If you want to talk, I'm a good listener."

"Thanks," I said, feeling no inclination to confide. It didn't portray me in a good light.

The cocktails slid down our throats. The sweet exotic flavours stimulated our taste buds, cultivating a desire for more.

At first, Lucy spent most of the time talking, telling me about her life in Brighton, friends, work, exes and an extremely hectic social calendar. Lucy and Jen had been friends since childhood, living next door to each other. I laughed at some of her anecdotes.

I knew the time had come to confide in Lucy. I needed to get it out of my system even if she did think badly of me. I told her about my first meeting with Theo right through to him dropping me off that evening.

"What are you going to do?"

The barman hovered, watching the level of our drinks. Apart from an elderly couple who seemed to be nursing the same drink all evening, we were the only people in the hotel bar.

"There's nothing I can do." Disappointment threaded my words like veins. "He has a girlfriend."

"There seems to be a connection between you both." Lucy reached over and stroked my arm.

"How can I have such strong feelings? I know nothing about him. I've never believed in love at first sight; it can't be that."

"So where does that leave you?"

"I'm just going to have to try to forget him. Two more, please, barman."

Theo

"Double whiskey and two pints," I told the barmaid.

I felt Jake's eyes on me while I knocked back a double and handed him his pint. It was two nights since meeting Gemma, and I'd spent both inebriated.

"Steady on, Theo," Jake cautioned when I ordered another double. "This isn't like you. What are you trying to do?"

"Just enjoying my freedom."

The nights and days passed in a drunken stupor. I drank to forget what I didn't want to face, but nothing seemed to blot out my thoughts. My nightmares merely sharpened. I told myself I was suffering from sexual frustration, but I couldn't achieve relief no matter how hard I tried. If I were more like Jake, I would have slept with Gemma and got her out of my system, and not given another thought to my pregnant girlfriend. In fact, Jake wouldn't have been stupid enough to be in my predicament. At this thought, I ordered another whiskey chaser.

At first, Jake turned down a dozen or so tempting offers, to accompany me back to the hotel room and keep a watchful eye on me. I think he'd had enough by the third night; he took up his pursuit of the fairer sex with renewed vigour.

Sunday mid-day dawned. I lay in a virtual comatose state in my bed and realised I'd been out of it since seeing Gemma on Wednesday. Sickened by this display of self-pity and the waste of my holiday, I reached for my mobile phone and collapsed back onto the pillow. Switching the phone on, I waited while it picked up the local Greek network. Message after message burst through. Each loud ring tone penetrated my skull, hurting an already tender brain.

Claudine's texts seemed never-ending. I'd

promised to contact her daily and hadn't done so for five days. Messages ranging from, *Hi Theo. How's your holiday? I'm missing you like crazy. x Claudine to Why the silence? You'd better have a good explanation. This silence isn't good for the baby.* I hated the ease with which she used the baby already as a guilt trip.

Another text followed from Cass: *Theo, C's worried. Bet u havn gud tme, txt me let me no u ok.*

A voice message beeped through. I listened with growing concern. *"Claudine's just told me the news. I can't believe it. I think I can understand you going off the radar but please let me know you're all right. We can talk about your impending fatherhood when you get back."* Anger ripped through me. *How dare she tell my sister?*

Havn gud tme, soz 4 silnce, spk soon. I sent this to both Claudine and Cass.

I spent the remainder of the afternoon by the pool soaking up the sun, shades pressed close to my delicate eyes. Jake joined me later.

"Back to normal?" He threw himself down onto the empty sunbed next to mine.

"I think I'll take it a bit easier tonight," I said.

"Yeah, I think I could do with a quieter night myself."

"Are you flagging?" I grinned.

"You could say that."

"A few beers in the hotel bar?"

"Sounds good."

I stood outside the hotel, the warm morning sun filtering through the scattering of meagre clouds. This purpose-build resort was characterless. No white-washed walls or blue-domed roofs coloured the vista. Buildings specifically built for the drunken crowd who visited and on whom culture would be wasted, most of who wouldn't even see daylight. Jake had turned down the opportunity to see a bit of the island. *And you've been better?*

I stepped up onto the coach; one seat at the front

remained. We drove to Aghios Nicholaos to catch the boat that was going to take us across to the island of Spinalonga, the last leper colony in Greece. The forty-five-minute journey passed quickly as I relaxed and enjoyed the scenery. We drove through craggy mountain ranges battered by age and the elements. One caught my eye. It was etched on the skyline as though it were painted in watercolours.

The harbour bustled with activity. Vessels ranging from tourist excursion boats to private yachts were moored there. A sleek white liner towered above all the rest, bobbing in the cool blue water.

A strange prickling sensation washed over me, as though I was being watched. I swung around, my eyes sweeping the length of the coach. I turned back to gaze out to sea but this time I failed to appreciate the sun highlighting the waves, the slap of the water against the sides of the boat, or the clank of the rope against the mast. We'd be spending another day together. *You can always sit at opposite ends of the boat.*

"Hello, Theo," Gemma said, coming to stand

beside me.

We stood in companionable silence staring out to sea for a while.

The guide indicated our boat, and the group surged forward to board, all eager for the best position. Without hesitation, I reached across and took Gemma's hand. My resolve and beliefs all seemed in that instant unreal and unreasonable as I slipped towards the path that destiny had laid before me. This was when I should have insisted upon separation. I helped Gemma onto the gangplank and was rewarded by a glimpse of her firm upper thighs and buttocks. I followed behind her like a slavering dog trailing its master.

"What made you pick this trip?" I asked as we settled on Gemma's beach towel.

"Well, it has it all: culture, sea and sun; a must-have for a sun worshipper."

"A sun worshipper?"

"Oh yes. Hours in the sun – pure heaven." She adopted a breathless voice that made me smile.

"Is this your only trip?"

"I went to Samaria Gorge, too – which was incredible – and brought back dozens of souvenir blisters as a memento."

"I take it you won't be handing them out as gifts when you get home."

Little lines crinkled at the side of her eyes, which danced with amusement as she parried my thrust with ease.

"Only if you help me pick them."

I roared.

"It wasn't that funny." She giggled.

I watched, mesmerised, as she removed her dress and, with expert precision, massaged sun lotion all over her exquisite body.

"Do you want some?" she broke my erotic train of thoughts.

I looked at her, perplexed.

"Do you want some lotion?"

She watched me with amusement. I got the impression that she'd known the direction my thoughts had taken. I took the proffered bottle without a word and made a ham-fisted attempt at covering my back.

"Here, let me."

I lay down on my stomach. Long fingers massaged cream into my back and legs, causing me to tremble.

"That'll do," I said, struggling for control.

"Dolphins!" someone exclaimed with a high-pitched squeal.

Gemma jumped up and rushed to the side of the boat. "Come on," she invited with an expression of rapt excitement as she reached for my hand.

The captain switched off the engines. The dolphins swam up, playing hide-and-seek with us as they rose out of the sea and dived under again. One flipped over in a perfect arc before descending below the surface again.

Gemma's face broke into a grin as she turned to me. On impulse, I pulled her into my arms. My barriers crumbled as I succumbed to the exquisite sensations. Her eyes glazed and her parted lips trembled. I pulled away as reality hit me.

I stayed where I was while Gemma returned to lay stretched out on a towel, face down, looking out to sea. My knuckles whitened as I gripped the thick, knotted rigging. I watched without interest as the boat cut through the waves while I tried to control the sensations coursing through me.

The boat pulled into a secluded cove. I dived with exhilaration into the clear water. As I resurfaced, I flipped over onto my back and floated. I saw Gemma preparing to dive off next. Her body made a graceful bow as she descended through the air before hitting the water, breaking the surface. I held my breath until I saw her head come up. Her long blond hair had come loose and floated around her like a halo. I flopped back onto my belly and began a frantic swim in an attempt to block out my sensual fantasies. Minutes later, I pulled my exhausted body out of the water, my breaths coming in gasps from the exertion. Overindulgence of alcohol and lack of exercise were taking their toll. My toes curled into the warm sand. The coarse, grainy particles clung to my wet legs when I sat down.

Is This Love?

I'd thought that the water and exercise had cooled my ardour until I saw Gemma reach the shallows. I watched spellbound as she strode like a *Bond* girl, through the shallows, water dripping from her bronzed body. She tossed her hair back, lifted her arms and brushed the clinging tendrils from her face. Her breasts tilted upwards, pert, taut nipples showing through the flimsy material of her bikini. I groaned, my fingers aching to touch her satin-smooth skin. I hardened in response to this image. Her face lit up with a smile. I'd never met a woman so delighted with the simple things in life.

"That was great," she gasped between breaths.

The fortress at Spinalonga was built in 1579. It was occupied by the Venetians and the Turks before it became a home for the lepers from Crete and beyond. The sun blazed down on the Venetian fortification that rose majestically in the sky and was the main focal point of the island. We walked through a dark, dismal tunnel with iron gates leading out into the bright sunshine and to a large house with wooden doors, shutters and a balcony. Ruins and long-forgotten shops with blue and green shutters were now faded from age and neglect.

We hung back, trying to get a sense of the island. It was humbling to walk in this place that had seen so much suffering. These people had carved out their own way of life away from the rat race. People had fallen in love, married and had children, a question mark hanging over them; we all know one day we would leave this earth but these people already had their warrants signed – no doubt as to their cause of death. They'd chosen to fight, to make conditions better for themselves. I wasn't sure, had I been in their place, I would have had that strength.

The island was known as the island of pain. I couldn't help but think the lepers had at least suffered in an environment of great beauty. Other people through the ages had lived out their agonies in much less savoury places.

"Will you come out to dinner with me tonight?" I asked on impulse.

Chapter 8

Gemma

I stepped off the coach in Aghios Nikolaos and walked towards Theo, whose back was to me. A white ribbed t-shirt cleaved to his torso, showing off the muscles on his arms. We greeted each other with a reserve borne of the situation we found ourselves in.

When he reached for my hand, it felt like the most natural thing on earth, but I paused. From that viewpoint, it made my behaviour worse. It wasn't as though I acted on impulse – on the contrary, I did think, and yet I still curled my fingers around his.

We walked together like any other couple, except we weren't. A proprietorial surge flooded me as I spotted two women eyeing him. But he wasn't mine. This moment was stolen, and I was the thief. *What a gentleman,* I thought as he handed me onto the plank that led to the boat.

Slathering sun lotion on, I was conscious of Theo's scrutiny. He made a mess of rubbing it onto his back so I commandeered the bottle. I discovered my mistake the moment my fingers encountered the warm, soft skin on his back. I tried to be professional, imagining I was giving an impersonal massage to a client at the salon; it didn't work.

I visualised my lips blazing the same trail down his back that my fingers had taken. My hands travelled along the taut, quivering muscles at the back of his thighs and calves. Theo moved away, breaking my erotic train of thought; I was sure he, too, was disturbed.

Someone sighted dolphins, so I dashed over to

look, calling for Theo to follow.

The dolphins put on a wonderful aquatic display. Theo pulled me closer, holding me in an embrace as we shared this moment. I clung to him, legs trembling. Tilting my head upwards, I longed for his lips to descend on mine. Theo dipped his head then, eyes dilating, pulled away. He apologised. *Is he apologising for holding me or that it can go no further?* Theo stayed away from me after that.

I watched as Theo's body cut through the air and broke the surface of the water. My turn to dive came next. I stood at the edge of the boat, frozen. An attack of nerves fluttered inside my stomach as my brain registered fear. I wasn't scared of swimming in the sea, just diving in. Normally, I would climb down the steps and ease myself in, but when Theo flipped over onto his back, I gritted my teeth, hardened my resolve and threw myself off the boat. The warm salty water stung my eyes and throat.

The sheer beauty of the imposing stronghold rising up

out of the island caused my breath to catch in my throat. The sun shone down on the sand-coloured stone of the fortress, peeping through the open archways. A shiver swept down my spine as we walked through the tunnel; was this where the lepers entered when they arrived on the island? Were those imposing iron gates a bar to stop people leaving? We ambled along, soaking up the atmosphere.

I reached out a hand to touch the thick stone walls that held and hid thousands of stories in their depths. It could tell of the Turkish occupation of this island, which came to an end in 1903, to be replaced by a leper colony, of the brave people who suffered from such a debilitating disease that ate away at them.

They'd been feared by society, who believed the sign of leprosy was an indication of impurity. Society dreaded to be near these carriers in case they caught the disease, so they gave them an island to live and die on away from the rest of mankind. It was not discovered until much later that leprosy only spread through contact, from a wound on the leper to a fresh open wound of an unaffected person. Would such knowledge have changed the narrow-mindedness?

In many ways, nothing had changed. We thought ourselves civilised, better informed, but were the carriers of modern diseases and illnesses treated any better?

I enjoyed walking around the island with Theo. We talked about what we saw and how these people must have suffered. It was refreshing to find a man who was sensitive enough to care about other people's suffering and yet lost none of his masculinity in doing so.

"Come to dinner with me tonight?"

My answer was inevitable. He drew me like a magnet; I was powerless to say no.

I slipped the new black dress over my head. The soft material skimmed my body like silk. *Is this a date?* Wracked with guilt on the one hand, I was filled with excitement on the other. Applying a swathe of beige and browns to my face, with the customary slash of pink to my lips, I spritzed a generous cloud of Chanel no. 5 just as someone knocked on the door. *He can't be here this early.*

"Ooh, look at you," Jen said while Lucy smiled her appreciation.

"Come on in." I opened the door wider.

"We were just coming to see if you wanted to go out on your last night," Lucy said. "Looks like you've already got plans."

"I'll get the wine."

I poured three glasses of red wine and handed Lucy and Jen theirs.

"You've got a hot date with Theo, haven't you?" Jen smiled.

I filled them in on the details of our meeting while slipping into black heeled sandals. With time to spare, we took our wine out onto the veranda.

A knock on the door disturbed my equilibrium.

"He's here." My voice shook.

"Let him in, then," Lucy laughed.

"You look lovely," Theo said, smiling warmly from the

doorway.

My pulse quickened. He stood on the threshold before me, an approachable god-like man in tight black trousers and a white fitted shirt, the two top buttons open, showing tanned skin. After brief introductions, I walked Jen and Lucy to the door, hugging them tight amidst promises to keep in contact.

"Where do you want to eat?" Theo asked.

"There's Italian and Mexican down the road; I can recommend both."

"You choose," Theo insisted.

"Italian it is, then."

The dark-haired waiter held the chair out for me and, in a dramatic gesture, flung out my napkin before placing it on my lap. Theo ordered a bottle of red wine while I studied the menu. I ordered breaded mozzarella sticks, Theo plumped for dough balls, and we both chose Linguine.

"When are you going home?" I asked after the waiter departed.

"Monday. It'll be good to get back and sort myself

out; non-stop drinking is playing havoc with me. I was wiped out after that swim earlier. What about you?"

"The swim or when I'm going home?" I teased.

"Both."

"It wiped me out, too, and my flight is at midnight tomorrow night." I pulled a face. "I could do with another week in the sun."

"Greedy."

"Absolutely."

A single red Gerbera sat in a small white ceramic vase between us; a tiny droplet of water rested heavily on a petal, threatening to drop. I focused on it for a few seconds as I tried to stop myself from grinning stupidly. The linguine arrived on huge square plates, fresh and colourful. I was never at my best twirling spaghetti, and it provided much amusement. I watched as Theo's nimble fingers twisted the long strands like an expert, and the effortless way he brought the food to his lips.

"Dessert?" he asked as the dinner plates were cleared away.

I hesitated. *Dare I eat any more?*

"Come on," Theo cajoled, "you have to have dessert."

I held my hands up in defeat. "You've twisted my arm."

"Didn't take much twisting," Theo joked.

"Oh, well, in that case... I can't possibly eat a dessert. I'll get terribly fat."

"That's true; I can see your dress is straining to keep you in as it is," Theo responded with a twinkle in his eye.

"Oy, you." I kicked him gently under the table. "Are you saying I'm fat?" I grinned at this harmless banter.

"Has issues around weight," Theo gibed in the feigned-serious tone that a therapist might use. "I'll have to remember that in the future..." He trailed off as he realised what he'd said.

We had no future, and the jest seemed to sober us. Theo ordered another bottle of red, and we both made an effort to recapture the silliness from earlier, but the tension between us now was charged with a sexual quality. Dessert, a creamy mouth-watering ice-cream, was devoured, the last dregs of wine disappeared, and we each had an Irish coffee, the bottom of the glasses clear now the liquid had gone. We couldn't sit there any longer. I needed to be away from him before I broke every rule in the book.

I hadn't expected him to escort me back to my room. We stood outside the door, both of us unsure. His eyes blazed with raw hunger. He stepped tentatively towards me, trembling. Butterflies pranced inside me. I locked my hands together in a nervous clasp. I could feel his nearness, his lips close to mine. I tilted my head. The charge surged between us. Theo's warm lips descended on mine, soft and probing. The momentum built and the kiss deepened.

We pulled apart, reluctant and breathless. My fingers shook as I tried to insert the key into the lock. I felt his warm breath on my neck as he moved closer, reaching his hand out to steady mine. He emitted a soft groan when his lips grazed my neck. His other hand reached around my waist to pull me against his lean, firm body. Theo's erection pressed into me, and I longed to reach behind me to touch him. He took the keys from me and opened the door.

"We shouldn't be doing this," he whispered in a voice choked with emotion.

"I know. I've never done this kind of thing before." I didn't want him to think I was that kind of woman.

"Me neither."

It was as though we believed that, by saying those words, it became acceptable.

"We can stop now if you want," I whispered, holding my breath, waiting for his response.

He reached out and took my hand, drawing me to him. I stretched up to trace his face and took his upper lip between mine, sucking tenderly. His hands encircled my waist before sliding down to caress my buttocks, pressing me closer to him till our bodies cleaved together. His fingers ran down the backs of my thighs. He tugged my dress up while my tongue slipped into his mouth, teasing him.

Theo lifted me up, my legs wrapping around his hips, the heel of my sandals pressing into the back of his thigh. His hand trailed over my back, shoulders and neck. Light, gentle caresses alternated with strong, firm strokes. With a charming reverence, he slid the strap off my shoulder and traced a path from my collarbone to my breast. Theo growled low in his throat, murmuring my name. He pulled me up higher, lowering his head to flick his tongue over my taut nipples.

He strode towards the bed and lowered me down. With slow, deliberate movements I unbuttoned his shirt, placing kisses down his torso. Holding myself back, I aroused him with my lips and tongue. Theo reached for my hair and pulled it from its bindings. As my light touches travelled towards his navel, his fingers became entwined in my hair, and he jerked them, pulling my head back.

Theo's intense gaze burned into me as he reached down, gathering up a handful of my dress and slipping it up and over my body. Languorous fingertips, lips and tongue stimulated me. I arched and writhed under his probing, longing to be joined in the ultimate ecstasy. When I couldn't take any more, I pulled him to me. Our bodies twisted together, rising and falling, arching and pressing together, giving and seeking pleasure.

We lay back sated. I gazed at Theo, basking in our pleasure. Theo's expression mirrored mine. I snuggled into his arms, placing my hand on his chest in a proprietorial manner. Theo's fingers idly traced a path along my arm. A comfortable silence enveloped us. I had never been happier. Like all stolen moments, though, it couldn't last, and there had to be recompense for the offence committed. Gullibility is not a trait I would credit myself with but laying there in his arms, I assumed everything had changed.

Lazy fingers trailed up his chest. "How are we going to manage the long-distance thing?"

His expression changed. He didn't exactly pull away from me, but his fingers inched away from my skin, and I noticed the ever-so-subtle tightening of his jawline.

"What do you mean?" His voice was guarded.

Like the sharp crack when a tree lost a bough in a storm, the realisation struck me. "This is a one-night-stand."

My fingers ceased their exploration, now hovering like a question mark over Theo's body. I'd presumed my feelings were shared in equal measure by Theo, which had led us both to betraying our morals.

I laughed; a mirthless snort. I'd swallowed everything he'd fed me. I rose from the bed, the desire to cover myself strong. Perhaps he hadn't fooled me; maybe I'd fooled myself. His hand reached out to touch me, but I shied away.

"You should go." I tried to keep my voice even.

"I asked you to come back with me that first night." His voice charred the air between us.

Spinning around in disgust, I snarled, "I can't believe you just said that."

"I didn't mean that the way it sounded."

"Just exactly what did you mean? Actually, I don't

think I want to hear it. I want you to go."

Theo rose from the bed. With hasty, disjointed movements, he pulled on his clothes. Despite my anger, I couldn't help but watch his bronzed body as it disappeared under layers of clothing.

"I do want to be with you." His words were faint. The poignant way they were spoken pulled at something deep within.

Looking at him was nearly my undoing. I clenched my jaws. I wasn't going to let him see my tears. He walked towards me. His next words opened up a chasm that I plummeted into.

"My girlfriend... Claudine... is pregnant."

"What the...?" Tears engulfed my cheeks as I pushed him away from me. "Get out!"

I couldn't believe what had just happened. My stomach churned as huge sobs streamed out. I turned into my pillow, seeking comfort only to be assailed by the scent Theo had left imprinted on it. I gathered it to me, holding it tightly, inhaling. My breath became trapped in my throat as I struggled for air. I wouldn't see him again. I wanted to hate him. I think a part of me did but, somehow, it didn't stop me wanting him.

Theo

I arrived at her hotel five minutes early. *I shouldn't have come.* Unwilling to let it end there, I convinced myself that I'd act like a perfect gentleman. My convictions were reinforced. I believed I was armoured against the assault of desire and temptation. Gemma opened the door wearing a black slip dress that moulded to her incredible figure, and black high-heeled sandals. *What am I doing here? Maybe I should leave now.* I made the mistake of looking at her long, lithe legs and found myself drawn further, like gravity making the planets orbit the sun.

Gemma led me to an Italian restaurant that

couldn't be distinguished from any other on the strip other than by the name. We talked and laughed, comfortable in each other's company. For a while, I forgot everything else but the pleasure of being with her. I fooled myself into believing I was a single man who was able to enjoy the company and charms of another woman. Everything was flowing until I made a throwaway comment about 'remembering it in the future', a joke that had started around whether she'd indulge in dessert or not.

I was captivated by her beauty and the sensuousness of her movements. Tears filled her eyes from the laughter of a few moments ago, her elbows resting on the table, one hand cupping her chin while the other raised the wine glass to her lips. Her breasts tumbled forward as she leaned further on her hand, the creamy skin inviting. Whatever the consequences afterwards, I had to have this night with her. I ordered another bottle of wine. Although I'd decided, I was nervous, barely focusing on what she said as I shifted gears. I visualised undressing her, feeling her soft skin against mine, and ultimately sliding the length of my cock inside her. I shifted whilst trying to appear normal.

The warm night air was punctuated with a gentle breeze. We strolled, the pace dictated by Gemma in her heeled sandals. I'd waited so long for this moment that when I stepped forward I was tense as a schoolboy about to have his first sexual encounter. I kissed her hesitantly, almost expecting to meet with resistance. Gemma's response was immediate and welcoming. Her arms wrapped around my neck. Gemma's body strained against mine, her breasts skimming my chest.

Gemma's calm demeanour fled as she fumbled with her keys, attempting to open the hotel room door. My hand closed over hers to steady it. Smelling the perfumed skin inches from me dispersed any lingering doubts. Wrapping my arm around her waist, I pulled her close. My erection strained against my trousers. I buried my lips into her neck, pressing little kisses.

Gemma's hand reached out to touch my face. She

took my upper lip between hers and sucked, gentle but firm. I found this incredibly erotic. Drawing her towards me, I slid my hand over her firm buttocks. Pushing the dress up, I revelled in the soft texture of her skin. Gemma taunted me with her tongue, causing little darts of pleasure to run through me. I lifted her onto my hips. With something akin to awe, I stroked her breasts, toying with them, delighting in the puckered texture.

Her body trembled as I laid her down on the bed. Moving lithely, she got to her knees. I longed to guide her towards my erection but watched instead while she undid my shirt, teasing me with her mouth. Red molten lava flowed through me at her gentle touches, shy yet confident, eager yet restrained.

I ran trembling fingers down the length of her body, sliding them between her open thighs, seeking out the sweetness between her legs. When I couldn't stand the exquisite agony any more, I entered her. Our rhythms merged, positions changing as we fought a silent sweet battle for supremacy. We both came together, fingernails clawing, teeth biting, backs arching until the tempo slowed to a mellower beat. Laying back, sated and replete, I toyed with her skin, tracing my fingertips up and down. I wasn't immediately hit by the guilt stick, lulled into living only in that moment, believing that we could freeze time and be like this forever.

"How are we going to manage the long-distance thing?" A bullet tore through the illusion.

My fingers stopped wandering, frozen.

"What do you mean?" I was playing for time.

I hadn't consciously thought of this thing with Gemma as a one-night-stand until she said the actual words. The truth was I hadn't thought at all. Sleeping around wasn't something I did. If Claudine hadn't told me she was pregnant, I would've finished with her, and this thing with Gemma could have been more. She rose up, anger dripping from her. I reached across, needing to make contact, but she moved away from my touch.

"I think you should go." Her voice trembled.

"I asked you to come back with me that first

night." As the words left my mouth, I regretted them; they were the mere ramblings of a disjointed thought process.

She swivelled to look at me, eyes filled with unshed tears I'd caused, as she demanded I leave.

What can I say or do to persuade her? My brain was whirring with the frenetic craziness of a theme-park ride. What would I be trying to convince her of? I pulled my clothes on while attempting to make some sense of what was in my head.

I walked out of the open door. I cringed as I thought about my comment with regards to the first night we'd met. In my mind, I'd thought that if we'd got together that night, I wouldn't have succumbed to Claudine's charms. But Claudine would have still been pregnant. *How bloody long has the bitch known?*

Dazed, I stumbled along the road. *Why did I take her out? Why did I think that I could exercise such iron control? And yet why hadn't I?* My brain screamed, emitting noises that hurt; I longed for release from the hammering pressure that was building. Over the space of a few hours, I'd had a complete metamorphosis.

The bar was crowded. Cigarette smoke and body odour mingled with alcohol while the darkened bar flashed with strobe lighting and people were gyrating on the dance floor. I lurched through the throng, looking neither left nor right. The bar became my refuge, the barman my best friend as I knocked back one shot after another. The more I drank, the more acute my pain became. I tried to forget, but I wasn't allowed to reach that state. I hovered in a place where I was dead drunk but my mind stayed alert. I kept seeing Gemma's face and the pain I'd caused her.

I stumbled out of the bar when the barman refused to serve me and walked straight into a barrier of the human kind. I slurred an apology. As drunk as me, he seemed intent on a fight. Had I been myself, I could have diverted him, but I, too, had pent-up anger that needed to fight free. Each punch I laid into him felt good, cathartic. Every blow I took seemed like natural justice, a punishment for my wrongdoing. We ended up on the floor, side by side, bruised and inebriated.

Strong arms lifted me, forcing me from the ground, to stand, to walk. Bleary-eyed, I tried to focus. Shapes drifted in and out of my line of vision. Jake's voice registered as he attempted to hail a cab, but they refused to take me. His wordless support lulled me into a false sense of security; a buttress to my weight as we stumbled home, his hand shoved at me when we reached our room. I fell onto the bed.

"Now, are you going to tell me what's going on?" His tone was like a dash of icy water.

"Fuck off!" I slurred.

His succour of a few moments ago forgotten, I was ready to fight again. *I don't need him. I don't need anyone.*

"Theo, what's happening to you?"

"Just leave me alone, Jake." Bile rose in my throat as my stomach heaved.

"I should have left you there in the gutter for the Greek police to pick up," he shouted.

"Yeah, maybe you should have."

The next night saw me in a bar alone, knocking back drinks. I was trying to numb the physical pain as well as the mental and emotional torment. Jake joined me, resting his elbows on the wet bar top. He ordered a beer, sipping at it, sitting beside me like a lonely sentinel guarding something precious. She'll be flying home now. Pictures of her invaded my head; I saw her lying naked on the bed, waiting for me. I shook my head. *This is torture.* My shaking hand reached for the glass in an attempt to drown these erotic visions.

Jake acted as my silent, stalwart protector again that night on our walk back to the hotel. When he saw me home safely, he walked off to fulfil his own needs. Friday and Saturday followed the same pattern, and each night Jake abandoned his own pleasure-filled existence until I was safely ensconced in the room.

Our flight was leaving on Monday morning, and even in my stupor, I couldn't face the journey drunk. The trip home was about as different to the outward journey as it could have been. There was no laughter, no conversation. We were like two strangers. Playing it over in my mind, I figured that whatever happened before, I had to focus on the here and now. The only thing I was sure about was that I would need to put this baby first, before me, before all thoughts of my relationship with Claudine, whatever that might be. It certainly needed to go before my guilt over the way I'd treated Gemma and any lingering feelings I may hold for her.

"Claudine, I've just got in."

"I need to see you. I'm coming around." The phone went down before I could protest.

I opened the door, then followed Claudine as she swept past me into the living room.

"So did you have a good holiday?" she snarled.

"You didn't rush over to discuss my holiday," I replied, unwilling to play her game.

"Was it was worth the sacrifice?"

"What are you talking about? I'm tired. Admittedly, I've over-indulged on holiday so my mind isn't on par with yours at the moment. So why don't you just spit it out?"

I watched as tears welled in her eyes. My mind strayed to another woman whose eyes had misted with tears. I found myself unmoved by Claudine's tears. I was sure they were available on demand as part of whatever game she was playing. In that moment, I knew that while I'd be there for my child, I couldn't do it as her partner.

"Was it worth the sacrifice of your baby?"

"What do you mean?"

"I was distressed when you ignored my texts, and knew you didn't want anything more to do with us."

"What have you done?" The accusation flew off my tongue.

"I didn't do anything. It's your fault… it's your fault I lost the baby," she sobbed.

I felt as though someone had taken my knees out by a chainsaw as they gave way. I bent my head down and wept.

"What happened? What did the doctor say?"

"I told you, it's your fault."

"Claudine, don't put that on me. I know I've been an arse, but I don't deserve that."

"The doctor said that it was caused by stress."

I looked up at her from my position on the floor and knew that the world as I knew it had crumbled; my own personal Armageddon.

"Oh, and in case there's any doubt," Claudine, whose tears had disappeared, threw me a withering look, "we're over."

I clenched my hand into a fist, smashing it into the floor. My stomach heaved. I ran to the bathroom, where I proceeded to empty the contents of my stomach.

The pub was quiet. Only a few locals propped up the bar. A senior couple sat in their usual place before the open-fire grate that, at this time of year, held no flame. Pewter tankards emblazoned with the names of long-past locals sat on the shelf above the fire.

"A pint, please, Bob."

"You back from holiday, then, Theo? You don't have much of a colour this time. Bet you spent most your time in the bars if I know that Jake."

"That's it, Bob." I wasn't sure why I'd come here – only that I couldn't stay indoors.

"Who are you meeting tonight?"

"No-one."

"Not like you, Theo."

I took the drink and headed for a table lest he tried to engage me in any more unwanted conversation. Thoughts raced through my head until I was no longer sure about anything. I'd sought to lead an honest life, to be a decent person, but I'd failed. In my childhood, my parents had cared nothing for Cass and me, which had hurt. Cass had learned to cut them off. She used to say that if you don't care, you can't get hurt. Perhaps I could learn from that.

Every day followed the same pattern. I worked by day and drank by night. An atmosphere pervaded the office as Jake and I found little to say to each other.

Is This Love?

Sometimes I felt his speculative gaze on me as I pored over the accounts. Friday night differed only in that Jake, Tom and Stephen joined me in the bars.

"Hope I'm not going to have to make sure you get home in one piece again," Jake sneered.

"No one asked you to before," I retorted.

"I should have left you for the police to pick up." Jake's eyes flashed.

"Piss off," I retorted, and then had to laugh at the twin expressions on Tom and Stephen's faces, eyes dilated and mouths agape.

Jake, too, laughed, and our mutual anger at each other melted.

"So how come you're not out with Claudine tonight?" Tom asked, evidently perplexed. I'm sure he wanted the low-down but didn't dare ask.

"We're finished."

"Then what's the problem?"

"There is no problem." I worked at keeping my voice even.

I woke up next to a brunette whose name I couldn't remember; it didn't seem important. She asked if she could see me again. I was honest and told her I saw no reason why we should. I felt a little stab of guilt when she flinched. I was only just learning the art of not caring. As the brunette headed out, my sister marched through the open door. My insides shrivelled.

"Who was that?" she demanded.

"I can't remember her name but if you run after her, you can catch her and ask her yourself."

Her mouth dropped open, and her green eyes flashed a warning.

"What's wrong, Theo?" She decided to give me the benefit of the doubt. "I've been trying to contact you since you got back. What are you doing with that woman when your girlfriend is carrying your baby?"

"Would you like me to draw you a diagram?" Sarcasm dripped off my tongue.

I turned away so that her hurt expression wouldn't rip through my newly built guard.

"I'll go and speak to Claudine, then, shall I?"

I could just about cope with her hating me because I was acting like a prick, but I couldn't bear her knowing that I was to blame for my baby's death.

"She won't want to talk to you. She lost the baby."

"Oh, Theo, I'm so sorry."

"Close the door on your way out."

She frowned as she took me in and pondered what she should do.

"I'll leave you alone for now."

I stood back against the door. A deep chasm opened up inside me.

Chapter 9

Gemma

My brain only started to function when I stood at the luggage reclaim, watching the endless rotations of the carousel. Soon, I'd walk out to the beaming face of my best friend, Susie, whom I'd betrayed. It was Claudine whom I'd really betrayed. In that moment, I hated her, this woman I didn't know. She had until that moment been nameless, and was still faceless, but now it was Susie's face I could see, and the two became indistinguishable from each other. *How can I face her? She must know what I've done.*

I couldn't avoid the inevitable. The sliding doors parted. I scanned the crowd. My mouth went dry. Tiny palpitations agitated inside my chest. Susie wore an enormous smile displaying perfect white teeth. An unruly strand of hair flopped over her right eye. She rushed over and enveloped me in a warm hug. Would she still hug me if she knew? Surely, she must hate me.

"Welcome home, Gemma. I've missed you so much." She pulled back. "Come on, let's get you home. You're looking tired."

"Hope you didn't have to wait too long."

"So tell me all," Susie gushed as she settled into the driver's seat.

Even to my own ears, the account I gave of Crete was wooden. Samaria Gorge in all its glory sounded like a dull, endless trek, and when I mentioned Spinalonga, a lump formed in my throat so I trailed off.

"What is it, honey? You're awfully quiet."

"I'm just tired. You know how awful those late-night flights are."

We sat in silence. I was plagued with jumbled memories playing back like a recording. Theo swimming through the water, his lips on mine, the warm breath on my skin, against my neck. I fought to keep the tears at bay.

"It's just that you're ordinarily brimming over with news."

I forced a smile and threw in a jaunty tone of voice, "I guess I've just got to face the truth that two weeks of heavy clubbing is too much at my age. Honestly, Sus, I'm fine. I met a couple of lovely girls from Brighton, and they wouldn't take no for an answer, so I was out all the time."

"If you're sure…" Susie didn't sound convinced.

"Wait till you see me next. You won't be able to shut me up."

"Hey, why don't I come over tonight, when I bring your car back? I could bring a take-away and a couple of bottles."

"Oh, I don't know," I temporised, "I really am exhausted."

"Gemma, you can sleep all day, and you've still got tomorrow off work."

I gave in. As she drove away, I realised that I hadn't even asked her what was happening with Ted. *What kind of friend am I? Indeed, what manner of person?* I leaned against the front door, closed my eyes and inhaled a deep, ragged breath. *How can I cope with this secret? My friends know me too well to be fooled by an excuse of tiredness.*

Loneliness descended on me as I sank into my bed. *I'll never see him again.* Silent droplets formed in my eyes and tumbled down my cheeks. I awoke disorientated in the middle of the afternoon. A tension headache hammered my skull, which provided me with the perfect excuse for cancelling out with Susie. Her sympathy made me feel worse.

Voices drifted through from the living room as I slid the key into the lock. I thought I could get away with a quick hello to Carla and Joanne until I heard Jackie's short bark of laughter. *Everyone's here. I'll never get away.* A moment of panic swamped me. Taking a few deep breaths, I managed to switch to a less than impressive acting mode.

"This is a nice surprise," I announced, flinging the door wide.

"Where were you?" Jackie demanded. "We've been so worried."

"What are you talking about?"

"Our lunch date," Jackie huffed.

"What lunch date?"

"The note on the table with your keys. The arrangements were all written there. It said to contact Susie if you couldn't make it," Carla added.

"I grabbed the keys this morning. I didn't see a note."

"It was gone when I got up this morning," Carla insisted.

"It must have blown off the table. Let me go and see if I can find it."

"How are you?" Susie's voice startled me.

I jumped guiltily from my position on all fours.

"Oh, much better, Sus. Look, I've found it."

"I thought you might have rung and arranged to meet anyway."

"I was going to call tonight," I lied, wincing at how easily it came out. "I spent the day catching up on chores."

"Come on, grab a glass. We've got a bottle of red on the go," she said, walking back to the living room.

"I found the note half under the fridge," I repeated.

I looked around at my friends. Jackie, Amanda and Carla squeezed into one of the battered cream two-seaters while Joanne and Susie sat more comfortably on the other. I perched on one of the dining chairs. The cold, hard wooden slats pressed through my thin cotton skirt. The positioning of my seating with regards to that of my friends was a metaphor for the positioning inside my head. I was left on the outside of this intimate circle even if that was of my own making. The urge to confide swept over me until I pictured the expression of disgust from Susie. Instead, I smiled at them with a heavy heart and threw an overdose of enthusiasm into my voice as I answered their questions about Crete.

Theo

The next few months were spent drinking to excess and sleeping around. I found no release from my misery in these encounters, just a strange sense of disappointment. One night, after leaving the pub, I glanced through the window of an Italian restaurant and saw Claudine there with Caroline. They seemed to be engaged in an argument. The door opened and Caroline stalked out. I hesitated, wanting to move but unable to. She turned in my direction. Her face dropped when she spotted me.

"Theo. How are you?"

I shrugged, not wanting to talk to her. "Oh, you know."

I got the impression that she was going to say something else but then she shook her head and walked away. This only served to reinforce my guilt. I headed off to a pub with a renewed determination to get slaughtered.

"This is the second time this month that you've messed up, Perkins. What do you have to say?"

I noticed that the filing cabinet in the corner wasn't shut properly as a file stuck out, jamming it, and that Martin's tie was off centre. I shrugged my shoulders. My expression remained blank, bored. He blustered and his face reddened as he blew out a verbal warning, expecting a reaction.

"Have you finished now?"

"Get out of my sight," he hissed, knuckles white as he balled his fists. I was sure he had a hankering to punch me.

I turned on my heels and yanked the door open.

"And... sort out your appearance," he shouted, determined to get the last word.

I pulled the door hard, shaking the frame, and the noise reverberated around the office.

"What the fuck has got into you?" Jake snarled as we left the accident and emergency department.

Jake had a split lip, stitches above his right eye and some nasty bruises. I had a broken nose, various cuts and bruises, and no one but myself to blame. I could understand Jake's anger. We'd left work and headed to the pub; beers and chasers had followed as night pursues day, except at a swifter pace. I made a derogatory comment about a couple of women who were standing near us. Unfortunately, I hadn't spotted their two beefy boyfriends, who overheard my comments.

The inevitable fight broke out, and once more, Jake found himself beside me. Tom and Stephen bolted out of the way of flying fists. I didn't blame them. These guys were huge rugby types, and only someone who cared little for life would have contemplated taking them on. I had no choice in the matter, but Jake did. He wasn't going to leave me with the odds stacked against me.

"I don't want to talk about it." *Jake deserves better than this.*

"You know you've become like me." Jake meant it to hurt; it bounced off the metaphorical metal armour plating that I wore.

"Then you should like me," I responded flippantly.

"I liked you for who you were, for the strong morals that you stood for, not in spite of them," Jake continued undeterred. "I don't like seeing you doing a second-rate impression of me. I know what made me this way, and it's too late to change who I am. If you'd only just tell someone what happened, you could go back to being yourself."

He stopped to see if he'd made an impression.

"Do you realise how many people you've hurt? I saw Cass the other day, I've never seen her cry before. She told me that Claudine had lost your baby. Why didn't you tell me she was pregnant?"

I shrugged as a lump formed in my throat, rendering me unable to speak. A sharp pain stabbed at me hearing of Cass' distress.

"What about Toby, Jason and their families? Personally, I'm not into the whole kid thing but you seemed to dig it. Those kids want to know why they don't see their Uncle Theo." He stopped as though pondering something. "Is that it? Is it because you lost the baby? No, it can't be. You started acting strangely in Crete, and you didn't know about it then." I could see his brain ticking; he was trying to join the pieces together. "Talk to someone, for fuck's sakes, before you lose everyone."

I'd never known Jake to make such a long speech. I didn't particularly like what I'd become, but there was nothing I could do about it. I'd changed my thought processes irrevocably. I couldn't let them in now; I didn't know how. Jake looked expectantly at me.

"There's nothing to tell," I retorted, drawing the shield firmly back around me for protection.

"Then there's nothing more I can do for you, and I'll be damned if I let you drag me down further," Jake exploded and walked away.

A few hours later, the pounding on the door made me jump. The lights were off. *If I stay quiet, they'll go away.*

"Theo, I know you're in there." Jake's words destroyed that illusion.

"What do you want now?" I demanded as he pushed past me into the living room, flicking the light switch on.

"I know."

"What do you know?" I hedged.

"About a month ago I bumped into Chris, Gemma's friend. We exchanged numbers." He watched me.

I remained silent, wondering how much Gemma had told her friend.

"When I left you earlier, I rang her, to talk to someone who didn't know you, who could be objective. I needed to know whether I'd done right by you. We talked for a while, and she said that Gemma was in Crete the same time as we were. But I think you already know that. Chris also said that, since she's come back, she's become a recluse, blocking out all her friends."

It surprised me to hear that she hadn't confided in her friends. Little frissons of something passed through me. *How many people have we hurt?*

"I didn't have to be a genius to work out that you slept with her. Also, putting the pieces together, I'd say Claudine told you she was pregnant before you went away. When you got back, she must have told you that she'd lost the baby, and you blame yourself. Am I right?"

"It's my fault."

"I know you have some misguided sense of morality, but sleeping with another woman doesn't cause a miscarriage."

"The doctor said it was stress, and I was responsible for that stress."

"Did she tell you that?"

"Yes."

"Mate, she was lashing out. Look, I don't know much about pregnancy and all that but if women lost their babies because their boyfriends acted like arseholes, we would be severely underpopulated."

"I still cheated on my pregnant girlfriend." But his words had penetrated my defences.

"You forget we're all only human, programmed to make mistakes. Everyone who knows you wouldn't have thought less of you. You needed some reward after putting up with Claudine."

Huge stone chunks were now falling; Jake's battering ram had breached my walls. I'm ashamed to say I cried. Not quiet, discreet tears, but huge blubbering sobs. I became aware of Jake beside me, his hand rising to comfort me. It hovered in the air and then settled back down onto his lap. Women hug each other to give support without being self-conscious or creating fears of homosexuality. Most modern straight men will tell you: There's nothing wrong with being gay, but the moment there's even the slightest question mark over our sexuality, we run a mile faster than any Olympic athlete. So I sat there alone in my misery, while Jake juggled in his mind what he should do. I took heart from this indecision. It gave me the comfort I sought, and my embarrassing episode came to an end.

"Sorry 'bout that," I mumbled.

"Nothing to be sorry about." Jake could afford to be magnanimous now that I'd stopped.

I told Jake how I was going to split up with Claudine until she had landed that news on my lap and how I had bumped into Gemma in the village and spent the rest of the day together. "The chance meeting on the Spinalonga trip sealed the deal."

"Sounds like you're in love with her," Jake observed.

"No... at least I don't think so."

It was a week for making amends. I began with Cass. At first, she wouldn't even open the front door, but it soon became apparent that I wasn't going anywhere. Ordinarily, she could have left me there all day but she made the mistake of peering out of the window and spotted my battered face. The bond between us was too important to allow her to ignore that.

"It had better be good," she threatened.

I cleared my throat and looked down to the stripped wooden floorboards as I falteringly told my tale.

"The bitch! How could she have laid that on you? How could you have let her? Did you honestly think I would think any less of you?" she demanded, outraged. "Have all our years led you to believe that I wouldn't support you?"

"To be honest, Cass, I wasn't thinking at all. Yes, looking objectively, there's no reason I shouldn't have told you. When you hate and can't forgive yourself, you don't think other people will be any more charitable."

"It wouldn't have been charity. No, no." She held up her hands to stop me speaking. "You always had a misguided sense of right and wrong. Not quite sure where you get it from. I'm warning you... don't ever do that to me again." Tears settled in the corners of her eyes.

"Scout's honour." I held my hand up doing the scout's sign.

"You were never a scout, you clown." She hugged me before pushing me toward the kitchen. Switching on the kettle, she proceeded to tell me what I should do, which coincided with Jake's opinion.

I arrived at the Dog & Duck early on Wednesday night, and despite my determination not to drink, I felt the need for a couple of pints for Dutch courage. Jason and Toby turned up together. There was a definite chill about their demeanour. They greeted me in a reserved manner. They listened in silence and accepted all I told them without a word, which, I have to say, unnerved me.

"So when are you coming back to the club?" Jason's tone was matter-of-fact.

"I haven't been to practice so long now I doubt I'll be picked for the team, but yeah, I'll come to practice."

"You might. We're terribly short of men at the

moment. Stu's on holiday with the missus, both Simon and Joey are off with the flu and… oh yes, Andy broke his ankle in the last match." The perplexed look shifted from Toby's tightly knit eyebrows.

"I warn you, I'm seriously unfit. I doubt I'll make a meaningful contribution to the match."

"Did you ever?" Jason ribbed, thumping me on the back.

"Hilarious. Have you been taking lessons from the kids?" I retorted with a grin, grateful to them both for the easy way they'd accepted all I'd told them. Toby spluttered into his pint, amused.

They filled me in on their families. Jack had been accepted into his school's football team. Toby's twins had started school. I was ashamed to realise that I'd distanced myself so much that I hadn't been to wish them well on their first day.

"Tell us some more about Gemma," Toby surprised me.

I tried to give an honest account of Gemma from when I had met her to the chance meetings in Crete. I wanted to capture her essence so they could picture her – how she made me laugh, her adventurous spirit, the depths of her compassion and understanding.

Before we left, Jason said, "Sorry that you lost the baby. You'll make a good dad one day."

The snooker club was quiet. Only Cass and Keith played on a table while they waited for me.

"I rang Jake. He's coming to make up the numbers."

"Does that mean we've got to wait hours while he makes himself beautiful?" Cass teased.

"He's already beautiful." Jake snuck up on us.

Cass and I teamed up, trouncing Keith and Jake, who were despatched to get the next round in.

"What do you mean, orange juice?" Jake guffawed. "From one extreme to the other."

"No," I assured him, wrinkling my nose at the idea of an alcohol-free existence. "I've got a match tomorrow, and I'm already unfit."

"We'll come," Keith said, "see if loud cheers and

positive thinking can improve your game."

"You're funny."

"Count me out." Jake grinned. "Hot date tonight, and I'm hoping to be otherwise engaged tomorrow." His eyebrows twitched suggestively.

"A date?" Cass queried. "I didn't think you bothered with the niceties. This one special, is she?"

We grinned at each other in anticipation. Was there a woman alive who could tame Jake?

"They're all special." Jake winked.

When Jake had departed amidst a flurry of innuendo and risqué comments, I put my idea to Cass and Keith, enlisting their help.

The match on Sunday was, as predicted, a veritable disaster. We were trounced four-nil. The supporters cheered, trying to rally us. Our best players were absent, our morale was at an all-time low, so we never stood a chance. The beer garden was shrouded as dark clouds swamped the sky. The kids ran off to the play area: swings, a climbing frame and an old bus dominated the yard. I put my proposal to both sets of parents, who laughed and wished me well, exchanging knowing looks. Keith, Cass and I were bemused, waiting to be filled in, but they remained steadfast in their silence. *How hard could it be to take a few kids out for the day?*

Keith, Cass and I picked up all four kids in the borrowed seven-seater Sharan. A five-year-old, four-year-old twins and a three-year-old all pumped up in the middle and back rows. Our destination was a pet farm and activity centre. The mere forty-five-minute drive took on a whole new appearance as Tim and Joe bickered the entire journey.

"Come on, guys," Cass attempted to mediate.

"It's him," Joe grunted.

"No, it's not. It's him," Tim whined.

"I hope you're not going to be like this all day," I threw over my shoulder as I drove, wondering what I'd taken on. They always behaved impeccably when I was around, but then that was for short periods of time and always with their parents present.

"No," they piped up, "we never get on in a car. Dad makes him sit there." They both pointed in opposite directions.

Nice of them to warn us. We're in for a day of it.

Meanwhile, Jack talked non-stop as though the twins' argument wasn't happening.

"Wee-wee." Katie's quiet timbre was spiked with urgency.

Cass screeched in horror while Keith and I laughed from the comfort of the front seats as I pulled off the road so Cass could help Katie.

"Whose clever idea was this trip?" Cass growled.

"I know. I owe you a drink."

"You won't get off that lightly, Theo Perkins," she warned.

"Take your thumb out of your mouth, Katie," Jack said in an exasperated tone, mimicking Cathy. "Mummy says you'll have buck teeth like Bugs Bunny."

"Won't!" Katie pouted.

The twins took up the chant, the telepathy between

them acute, "Katie's got buck teeth."

"Leave me lone." Katie burst into tears.

"Lads, cut it out."

"Katie has buck teeth. Katie has buck teeth."

"Leave my sister alone."

"Right," shouted Cass, commanding respect by her forceful tone. "The next person to say a word will not be going on the go-karts."

For the last ten minutes of the journey, peace was restored.

"Okay, kids, we're heading for the indoor play area." The boys raced ahead while Katie snuggled into my arms as we walked at a more sedate pace. "Let them expend some energy before we inflict them on the animals," I said.

"Twelve o'clock is feeding time for the animals," Keith read out, adding, "We can buy feed."

"Uncle Feo," Katie whispered in my ear, "can I hold a rabbit?"

"Yes, sweetheart."

"Uncle Feo, a ball pool."

I removed her shoes, depositing her in the middle of the ball pool amidst squeals of pleasure. The boys were already in full swing, running around, stirring fear in the parents. As they started to tire, we headed to the animals. They seemed content petting and feeding them. Katie got to cuddle a rabbit. They all rode on the back of the Shetland ponies – a small circuit around the pet farm.

Jack squealed, "Look at me, Uncle Theo. I can ride a horse."

Both Tim and Joe said they wanted to be cowboys, and Katie clung to me and asked me to walk around with her. Burger and chips were followed by another tumble in the play area and the go-karts, which proved to be a firm favourite with us all.

"Don't ever ask me to do that again," Cass warned.

"You enjoyed it, really."

Her left eyebrow rose menacingly, but she smiled as she lifted the glass to her lips.

"You'll make a great mum." Keith grinned. The glass hid Cass' grimace.

I must have shown some residual sadness, as Cass' hand reached over and covered mine. "You'll have another chance to have a family, and when you do, you'll make a great father."

I sensed rather than saw someone hovering behind me.

"Theo."

I turned and frowned as I saw Caroline, Claudine's best friend, standing above me. A prickle ran down my spine.

"Caroline."

"Can I talk to you?" She looked at Cass, discomforted.

"Go on."

"Alone."

"There's nothing you can't say in front of Cass and Keith."

"Please." Her normal sneer was missing.

I nodded.

"Can we go back to yours?" she asked as we walked away together.

"Really?" I couldn't disguise the scathing tone of my words.

"You don't want to do this here." She returned my look with a steely one of her own.

I conceded with a sigh.

Chapter 10

Gemma

Over the next few months, I withdrew from everyone as I couldn't slip back into the easy friendships while this deceit hung over me, yet I couldn't tell them. I began to invent excuses as to why I couldn't meet my friends, but I couldn't always avoid them. Perversely, I found myself lonelier in their company than I did when I was alone. I felt as though I was watching everything from a distance: Susie's heartbreak over Ted, Amanda's blossoming relationship with the managing director, and Jackie's with Rory. I retreated further into myself, warding off their enquiries, pretending not to notice their hurt and confusion, until they stopped trying.

To fill my time, I went on day trips, meandering through castles and cathedrals, roaming through cobbled streets or high streets teeming with gorgeous shops.

As soon as I stepped out of the station I grasped that I was in the middle of nowhere – no people, no movement. I found the emptiness of the place unnerving. *Well, you're here now. You can't just turn around and go home, so make the most of it.*

I set off with a purposeful step, heading towards the castle.

"Public footpath to Hever." I read the sign out loud, attempting to shatter the silence.

The pathway opened up before me, surrounded by trees. After a few moments of walking the path, I pulled up short, letting out a stream of colourful invectives when my new boots sunk into squelching mud. I considered turning around, but the damage had already been done, so I plodded on in the hope of seeing some sign of life. In spite of the big houses, I still hadn't caught sight of anyone. The leaves crinkled beneath my feet as I sought to avoid the worst mud patches. Despondent and cold, I trudged on, but I couldn't escape the dawning realisation that I was in an isolated copse in the middle of nowhere.

A twig snapped underfoot. My heart raced. I looked around with frightened eyes, trying to walk faster but hampered by the mud. Images careered helter-skelter through my brain – of my body being found weeks later, unrecognisable, by a man out walking his dog. Skidding on a wet leaf, I pitched forward. My arms thrashed out for something to grab onto. I just managed to stay upright.

I laughed; a hollow sound in the deserted thicket. It was silly letting my imagination run away like that. It was rather like the irrational fear you experience at night from a slight sound. In the cold light of day, it all seems stupid. I was in a vulnerable position, but there was no need to panic.

The pathway widened ahead, leading into a field,

which I walked through before climbing over the locked gate on the other side. I found a pub and sighed. *I'll come here later.* As I rounded the corner, I saw a stone archway leading to an old church, and just further on, a sign for the castle. *Here at last. Damn it!* A sign proclaimed the castle closed until March. *I should have checked the opening times online last night.* I wandered back towards the church. Beside the beautiful archway was a sign that said 'footpath to Chiddingstone'. *I know all about those damn pathways.*

The church held the tomb of Thomas Bullen, father of Anne Boleyn, the second wife of King Henry VIII. My fingers were cold as I flexed them against the heavy door and pushed. A sense of peace descended over me as I walked around the tranquil environs of the church. I sat in a pew and tried to figure out what had brought me here. I don't mean I saw any blinding lights or had any religious conversions, but I felt that a stronger being had lured me here today.

Once I was outside in the frigid air, I thought again

about the path to Chiddingstone. *Maybe there's a little village there with some shops I can explore.* With that in mind, I headed through the graveyard. My expedition was no more fruitful, the path was the same as the last, and once again, I chided myself for placing myself in an exposed position. I slipped on the mushy ground while contemplating my friends' reactions if I fell face down in the mud. My laugh froze in the air as I remembered they would never know.

I reached a gap in the trees, beyond which I glimpsed a glistening cobalt-blue stream. Standing still for a few moments, I drank in the view. The realisation came to me. I had been drawn there that day, in this distraction-free environment, to put things into perspective. Sleeping with Theo hadn't been the reason I'd failed my friends. Not trusting them to understand me was. The ultimate betrayal of his pregnant girlfriend was his, as I hadn't known she was pregnant. This didn't mean I was blameless.

It was time to rebuild my bridges.

The pub was empty. Neutral ground, Susie had called it. Rather than estranged friends, it made me think of enemy nations getting together to settle on peace terms. My stomach somersaulted as I waited, nursing my second vodka.

I glanced at my watch. *They're late. Will they show? No, they're not vindictive.* Jackie would give me a tongue lashing. In fact, she was probably rehearsing it now. Susie would try her hardest to understand, and Amanda... she'd take her time, let it sink in, but then I couldn't be sure.

They all walked in together. *Lamb to the slaughter.* I smiled, a nervous, awkward movement of the lips. Susie was looking better, less like someone who'd been dealt a bad hand, Jackie was the same, but I couldn't help but notice that Amanda seemed tired. I wondered as to the cause. It struck me anew that I'd missed out so much in their lives. Nausea rose from the pit of my stomach, hollowing upwards till it lodged in my dry throat. I reached for my glass but it was empty. The girls were getting closer. They didn't stop at the bar for drinks, so I couldn't go and buy one.

"Does anyone want a drink?" I asked.

Three heads shook in unison. They sat down with stilted greetings. I launched into my tale.

"Was he still with his girlfriend?" Susie interrupted.

I nodded. I'd just been telling them about our chance meetings, the strange magnetism, and how being together was like fitting together the last pieces on a jigsaw. Her interruption, the question she asked, the answer I gave, all brought it down to a tawdry level.

Amanda's eyes misted over. "Go on," she urged in a soft voice.

"We went out together that night."

"A date? You'll not have us believe that was a third coincidental meet." I couldn't blame Susie for her antagonism.

I nodded. They knew what happened next, but they weren't going to make it easier for me, they wanted me to say the words. "We tried to resist the..." I struggled for the right words. "The attraction was too strong. We slept together."

"And now?" Amanda asked.

I shook my head, the memory too intense. "He told me… his girlfriend's pregnant." Tears fell, silent globules blazing a trail down my cheeks. "I cried myself to sleep. It was the next day that I left Crete. I spent the whole day numb, not prepared for what would happen when I got home."

"And you didn't think you could tell us? Didn't you think we'd understand?" Susie snapped, her puppy eyes full of scorn.

"I wasn't thinking much that day. It was only when I reached the airport that I remembered you were picking me up." I looked at her, my eyes beseeching. "I remember feeling that I had betrayed you, especially after… Ted."

"I can understand that, but it wasn't just that day. You've pushed us away for over six months. You should have trusted us," Amanda added.

Jackie stayed silent.

"I may not have understood, but I would have tried." A tear formed in Susie's eye.

"Even if you didn't want to confide in us, you could have kept it secret. Or didn't you think enough of our friendship?" Jackie added.

"I didn't set out to distance myself from you. You all know me too well to think I could cover anything up. The longer I went on not saying anything the harder it became. I should have told you, but you know what they say about hindsight." When I didn't get a response, I ventured, "Is it too late now?"

Susie rose to her feet, swept me with a contemptuous glare and stalked out.

Amanda and Jackie rose, too. *I've thrown away my best friends.*

"Sorry, mate, we need to find Susie." Jackie's tone held a trace of regret.

"Give her time." Amanda squeezed my arm. "Give us all time."

Theo

Over the next few months, I kept busy by throwing myself into a dizzying round of activity. Although I was moving on, it was incomprehensible to me that anyone could be so evil. It didn't mean I was blameless but had I known this beforehand, I'd have been a free man. The conversation with Caroline still reverberated around my brain:

"Okay, Caroline, I don't mean to be rude but what's this about?"

"Theo, there is no quick or easy way to say this." She held a hand up to stop me from talking. *"We're here now; you might as well hear me out. You've never liked me, and I don't think much of you either, but you're a decent man. I haven't known this all along, and how I found out is private."*

I was starting to regret allowing her to talk me into this until she uttered her next words, which blew me out of the water.

"The baby wasn't yours."

"What rubbish is this, Caroline? Is this some elaborate revenge you and Claudine have plotted to hurt me more?"

"Theo, this isn't a plot. Claudine and I are no longer friends, and we won't be again."

She had my full attention.

"Claudine wasn't carrying your baby. She'd been having an affair with her boss since almost as soon as she started working at the bank."

"But that's about sixteen years ago," I interrupted, incredulous.

Caroline nodded. *"She's been waiting for him to leave his wife."*

"Why did she get involved with me? Was it an attempt to leave him?"

"No. You were the last in a chain of men used to divert attention. He insisted on it. Until his children were old enough, he couldn't risk anyone finding out. The deal was that as soon

as they'd left school, he'd tell his wife. Claudine left you as she'd just discovered she was pregnant. She knew that it was his, as they'd become sloppy with protection. He reneged on the deal and refused to leave his wife. Claudine panicked and ran straight back to you."

"Oh my God, I can't believe it."

"That's not all. She decided you would stick by her, as we all know how moralistic you are. She knew you didn't love her. She often wondered why you stayed. Before you went on holiday, she feared you were going to finish with her so she blurted it out. She knew you wouldn't be happy but thought you'd cancel the holiday. While you were away, you went off the radar, and she knew that, while you would support her, she would be stuck with this baby alone. By this point, her ex had transferred to another branch and made it clear he wouldn't acknowledge her or the baby. He'd been supporting her all along to stay in that flat, which she couldn't afford on her salary."

"Wait... That was money left in her mother's will," I challenged.

"Her mum is alive and works two or three jobs to keep her head above water."

I felt as though I'd been pushed out of an airplane without a parachute, free-falling to earth and knowing it would all be over when I hit the ground. Caroline reached a hand out to me, placing her chubby fingers on my arm, and I knew I was about to crash.

"She aborted the baby."

I won't dwell any more on that night. Caroline left me hunched up on the floor after trying to comfort me. I drank myself into a stupor but woke up with a determination not to let her send me into another downward spiral.

"Merry Christmas." The roar broke out in the crowded club as the midnight hour struck.

Cass kissed Keith and then flung her arms around me.

"Happy Christmas, big bro."

Jake stood chatting with Chris, Gemma's friend. It had given me quite a jolt to see her. A flicker of something I'd thought was buried rose to the surface. There was a spark between Jake and Chris. I was sure he treated her differently than the hordes of other women. Light touches from a guy whose idea of tactile was a quick grope in the dark.

Stephen and Tom came over bearing beers and Flaming Sambucas before heading back out on the prowl. "Taking advantage of the dim lighting to detract from their deficiency in the looks department," Cass said.

My focus moved to a brunette. Paige appeared to be one of those women who laughed at life, which was emphasised by the deep laughter lines at the side of her eyes and mouth. Honey-coloured eyes looked out from long lashes which, along with her long silky hair, were her only claims to beauty. A pinched nose and wide lips gave her face a distorted, asymmetrical appearance. At the end of the night, we exchanged numbers before I staggered home with the sharp, stale smell of cigarette smoke clinging to me.

Nervous tension gripped me. *A first date. I haven't done this in a long time.* Being out of the loop for so long had made me forget how hard it was. With Gemma it hadn't felt like a first date. It was more like we'd always known each other. I shrugged off this thought.

"What a lovely restaurant," Paige exclaimed, her voice a tad overloud.

"Shall I pick a wine?" I asked.

"No. I don't need a man to make my decisions for me. I'll choose my own."

Oh God, what am I doing here?

"I'm sure you can. I'll have whatever you choose, then."

"I don't need you patronising me either, Theo." Her voice rose an octave.

"I wasn't."

Sod this. A fleeting vision of another meal, almost another lifetime ago, flashed in front of me.

The rest of the date wasn't too bad, after Paige had settled her feminist issues. I can only thank whatever demons possessed her at the start of the night, as they'd given me a warning to the other facet of her personality. She invited me back home, but I declined with feigned regret.

"It's nice to meet a real gentleman." I couldn't help but think that this statement was at odds with her previous opinions. She leaned forward on impulse and kissed me on the cheek. I could have told her the truth, but cruelty was no longer part of my repertoire. Instead, I said goodnight and told her I'd call, although I had no intention of revisiting a high-maintenance relationship.

I did my homework; researched my areas, prices, what were considered good neighbourhoods. After my disastrous date, I'd decided it was time for me to put a foot on the property ladder. Cathy told me I should consider good catchment areas for schools. I gave her a wry look before escaping any more unwarranted advice.

"It may be useful in the future," she'd called after my departing form.

"Then I'll ask for your advice on that matter in the future," I threw back over my shoulder.

From the outside, in my amateur estimation, it looked structurally sound but in need of some attention. *It needs repointing.* It had a neglected air. The door was opened by an elderly gentleman.

"Who is it, Alfred?"

"I don't know, Doris." The man's eyes twinkled with amusement and his moustache twitched as he continued, "I've only just answered the door, but my guess would be the five-thirty viewing for the house. Am I right, young man?" He winked at me grinning, showing teeth worn and yellowed with age.

A musty smell permeated the walls. As I wandered around, I found myself impressed by the generous size and character of the rooms. I knew I'd have to register my interest fast as they'd had five viewings already that day. I looked past the faded flowers on the wall, the chintz curtains and vulgar patterned carpets that were threadbare in places. I pictured crisp whites, burgundies, wooden and stone floors. *I could live here.* They invited me into their tired old kitchen. *It needs to be gutted.* I watched Doris fussing around with tea and cakes. I tried to refuse politely, but she wouldn't take no for an answer.

"Easier to give in." Alfred beamed.

I did just that. The couple talked with animation about the house and area.

"Lucky with neighbours, we are. Aren't we, Alf?"

Alfred nodded and went on to tell me how sad they were to be leaving, but their daughter and her two kids lived near the New Forest, and they wanted to spend more time with them. "Before it's too late," Doris said.

"It would be nice to see you living here." Doris turned light blue eyes on me, creased around the edges, but a glimpse of her earlier looks lingered in the flirtatious irises that age hadn't dulled. "I can see you'll love it as we do. We've had some wonderful times here." A poignant note touched the air. "I can see you here with a beautiful young lady."

"Doris, you're embarrassing the lad."

"Nonsense, Alfred," she declared and winked at me.

"I don't have a young lady, beautiful or otherwise."

"You will." She was about to add something else but stopped. A shiver of unease swept through me, and I found myself eager to leave this eagle-eyed old woman. Once outside, I laughed at my own fancifulness.

"It's going to take a lot of work," Cass said after she'd accompanied me for the second viewing at the house.

"I need that."

"You still think about her, don't you?"

I wasn't willing to go down that road again. "So you like it?"

"I'll help you."

"You mean with colour charts? I bet you won't strip any walls."

"Well, of course, with colour charts and furniture. I have to make sure you don't do high-street. Only high-spec bespoke will do."

"And how do you propose stretching my finances to a mortgage and designer suites?"

"You're an accountant, so do your job and advise

yourself financially."

"Accountant, not financial adviser. If I were, I'd say don't commit to too much debt."

"Then we'll have to resort to Plan B," she declared.

My eyebrows rose in question.

"Sourpuss and Grumps." I laughed at her not-so-affectionate names for our parents.

I waited for her to continue, although as yet Plan B seemed to be no more promising than her previous idea – that I could finance it.

"We tell them that you're plumping for cheap and nasty due to lack of funds, then we tell them that we're throwing a house warming…"

"Go on," I growled.

"We tell them that we're going to invite that bunch of toffs they hang out with, and their innate snobbery will do the rest. They'll throw money at you, the best of everything."

I threw back my head and laughed. Only Cass could think this was a way. Although she was probably right; they would rush in with assistance at the very idea that we might show them up by not being totally top-shelf.

"All right." She threw her hands up in mock despair. "But we still browse the showrooms. We can pick up bargains buying the show pieces or the end-of-range items. Oh, brother dearest, you are so in the best hands."

Cass dragged me around for hours poring over different stone slabs, exploring textures, which all felt the same to me. Floorboards of all different wood types and shades were inspected. Suites of furniture were exclaimed over until I pleaded for release from this torture she made me endure.

"I was exploring my feminine side," Cass disclosed.

"Wasn't aware you had one," I teased.

"Admittedly, mine is less developed than yours," she quipped. "Pub?"

I gave her a playful shove.

Saturday, 14th of February 2004. It was the first time in a few years when I didn't have to worry about getting flowers or booking a romantic overpriced meal. I headed to The Crypt with Tom and Stephen. It was decorated with red hearts suspended from the ceiling on different lengths of ribbon. I'd only just noticed it; it was trivial, really. Before me, on the end of a key ring, was a dolphin.

Pictures flooded my brain, memories of a perfect day crowding in. I tried to block her out, but my mind rejected this attempt. Her outline lay sketched inside my brain, her long blond hair a vivid slash of colour. A set of blue eyes stared defiantly at me, dancing with excitement, filmy with passion, and then clouded with pain, all of which I'd caused. The noise in the club seemed unbearable, so I left Stephen and Tom deep in their chat-up lines to a couple of unimpressed brunettes.

I took a deep lungful of the cold winter air. *Why do I feel so strange? Am I coming down with something?* I walked in the direction of the quays. The water lapped against the concrete walls, only disturbed by the street lamps reflected in the dark water. A couple were framed in the distance, heading towards me. They huddled together. Something about them was familiar. She threw back her head, laughing at something funny.

I longed to be in his place as he pulled her to him for a kiss – not with her, but with Gemma. That realisation was like a knife thrust. *Does she still think of me? She must hate me. Does she have someone new in her life?* Thinking of her with someone else ripped through my guts.

To divert myself, I turned away, but my attention was taken back to the two lovers. I was almost upon them when they parted from their embrace. They were so wrapped up in each other they didn't notice as I slipped past. I figured the last thing that Jake would want was me interrupting this intimate moment with Chris.

I rubbed my hands vigorously in front of the blazing, open fire.

"Remind me why we're playing in this weather. It's

cold enough to freeze your balls off."

"Because we're crap and we need all the practice we can get," Toby answered. "Changing the subject, I've got some news."

"You've won the lottery and you're planning on splitting it three ways," I joked.

"Not exactly, but I wouldn't mind divvying up the sleepless nights with you."

"Lisa's pregnant?" Jason, being a father of two, understood the reference to sleepless nights.

Toby's smile lit up his face.

We called the landlord to bring over another round to celebrate.

"I was content as we were, but Lisa wanted another baby to fuss over now that the boys are getting bigger."

"Better watch out that Cathy doesn't become broody now," I teased Jason.

"Not a hope. Actually, Cathy's going back to work. Apparently, she doesn't find being a full-time mum fulfilling enough."

"It'll do her good to get back into work, and surely,

the extra money won't go amiss."

"She never seemed discontent to me." Toby's brows furrowed.

"I wouldn't say discontent. She loves being with the kids, and she's only going back part-time. She says she needs to use her brain again."

"You don't seem too keen on the idea."

Jason confided his concerns about her being back in the law firm, meeting like-minded people and outgrowing him.

Chapter 11

Gemma

I was left reeling from Susie's reaction. I'd assumed I'd be forgiven and hugged to death. I tried to place myself in their shoes and, depressed with my findings, I headed to the bar and ordered a bottle of wine. Knocking back the first glass, I felt an immediate head rush. *What have I done?* Tears stung my eyes. The wine bottle became emptier, and my woe-is-me attitude heightened. Scalding tears poured down my face.

My head spun and the room blurred. I reached for the bottle to pour the last of the wine but my hands were unsteady and I clipped the bottle. It hit the table as my reflexes were slow. I watched transfixed as rivulets drained from the bottle and ran full speed the length of the table, splattering me. The smell of the wine soaking into my jeans made me nauseous. My head felt too heavy for my body, and all I wanted to do was lay it down.

"Come on, love, you've had enough. Time you were leaving." Strong fingers dug into the soft underside of my arms, his nails ripping into my skin.

The freezing cold air came as a shock as I staggered forward, the ground shifting beneath me. I could just make out the shape of a black cab coming towards me. My arm went out, followed by the rest of my body, but the taxi shot past.

"Shit."

I stumbled backwards and would have fallen but for the hands that encircled my waist, pulling me close. Stale smoke and rancid body odour wafted from my dubious rescuer. I felt the scratchy roughness of a beard as he pulled me closer. I was helpless to push him away.

"Fanks," I mumbled.

"I'll take you home," the husky voice leered at me.

A warning prickled inside my head. I didn't want him to take me anywhere.

He led me along, half carrying me as my legs felt hollow and weak. The wind whipped his offensive body odour in front of my nostrils causing fresh waves of nausea to sweep through me, and this time I failed to control the vomit that sped up my throat. Alcohol and remnants of my earlier meal splattered his light-coloured coat.

"You bitch!" He lashed out with the back of his hand, striking me across the face.

Stumbling back, I reached out to break my fall. I sobered as I realised the danger I was in, sprawled on the floor, hands stretched out behind me, the vile wretch towering over me. I looked around for help. Music pumped out of the once quiet bar. Any cries for help wouldn't be heard. He removed a tissue from his pocket, wiping at the stain. *I have to get away*. Pushing myself up, I began to run.

"Come back, you bitch! You're gonna pay for this!" I heard him growl. His heavy tread sounded menacing as he thundered after me.

Fear drove me forward. Too scared to even turn my head, I was aware he wasn't far behind. I kept running. My heart jumped into my breast, pounding at a furious rate until my breathing became shallow. Adrenaline was exploding through me, but the excess alcohol was taking its toll. I couldn't keep up this speed for long. I heard a thud, followed by a vile invective. Risking a glance behind, I saw him sprawled on the floor. I didn't stop. Using his fall to my advantage, I forced my pace, shooting around the corner.

An alley a few hundred yards down led out onto my road. I was taking a chance by being so isolated, but if I could get there before he turned into the road, it might pay off. The alley was dark; no street lighting until I exited it onto my road.

I made it to the front door and fumbled with the keys. The lights were off. I remembered that Carla and Joanne were out on an all-nighter. Urgency washed over me as I realised that he could be anywhere. The key slid into the lock. Turning it, I pushed the door open. Almost falling through the door, I slammed it shut, locking it with bolt and chain. Terror still surged through me as I ran to my room, locked that, too, and sank down on the floor with my back leaning against it.

The enormity of my experience flooded into my consciousness like a tidal wave crashing on the shore. Huge sobs tore from me as I rocked back and forth. I should call someone. *Susie. I need my friend.* Bitterness stopped me as I realised I'd burnt that particular bridge. I didn't doubt that she'd rush around, but I couldn't use what had happened as a lever to rebuild our friendship. I heard my father shouting in my head to call the police. It was the right thing to do but fear kept me rooted to the spot.

I must have fallen asleep curled into the foetal position, back pressed against the door. Rubbing my aching neck, I stretched my back, cat-like. My head pounded. I climbed wearily into my bed and burrowed under the duvet, unable to block out my ordeal.

Touching the angry welt that had risen on my face, I felt a tiny cut imprinted from his ring. I could have been a statistic on a police record, a cold, clinical examination determining the truth of a certain brutal encounter. Lying there, contemplating it, I knew I needed to report it to the police. I couldn't live with the knowledge that by doing nothing I endangered another feckless female, alone and vulnerable.

I rushed home on Friday evening having decided to try out some singles' bars. Things didn't quite work out as planned, though, as I spied Chris sat on my doorstep, cold and shivering.

Chris stood up and stretched out her arms, pulling me into a hug.

"What are you doing here?"

"Let me in and I'll tell you. I'm frozen."

I bustled her in, happy to have at least one of my friends with me.

"I've got some wine. Why don't you order a takeaway, and then we can catch up?" she said, and on noting my hesitant expression, added, "I know the story. Jackie rang me. We're cool, and so will the others be soon. To be honest, I think Jackie and Amanda already are, but they're working on Susie. I think she's only taking so long because of the whole Ted thing. She thinks she needs to toughen up, which she does, but she has to realise for herself where and when it's appropriate."

"Oh, honey, you're a breath of fresh air."

"Oh, don't get me wrong, I was a bit put out, but then I'd guessed the story earlier." She shrugged. "I'll fill in the details later, but I've seen a bit of Jake, and we'd figured it out together so I've had time to get used to it."

I wanted to ask her questions but had to content myself with the knowledge that she'd tell me soon.

"So I put in an offer on the flat, and it was accepted. It was exquisitely decorated; no need for me to do anything."

"You're going to gut it and stamp your own mark

on it."

"Hell, yes."

"Come on, then, I want the low-down on you and the luscious Jake." Little flashbacks formed like bubbles inside my mind.

"There's nothing much to tell," she hedged.

I threw her an I'm-not-having-that look.

"Okay." She threw her hands up in surrender.

I listened, happy for her if not a bit envious. The irony was, Jake hadn't come across as the type to get serious. And Theo? He had a girlfriend and maybe even a baby now, but if he hadn't, would we have stood a chance together? She told me about the romantic Valentine's trip to a privately hired boat on the quays, with champagne and oysters.

"Ah, how lovely."

"I know." We grinned at each other between mouthfuls of pizza.

"Did Theo boast about his conquest?"

"No," she was quick to reassure, but hesitated.

"Come on, Chris. I can take it, whatever it is."

271

"He went wild after his girlfriend lost the baby. She blamed him, finishing the relationship."

"How awful." I imagined how the guilt would've messed him up. "Did he push everyone away, like I did?"

"No. Well, sort of. He went on a bender in Malia before coming home; that was before he found out about losing the baby. He came close to losing his job, friends and family, and he slept around."

The colour drained from my face. I'd meant nothing to him – a quick lay, and the first in a long line. Perhaps he realised that he didn't need to limit himself to one woman – maybe he never had.

"And now?"

"He's back on track. Jake thinks…" she trailed off.

"Uh-huh. What does Jake think?"

"He thinks he's in love with you but won't admit it. Don't get your hopes up."

"I don't want to be with a liar and a cheat," I assured her.

She hesitated. "I don't think that's his normal

behaviour. Jake seemed quite shocked that he'd cheated on Claudine. Not because he was in love with her. By all accounts, he was going to finish with her, and then she landed the pregnancy on him just before he went away."

It tied in with the guy I'd thought him to be and the words he'd uttered after our time together about wanting to be with me. It would have been easier, though, to hate him.

"When are you going to visit the girls?" I asked in an attempt to change the conversation.

Chris looked embarrassed.

"Of course you're going to see them; it's not often you're here."

My tired, weary limbs sunk under the water after a day's shopping with Chris. Lying back with a contented sigh, I closed my eyes, savouring the moment. My eyes drooped, until the key turning in the door brought me back to consciousness.

"Gem?" Chris' voice drifted up the stairs.

Why's she back so early? Has something happened?

Wrapping a towel around me, I got out. My wet feet touched the cold lino, leaving prints on the floor as I made my way downstairs.

"Why are you back so soon?"

"Come on down and I'll explain. Actually, throw some clothes on first."

Walking into the living room, I saw Chris with Jackie, Amanda and Susie. Tears welled up in my eyes. Susie stood up hesitantly and held out her arms. I stepped into her embrace. Jackie and Amanda stood waiting their turn as Susie apologised profusely for her previous reaction.

The wine flowed, as did the conversation. From time to time, I reviewed what was happening and couldn't help grinning. I'd believed this particular door was closed to me, and yet, now, I was back in the midst of my friends as though nothing had happened.

"I'm so sorry about walking out on you. It must have taken so much courage to admit to what happened," Susie apologised. "What did you do when we left?"

The question I'd dreaded. I didn't want to answer it because I knew how they would feel the inevitable guilt.

"What?" Susie's question took me by surprise. I'd forgotten how well she knew me.

I told them haltingly what had happened that night.

"Why didn't you call one of us when you got home?" Jackie demanded.

"We'd have been there for you," Amanda asserted.

"I know, but how could I force you into that position?"

The girls saw my predicament, and after making me go through the details again, we moved onto the details of everyone else's life. Jackie had got engaged. I nearly cried when she asked me to be a bridesmaid along with Chris, Amanda and Susie.

"Mum'll kill me," she laughed. "She's got her mind set on a meringue wedding with my cousins as bridesmaids."

I could just imagine Mae's reaction to us as

bridesmaids and the modern affair that Jackie would have.

"I was thinking of a weekend in Dublin," Jackie said, breaking into my thoughts.

"Huh?"

"The hen weekend… Come on, Gem, get with it."

"Sorry, I was picturing your mum's reaction."

Jackie rolled her eyes. "Well, you're going to see it first-hand at the hen weekend."

"She's never coming." I guffawed.

His fingers ran along my spine, teasing and arousing me. I strained closer to his warm, firm body. Our lips met again, a light, gentle touch. He trailed his fingertips lazily over my back, running down the hollow until both hands tightly grasped my buttocks. He pulled me toward him, and the kiss deepened. Tongues played, each one vying for precedence. My nails raked his back as I sought deeper contact. I pulled back to remove the last of his clothes, his trousers a barrier between us. Turning in my sleep, I came to slow awareness, aroused from the dream. I rolled over, hoping to step back in where I'd left off. At first sleep eluded me, but when I did eventually sleep, my dreams were quite different.

When I woke, the pale wintry sun was peeping through the curtains. My thoughts turned to my dream of the night before. As a one-off erotic dream, I could've coped, but these dreams were coming on a nightly basis. They always stopped at about the same time. Sometimes I was allowed a few more minutes, sometimes much less, but I was always left with a tantalising glimpse that never reached its natural conclusion.

A letter dated last year and post-marked Brighton was waiting on the mat just inside the front door for me when I got home. I inserted my nail under the flap on the underside of the envelope, ripping it open. My eyes scanned it, finding the signatures on the bottom, Lucy and Jen. I grabbed a quick coffee and scooted upstairs with my letter, then flopped down on the bed.

Is This Love?

The Willows

14 Barley Lane

Brighton

13/09/03

Hi Gemma,

We arrived back in Brighton after a six-hour delay in Crete. Still, can't

complain, the holiday was great, and we really enjoyed getting to know you. People bond easily on holiday, and promise to keep in contact, but the truth is, once home, that connection doesn't seem so real – a figment of the holiday magic, if you will. However, on arriving home we really did want to know what was happening with you and Theo. Jen says she thinks

you're together now, reading this. I'm sorry I booked Samaria Gorge for your last day. You were right – it was breath-taking, and I'm still popping the blisters, but we would have loved to have seen you off. Jen's interrupting me again; she says she bets Theo saw you off. I hope she's right.

We wanted to say to you, Theo is LUSH!

I stopped reading for a moment or two. The bittersweet memories came flooding back: the two of them, the fun we'd had, the night of my date with Theo and the subsequent pain. I jolted myself back to the present and continued reading the letter.

Jen and I are both finding it hard being back at work and in the increasingly colder climate. We long for the Cretan sun to warm our limbs. For the chance to sit on the balcony on a balmy night looking into a starless sky, the mountains as our backdrop and a bottle of wine or two on the go. Oh well, we'll have to dream some more until next year. For now, the cold, grey world we inhabit will have to suffice.

Must away now, people to see, places to go, etc...

Love, Lucy & Jen

P.S. Please write back

P.P.S. We're looking for our next destination!

XXX

They were on paper exactly as I'd remembered them in person, and I wasted no time in replying. It took several attempts to hit the right note with the Theo explanation. I added my email address so that our correspondence could be instantaneous. Once written, I posted it straight away.

Theo

"What was this barbeque in aid of?" I asked Jason.

"Does there have to be a reason to see friends?" he countered. "Have you got a drink?"

I held up my bottle in reply. "How's it going with Cathy working?"

"We haven't stopped arguing." Dark circles lined his eyes.

"Hey, how's it going?" Jake came up behind us, slapping us both on the back.

We shelved the inevitable conversation. Instead, we listened to Jake's verbal diatribe on just about anything and everything, from the politicians who ran the country to the dizzy tart who served him at the supermarket. We laughed, and yet I couldn't help noticing that Jason's amusement didn't quite register in his eyes.

"Are you still seeing Chris?" Jason asked.

A smile appeared on his face for the briefest instant.

"Is she the one?"

"Who knows? There are still so many skirts as yet left untouched."

Jake announced that he was going to brighten someone else's day and left us standing there. Jason's short bark of laughter was genuine this time.

"So?"

"We can't really talk here; if Cathy knew I was talking to you about it she'd kill me. Can you meet me tomorrow for a drink?"

The barbeque brought a few surprises to me that day, the main one being that I'd been blinkered. I'd naïvely failed to see what was going on around me. Watching Jason and Cathy interact with ease and loving devotion had been all I'd seen before, but now I saw their smiles didn't quite reach their eyes. I'd thought Jason and Cathy were the perfect couple, I hadn't seen beyond the obvious happiness, but now I saw the strain between them.

Through fresh eyes, I saw things differently, and it seemed to me as though the world appeared jaded and tarnished. Part of me wanted to turn the clock back and see things as perfect again.

Had it always been like that or was it due to the arguments over Cathy's return to work? I wondered whether other people weren't watching avidly the situation unfolding before me. *Is everyone else too busy plastering over the cracks of their own lives with fake smiles? Is this just normal life, with its smattering of ups and downs? Where had I got the fairy tale idyll from?* My parents had always seemed happy together; was that, too, an illusion? Their dissatisfaction had always been with Cass and me.

"What's up? You look like you've had your backside slapped." Jake's perceptiveness never failed to amaze me.

Jake had few illusions about life. Had they been stripped away early in his life or hadn't he possessed any? What made him so cynical, and cold to other people? And why had he singled me out as one of the chosen people who was allowed glimpses of a different side of his nature? We were so different, and that only intensified with this new perspective. What experiences in his life had taught him a lesson that I seemed only to be grasping after more than thirty years on earth?

"Can I ask you something?"

"Sounds deep; should I make a run for it now?" he teased, but he sounded wary.

"What happened to you?"

"What's that supposed to mean?"

When I said nothing, he added in a resigned tone,

"Okay, but not here. Meet me in that wine bar near the quays tonight at nine."

Jake sauntered into the bar half an hour late. His eyes wore a strained look.

"Before I say anything, this goes no further. After I've told you, I want you to drop it, never mention it again, no questions, and definitely no psychobabble required. Don't try to over-analyse me or fix me; I'm not broken. My lifestyle, the way I live, is a conscious choice, not a product of my upbringing. Finally, I don't want your pity. Have you got that?"

I nodded.

Jake took a deep breath. His eyes glittered hard, like polished stone, and his chiselled jaw-line tightened. He finally broke the tense silence.

"When I was five, my dad lost his job. At first, he went out every day, trawled every newspaper, went to countless interviews and beat a path to anything he could find. After a while, the fight went out of him. Six months of humiliation turned him from the jovial family man into a bitter one. Mum took on lots of jobs – cleaning other peoples' houses and schools, even taking in washing and ironing – to support us. Dad felt emasculated by mum becoming the breadwinner. She'd never had to work before; he'd seen to everything. She tried to console him, telling him he'd find something soon. A man with his abilities would be snapped up.

"Mum never stopped. When she wasn't working, she was cooking and cleaning for us. She may have taken over the role of breadwinner, but Dad said he'd be damned if he'd lower himself to the position of house skivvy. She didn't argue with him.

"After a while, he stopped bothering. He sat in front of the TV in his armchair, only getting up to change the channel, the newspaper beside him, though he no longer looked at the job vacancies. When Mum came in from work, he would demand his cup of tea be brought to him straight away. It didn't matter that she was dog-tired. *"Where have you been, woman? Where's my tea? A man could die of thirst waiting for you to do your wifely duties."* Off she would scuttle, stooped with exhaustion, to do his bidding. She'd leave a sandwich in the fridge for his lunch. At weekends, he wouldn't even get off his backside to get it. He'd send me. It wasn't long before he started drinking, frittering away the money Mum had slaved for, at the pub with his mates.

"Over the years, I went without. Shoes and socks full of holes, trousers that were patched so much you could barely see the original material. They flapped about my ankles as I grew. Some nights I'd go to bed hungry because he'd pissed off with the food money. When Mum dared to voice a half-hearted complaint, he hit her, something he'd never done before. After a while, the violence became a regular part of our routine. Mum tried to shelter me from it. She put herself in front of me but sometimes he would beat her till her lips split, her face was bruised and bloody, and then he'd do the same to me."

He paused for a moment as though there was worse to come. I sat stunned, appalled by the hell that had been Jake's childhood. My own hadn't been a picture of family harmony, but I couldn't imagine that kind of abuse, and I'd had my sister beside me.

"He broke my nose on my fifteenth birthday," he continued. "I left home that day, slept rough for a while. I found work in pubs and restaurants. I'd always looked older than my age. I would go to the public toilets to wash and make myself respectable." He paused, lost in the appalling memories of a past so horrific that it seemed more fitting as a work of fiction.

"I managed to get into this squat, where everyone was injecting as often as they could beg or steal the money for a hit. Once or twice, I was tempted to shut myself off from the misery of my existence, but I'm not a quitter. It seemed like the easy way of opting out of life. So I lived there, working all the jobs I could, saving money. I slept with one eye on the door and one hand beside the carving knife I kept under my pillow. I'd have cut anyone who tried to come between me and the new life I'd planned. I started night-college to take the exams I'd missed when I'd walked out of school. I spent many years working myself up to my degree. I'd always had a way with figures, and I wasn't going to end up a deadbeat like my father. Eventually, I managed to get a small studio flat. It wasn't much. I had cockroaches for company, but it was my own space, and I figured it was a step up from the drug squat I'd come from."

His hand reached for the glass, the only indication he was in the present. "I went back for Mum. *"It's not much,"* I told her, *"but it will get you away from him. We'll get something better together soon." "I'm sorry, Son,"* she cried. *"I'm glad you're doing well, and hope you get all that you deserve in life, but there's no question of me leaving your father. I love him. It's probably best if we don't meet like this again; he wouldn't like it. You know you hurt him when you left."* I couldn't bear the accusation I saw in her eyes, or that she blamed me. I haven't seen her since." He brought his tale to an abrupt end, his eyes wet and clouded.

"Wha...?"

Jake interrupted me. "There's no more to tell. I need to go for a slash."

When he came back, I could almost believe I'd

imagined the whole conversation, as he was so in control.

How had he lived like that and managed to get to this position? I knew the pressures of training for our chosen career, but I'd been sheltered. I tried to picture the five-year-old Jake, who'd learned life the hard way. It was no wonder he had no illusions about life. No matter what he said, I believed that his anger and treatment of women stemmed from the rejection from his mother. I sensed that this betrayal had hurt him more than the years of abuse, and had scarred him more than living in a house full of junkies.

I leant back onto the padded cushion on the bench in the Dog & Duck while Jason stood at the bar, waiting to be served. Still reeling from yesterday's revelations from Jake, I wondered what today would reveal. I'd hoped Toby would have been brought in on this, but I stayed the chosen one. I wasn't the kind of person who could give advice. My life had been privileged, a fact I was only beginning to appreciate. How could I be qualified to take on board such important details of people's lives when I couldn't comprehend them? The abused child and the married man who, until yesterday, I'd assumed lived the dream.

"Do you remember that American slime ball that Cathy was dating before me?"

"The solicitor guy, thought he was supremely intelligent? Bit of a bore. Had a double-barrelled surname and boasted that he could trace his family back as far as Elizabeth I. Didn't he claim that he was a direct descendant of Sir Walter Raleigh?" I laughed, remembering the day I'd met him.

"That's the one." Jason harrumphed. "He's back working at the same firm as Cathy. Started two weeks before she did."

"Jay, mate, you can't honestly believe that Cathy would... Well, you know. She's not like that."

"She's been working late. She was supposed to be part-time, but she's there all day."

"Cathy's probably trying to make a good impression. You know her meticulous attention to detail. Have you talked to her?"

"And say what? Are you and Mr. hot-shot-slime-ball-lawyer shagging behind my back?"

"That wasn't quite how I imagined the conversation going. You don't believe she would risk losing you and mess up the life of her kids for an unsatisfactory grope with an ex who couldn't cut the mustard the first time around?"

Jason slumped forward in his seat, his arms resting on the table. "But what if it's not meaningless? What if she's realised she still loves him? She did once, after all."

"Jay, she loves you. I can't believe she has feelings for him."

"Yeah, but you live in a sheltered bubble. Your equation of life is simple: Love + marriage = happy-ever-after," Jason gibed at my expense.

I decided to let it ride because it was true and he was hurting. He needed to lash out at someone; I just happened to be in the firing range.

It was decided that Jason was going to talk to Cathy

and tell her he wasn't comfortable with her working with her ex.

I arrived at the restaurant ten minutes late and flustered. I'd had a sinking feeling Cass was setting me up on a blind date, as she'd seemed unusually animated, but the table wasn't the intimate table for four I'd dreaded. 'The Parents' sat, looking unusually jovial, opposite what I can only assume must have been Keith's parents and a sulky, attractive woman in her early twenties.

We were obviously going to hear an announcement about my sister's upcoming nuptials. *How could she have kept that from me?* I stood there in confusion, my feet rooted to the spot. Cass saw me and grinned, but on seeing my expression hurried from the table toward me.

"I'm sorry I didn't tell you. Keith insisted we tell everyone together."

I smiled, trying to look magnanimous, but I couldn't help the little twist that my insides gave at being ousted from my position of the first and foremost person in Cass' life. Don't get me wrong, I didn't mean to be so immature about the whole thing. I really was pleased for her. Cass deserved happiness, but Cass had always been the only constant in my life so it was natural to have some minor misgivings.

"He knows how close we are, in theory, but can't quite grasp the truth of it in practice. I so wanted to tell you, big bro." She clasped my arm, giving it a little squeeze before pulling me towards the table. "I've kept you a space next to me, with Keith's sister on the other side."

Keith's sister, it turned out, was called Lily, a twenty-two-year-old raving nymphomaniac who kept grasping my leg under the table and giving me the kind of massage that was going to guarantee my embarrassment. *This can't be happening.* This is my future brother-in-law's sister who's groping me under the table. Relations between our families would be more than a little strained if I took her up on her silent but purposeful offer.

"I suppose some of you are wondering why we've dragged you all down here," Keith started. On seeing my expression, he added, "Some of you may have already guessed. I asked Cass to do me the honour of being my wife, and she has agreed."

There were smiles all around although his family did seem to be finding it hard to part their lips in so simple a movement. Cass had said Keith's parents were dour. "I would also like to thank Richard for granting me permission to ask his daughter for her hand."

Now I really am pissed. They knew before I did. My parents had very little to do with Cass' existence, apart from the happenchance of their co-habitation in the bedroom that had produced her. It was me who took care of her. As a two-year-old, I had taken notice of her, I'd kissed away her tears when she hurt herself and had been her willing slave ever since. I knew it was the 'done thing' to ask the father for his permission, but when had he ever taken more than a passing interest in her well-being? *Why had his permission been asked when I wasn't even told?* For Cass' sake, I plastered a smile on my face.

Chapter 12

Gemma

The next few months, Lucy, Jen and I exchanged regular e-mails, conjuring up images of Crete and Theo while stirring up varying emotions. I tried to keep mine light-hearted and laughed great belly rumbles over their amusing anecdotes. I painted a picture for them of the mounds of dresses we made our way through in our quest to get the perfect dresses for Jackie's wedding. Jackie's mother, Mae, stopped accompanying us after the first trip, as we'd ignored the hideous flouncy dresses she picked. She was only just getting over the disappointment that her nieces weren't bridesmaids.

What I didn't express in my letters was the overwhelming emptiness I felt. I wondered if I would ever be happy again, and yet I wasn't unhappy. I enjoyed my active social life, but there lingered a discontent, like something was lacking, and I didn't know what it was or how to fix it.

Susie was struggling to adjust to the overwhelming difficulties that accompanied her split from Ted. At times, the memories flooded in – the good times, remembering the plans they'd made for a life together. Then she would harden her heart, recalling his betrayal and the reality of how she was going to cope. She couldn't afford the mortgage alone, and yet she couldn't bear the thought of losing the house that she loved.

I dragged Susie out to bars at the weekends and roped her into joining the gym. It was amusing to see her out on the social scene. She'd never experienced it, as she had been with Ted since she was a teenager, so going out on the pull hadn't been necessary. Now she dipped her toe in the waters. With great reservation and a lot of persuasion from us, she'd gone out on a few dates. She declared that she didn't have a connection with any of them. I told her she didn't need to feel a connection, only to cut her teeth on the dating market.

So, together, we clocked up miles on the treadmill and exercise bike, knocked back many a drink and flirted with countless men. Our biggest problem was being single women in our thirties while most of the crowd were eighteen-year-olds. Running with a younger crowd was a great way to exacerbate our insecurities. Not that I would say we were actually running with them. With envy, we remembered our own pre-cellulite days.

Heathrow Airport was overrun by a rowdy crowd of thirty over-excited loud hens, all waiting to invade Dublin. It was strange to think of Jackie preparing to tie the knot; I'd always had her pegged as the last amongst our group to get married. Our party consisted of Jackie's close workmates, cousins, her mum and the four of us.

I hoped Mae wouldn't disapprove of the whole weekend: drinking to excess, crude jokes and the novelty sex toys. I could imagine her furrowed brows and pained expression, followed by a disdainful sniff of disapproval. In another couple of hours, she would wish herself anywhere but with us. She would be wondering how she'd reared a daughter so unlike herself.

One of Jackie's workmates, Lara, made a suggestive comment to Sam, the male check-in assistant who resisted her invitation. He oozed sexuality, and I'm sure he was more than used to being hit upon. The exchange caused Mae's lips to pinch together. My turn came, and while I couldn't help but admire his gorgeousness, I managed to avoid the example that Lara had set. He, on the other hand, decided that he was enjoying the attention and wasn't ready to be ignored. He flashed me his sexiest smile and flirted with me in the same outrageous manner that my fellow hens had turned on him. As he handed me my boarding card, he also gave me a piece of paper with his name and number on it.

"Call me," he suggested and blinded me with his overtly sexual smile.

The girls all around me howled their approval and teased me.

"Are you going to call him?" Amanda asked.

"He only wants one thing."

"Yes, and I bet he's good at that, too."

"You need some fun," Jackie added. I could see the girls were all in agreement.

"We'll see," I said in an attempt to quieten them.

"At least you didn't say no." Susie laughed.

"But I haven't said yes either."

I thought I might call him. Although I'd dated other men, I hadn't slept with anyone since Theo. Maybe this guy, who wanted nothing more than an enjoyable one-night stand, was just what I needed. Thinking about Theo caused a cloud to scud across my day. I fell back from the others, in need of a moment's solitude.

"You're thinking about Theo, aren't you?" Susie sidled up to me. "I recognised the look on your face. I wear the same one when I think about Ted."

"You think about him a lot?"

"Not as much," she conceded, "but still more than he deserves. I try to hate him, but now that the worst of my anger is over, I find I can't even do that."

"You wouldn't get back with him?"

"No, I couldn't do that."

We descended on Dublin like a herd of galloping horses, excited and playful. The one concession Jackie had allowed her mum was agreeing to stay in a respectable four-star hotel. I was sharing a room with Susie. Jackie had drawn the short straw and was sharing with her mum.

I remember little about our first night beyond the first few pubs where we had a couple of drinks each, accompanied by a seemingly endless supply of tequila shots. I do recall that, as a group of hens with pink satin sashes proclaiming our purpose, we received an inordinate amount of male attention. I also remember Jackie flitting around like a butterfly from flower to flower. Drinks flowed, faces blurred, the dance floor throbbed, and after that I don't recall anything else.

Our plan for Saturday was to separate and do our own thing during the day, meeting up again in the evening for our night out. We decided to hit the fashionable Grafton Street. Mae dragged her nieces out sightseeing when she'd received a grunt from a hung-over Jackie. It was gone mid-day when we headed into town on a bus. A mere five-minute journey managed to seem like hell in our delicate states. The whirling dervishes who'd planned to hit the shops of Dublin had become wilting flowers, dehydrated and in need of more sleep to revive their wilting petals. We headed for a first fix in a smart coffee shop that served our lattes in tall, slender glasses with a handful of chocolate gratings on top.

"Did you see the look on that man's face when you snogged him, Gem?" Jackie laughed.

"What bloke?" My eyes widened.

"You don't remember it?" She giggled, and the others followed suit.

"You're having me on." I sat back into my chair.

"Uh-uh. You grabbed him by the lapels of his jacket and brought him to your lips." Jackie spoke the words with evident pleasure, wagging her index finger.

"Like I'm gonna believe you lot."

"Susie, tell her," Jackie demanded. Susie was always the one who was called upon to advocate or back up a story, as she couldn't lie.

Susie smiled. "I'm afraid so, hon. I was mightily impressed. The guy looked like he'd been put in an electric chair."

"I must have been bad, then."

"Honey you weren't even talking to the guy, you just saw what you liked and took it." Amanda struggled to get the words out as the tears of mirth rolled down her face. "Never mind Susie. He was mightily impressed when he got over the initial surprise. He went in for round two, but you swatted him away as though he were a fly and walked on by."

My head sunk into my hands as I covered my face in shame. *I must have been slaughtered. I can't remember a thing.*

The girls grinned and sat back to enjoy their coffees.

That night we headed to the Mermaid Café, one of the hottest spots in town. It'd come highly recommended. I drank more cautiously at first as I remembered – or rather didn't remember – the night before and my scarlet behaviour. The food was superb and filling, so I figured it would soak up any inordinate amount of alcohol. I relaxed and joined in the light-hearted banter and teasing. We even managed the Herculean task of making Jackie blush. Now, if that had been suggested as a mission for a prospective loved one to win the hand of said maid, I would have deemed it impossible; it would have been easier to slay a fire-breathing dragon. After the main course, we handed Jackie the bag of goodies the four of us had collated.

"Cor. I wouldn't mind getting my hand on his

package," Jackie leered.

She referred to the picture of a half-naked male model who adorned the front and back of the goodie bag. Jackie placed her hand on the hunk's hidden package and grinned lasciviously. Mae had relaxed. The perpetual frown of disapproval had disappeared as her nieces had slipped a few shots of vodka into her orange juice.

Jackie dipped her hand into the bag and rummaged around. "Like a lucky dip."

"Was that a lucky dick?" Amanda quipped to much amusement.

Jackie pulled out an object and laid it with care on the table before tearing the Sellotape binding it. Her long, elegant fingers closed around the wind-up willy.

"Bit small," she cooed.

She wound it up and popped it in front of her to watch as it ran the length of the table. I took the spare one from my clutch bag and challenged her to a race. Jackie laughed with glee and insisted the loser down a shot of tequila.

We placed them side by side and watched as they made their way down the table to accompanying cheers. I groaned as mine stopped midway.

"Should'ha used Duracell!" Susie squealed as we howled our approval.

I knocked back my tequila while Jackie dipped into the bag. "Ten reasons why a cucumber is better than a man," the tea towel stated. We sat in silence to listen to them, commenting after each point. A pink, flashing feather boa and a pair of outsize boobs found their way onto the hen, and many more novelties followed, as did the glasses of wine and tequila shots. We ordered a slippery nipple apiece in an attempt to embarrass the poor young waiter. He seemed unfazed, and gave us his best I've-seen-lots-of-hen-nights-before-yours-is-tame look.

We didn't know where we were going, but that didn't matter, as there were bars in every direction. Within minutes, we'd trooped into a semi-full bar, making it our own. The blow-up life-size man caught lots of attention. It was amazing, but the men seemed to illicit more excitement from it than the women.

The DJ played *Girls Just Wanna Have Fun* and *I Will Survive*. I'm sure that was influenced by our large and loud crowd. It was timeless, get-the-crowd-on-the-dance-floor music; all he missed out was *It's Raining Men*. Tracks from the 1980's merged with songs from Beyoncé, Christina Aguilera and The Black Eyed Peas. We howled with the best of them, dancing, stomping and swaying. The dance floor vibrated from the throbbing music and pounding feet. Men flocked to the floor, drawn by a group of women having fun. Once more, the drinks flowed like a waterfall.

"Come on, you," Susie coaxed, "you've got to get up. We've a plane to catch."

I groaned, partly because of my swimming head and thumping headache but also because I couldn't believe that she could sound so cheerful. She'd been every bit as drunk as me. I could recall the vehemence in her voice as she'd sung the words to *I Will Survive*.

I even remembered her spinning around with her arms akimbo – not the easiest thing to do on a packed dance floor. She'd grabbed me and we sung to each other, each of us voicing the words to someone not there to listen to them. And now she was chipper. I twisted around and tried to bury myself under the scratchy wool blankets.

"Get up, Gemma." Susie's tone was insistent.

With a sigh, I attempted to rise, only to be hit by waves of nausea. Sheer willpower forced me into an upright position. My stomach heaved as Susie thrust a steaming cup of coffee into my hand, the strong smell wafting under my nostrils.

The hairdresser wound my hair elegantly to the top of my head, twisting the odd strand around her finger and leaving it loose, to frame my face. Susie sat beside me, lost in thought, as her unruly hair was forced to behave, for once. I realised that she was wearing 'the look'. *She's thinking about Ted. Well, of course she is.* The last time we were all congregated at the hairdressers' together would've been her wedding.

"So, Gemma," Chris interrupted my train of thought, "how did it go with Sam-the-super-stud?"

"Mm, he was good," I said with a self-satisfied smirk.

"You didn't?" Amanda choked out.

"We met for a drink, but after half an hour and two drinks it was obvious there was only one thing we had in common. We cut to the chase, headed back to his, and as I said, he was good."

The girls roared their approval.

"Are you seeing him again?" Susie asked when the furore died down.

"No. It was a perfect one-off, but I'd soon tire of him. To be frank, there wasn't much between the ears."

"Was there enough between the legs, though?" Jackie stifled a giggle.

"Oh, more than enough. As I said, a perfect one-off."

With that, my hairdresser and Susie's announced our hair was done and ushered us over to the waiting seats while they steered Amanda and Chris to the seats we'd vacated.

"Are you okay?" I whispered to Susie.

"Of course. Why wouldn't I be?"

"Oh, just *that* look."

"I was just thinking about the day I married Ted."

"I thought that might've been it."

"Has this Sam guy managed to dispel Theo from your thoughts?" Susie asked, trying to change the subject and shift the focus from her.

"No. Actually, that's why I didn't want to call him again. I kept comparing him to Theo, and the poor guy had no chance whatsoever."

"Not that good, then?"

"Not that good."

"Do you think any marriages have a chance these days?" she whispered.

"Hush. Don't let Jackie hear you saying that." I avoided answering, but her thoughts mirrored mine. *Is there such a thing as true love? If so, did it last or was it just a passing phase that you grew out of? Had we stopped working at relationships, become too complacent because the get-out clause was too easy?*

The church was decked out in ivory and dark red flowers, brightening up the gloom of the otherwise dark and staid building. Mae had been horrified when she'd realised Jackie was toying with these colours. *"You can't have red and white together. They're unlucky." "I don't buy into superstitions, Mum. You should know that. Anyway, it's ivory, not white,"* Jackie had retorted. *"It's something to do with hospitals,"* Mae continued as though her daughter hadn't spoken. *"The colours represent blood and bandages."*

A cloying smell of incense clung to the stones, mixed with the heady scent of roses. I could feel a tickle in my nostrils but resisted the urge to sneeze. The guests sat, waiting for the bride to appear, in their brightly coloured outfits. The men faced the altar, their faces chiselled into stony expressions. Many amongst them would rather have been anywhere than at a wedding. I was sure they wouldn't object to the reception afterwards. The women, in stark contrast, wore beatific expressions and somewhat gormless smiles. Some were remembering their own special days, while the singletons among the congregation imagined, at that moment, their own. The women watched Jackie's progression down the aisle, necks straining. They took in every aspect of her appearance, from her hair to her shoes and everything in between, in that one long glance.

Rory stood at the top of the church, waiting with a devoted expression for Jackie, who was sauntering up the aisle on the arm of her father. Her wild hair was perfectly coiffed, the sides held back in circular clips sparkling with diamanté pins, while the rest of it fell in ringlets over her bare shoulders. She wore a simple yet elegant dress of crushed ivory silk. Her hands, holding the dark red bouquet, trembled as she focused on walking up the aisle without tripping up; a nightmare she'd had all week.

We walked behind in our dark red, crushed silk dresses that were draping off the shoulder and moulding into the waists before dropping from the hips in a straight line to the ankle. The décolletage was picked out with cream satin rosebuds.

The service was blessedly short, although the same couldn't be said for the photographs. My jaw ached from smiling, and I wasn't the only one who was gasping to reach the bar.

The evening reception brought a shock to me that I hadn't anticipated, but I suppose it was natural since Jake was Chris' boyfriend that he would be there. My reaction to coming face to face with Theo's friend, after the amount of champagne I'd consumed, was embarrassing. I mean, how many women my age gasp and turn pale, which I'm sure I did? I remember blubbing something later to him about missing Theo. I can only hope that he'd have forgotten my words and not ended up repeating them verbatim to Theo a few days later.

Theo

Saturday 19th June 2004 was the day I moved into my new home. Cass roped Mother into helping us scrub the house from top to bottom. I couldn't believe it. For a woman who hadn't so much as chipped a nail washing up in all our years growing up, to don marigolds and start scrubbing my new house was beyond amazing. I was surprised she hadn't suggested sending Maria, the small middle-aged Hispanic woman who charred for them.

The windows were thrown open, and every nook and cranny was scrubbed by our three-strong team. I would've tried opting out, claiming some job that needed the male touch, if I could've got away with it but Cass would have downed tools and walked out.

Women clean so much better than men, or at least that's what we convince them in an attempt to avoid it ourselves. Am I spending too much time with Jake? *Traces of his influence could be detected in that thought.*

After Cass and Mother left, I headed to the supermarket to stock up the cupboards with essentials. These inevitably included a crate of beer and a bottle of wine. I'd need a drink to unwind, once I'd finished a day of physical work. The place was empty but for the few items I possessed. The whole house needed to be redecorated and walls needed to be knocked down to make it open-plan. It made me realise just how much work was involved.

A dilapidated old van was parked outside when I got home, and leaning casually against the bonnet was the lanky figure of my future brother-in-law.

"I was about to call you."

"Keith," I greeted him. "Come to help, have you?"

"No. But I do have one extremely worn and haggard sofa bed in the back of that clapped-out heap that calls itself a van. It seems to be causing quite a stir amongst your neighbours." Keith laughed and waved at the woman across the road, who dropped her curtains back into place.

Laughing, I wondered if I would have to contend with nosy neighbours.

"Where did you say you got that heap of shit?" I exclaimed.

"Ah, well now, if you don't want it…"

"Depends on whether you know the previous owners and can vouch for their personal hygiene or whether you trawled the local rubbish tip for such a tasty morsel," I joked.

"I can vouch for the couple who owned it but not for their brood of kids, who had exclusive use of it in their playroom." Keith chuckled.

I searched through my bags and slung a sheet over it before we sank onto it with beer in hand.

"You've got your work cut out making this place habitable," Keith said, pulling the ring on the can.

"I know. I think I'm just starting to appreciate exactly how much. Still, time is something I do have, and I relish having my own space after so many years sharing."

Those words were guaranteed to come back to haunt me, and it didn't take long. Keith left after one beer for a date with Cass. I sat, idly flicking through the television channels. Nothing grabbed my attention, so I switched it off. I pulled out the latest crime thriller that graced my meagre library selection, and started to read. I reached the bottom of the page before I realised I hadn't taken in a single word. I tried again, but the words wouldn't register.

The silence echoed eerily around me, making me uneasy. I wasn't scared of noises in the dark in the female sense, it was more an unease born of the utter stillness and silence that I wasn't used to. I'd been alone in the flat many times and hadn't felt this deafening silence. I should have been revelling in my new-found solitude but I wasn't. I felt restless.

Maybe I can't relax because it doesn't feel like mine. After a few hours of stripping walls, I might get the sense of belonging here. The main bedroom was my initial project. The sooner I had a room to sleep in, the better. So I laid into the musty-smelling aged wallpaper with gusto, only to discover another layer beneath, which was, if possible, grubbier; yellowing stains lay over it like a watercolour wash. I set about soaking it with water and scraping off the offending traces. The layers of faded and dusty paper gave way to a crumbling uneven wall underneath that required the skills of a plasterer. It was fortunate that I knew one, Jason, but I was disappointed that I couldn't just crack on without assistance.

I tapped on the white front door. The sweet scent of roses wafted up. I heard the sound of scurrying feet, and the door creaked open. Jack and Katie peered out, and on recognition, threw themselves headlong into my arms.

"Come in, Uncle Feo. Mummy and Daddy are upstairs, shouting again." Her welcome was punctuated by angry words coming from upstairs.

I hesitated on the doorstep. Jason and Cathy would

not want me to be a witness to this, but I knew the kids would tell them I'd been here. What would they say if I turned around and walked away? I stepped over the threshold as angry words rebounded between Jason and his wife like a ball between two tennis racquets. A door slammed with violence. The reverberations echoed downstairs and I heard the heavy tread of footsteps on the stairs. A petrified expression froze on Cathy's face. Her usually proud features stiffened as she prepared herself mentally to play a role.

"Theo. What a surprise. How long...?" The rest of the words caught in her throat.

"Oh, not long, Cathy. I've only just arrived." My own acting skills were not too convincing, but she smiled as I allowed her to save face.

"I came to see himself." I indicated upstairs with a short nod. "If you're busy, I could always catch him another time." I hoped for an early release from the oppressive tension wrapping around the house.

"No, it's okay, Theo." She smiled wearily. "Jay," she shouted up the stairs, though her tone had changed now for my benefit.

"What now?" His words were still full of anger but they also held a note of weariness. His voice hadn't adapted to the new situation because, as yet, he was unaware there was one.

"Jay, Theo's here." Her voice rang out as a warning. "I must get on with dinner. The roast won't cook itself." I doubted she had started dinner. There was no tell-tale smell of meat wafting through the house as there would normally be. "I only got a small joint this week or I'd invite you..." she trailed off as I waived my hand.

She fled through the archway that led into the kitchen. I suppressed a sudden urge to walk in and hug her. I knew, if I did, the floodgates would open, and she wouldn't thank me.

"Theo, mate, what a surprise."

I turned in his direction and was shocked by his appearance. A shadow highlighted his face where he hadn't shaved, giving him an unkempt look. Dark circles and grooves pulled at his eyes.

"Jay."

"What can I do for you?" His eyes pleaded with me to give him an excuse to get away.

"I came to ask a favour, but it can wait. I should have called." I edged toward the door.

"Don't go. Since when have we needed to announce a visit?" His bleak look matched the kids'.

"I need some plastering for my new house, but there's no rush. I just thought I'd pop in to see when you could fit me in."

"I'm free right now." He grasped the excuse with both hands.

"Oh, there's no rush. I don't want to spoil your Sunday." *Idiot.* I shuffled from one foot to the other, staring at the wooden flooring.

"No, really, I insist. You must be keen to get on. We've got many more Sundays to enjoy."

Who's he pretending to? He knows I know and the kids hear it all. Is it for his own benefit?

"Cathy, I'm just popping out. Be back later," he called out, and as an afterthought, stopped and kissed

Jack and Katie before rushing headlong out of the door.

Jason viewed the room in silence. The walls were bare now. If I didn't know him so well, I'd have assumed he was assessing the walls. It seemed like he was staring blankly at them. I wondered whether I should ask him about it, but felt it would be better to let him talk when he was ready. It didn't take long before it spilled out – the accusations that couldn't be unsaid, the hurt, humiliation and insecurities. Righteous indignation fuelled the flames further, and stubborn pride stopped either of them from backing down.

"I know she hasn't cheated on me," he finished.

"So why all this?"

"Once it was said, it was too late to retract it. My instincts tell me she didn't, but my paranoia and insecurities made me accuse her in the first place."

"Why not tell her that?"

"She won't listen now. She hates me for even thinking it."

"What about the kids?"

"What about them? They don't know anything."

I snorted in disgust. "You think?"

He looked askance at me.

"When I turned up, you were shouting the odds at each other. Jack and Katie answered the door to me. You didn't hear me come in; I could've been anyone. Katie told me that you two were shouting at each other again. They're not stupid, Jason. Jack, at least, is probably petrified that you're going to split up; he must have seen it with friends of his from school. Their world's been turned upside down. I know I'm no expert on relationships or children, but I do know you need to sort this out somehow for their sakes before they suffer any more."

"Bloody XL," I muttered.

"What was that?" Jake asked, studying me with a little too much interest for my liking.

"Just got the accounts through from XL again. They must have a child doing their books. It's a jumble, barely legible."

"Why don't they e-mail you the accounts?"

"Too advanced for them. They don't even use a computer for it. Look at these books; they're out of the ark. It's even got a bloody coffee stain. Can you believe it?"

Jake smiled but kept quiet.

I leant back in my seat. "Okay, out with it."

"What?"

"Whatever's bothering you. You've been uncharacteristically quiet all day."

"Are you free tonight?"

"I'm free every night." I laughed.

"I'll come around with beers and pizza." His voice sounded pensive.

"It must be serious, then," I said, trying to josh him out of his strange mood. When there was no grin forthcoming, I shrugged and turned back to the archaic accounts that gave me such a headache.

"Okay, spill," I exclaimed, taking another mouthful of

the pepperoni pizza.

"I don't quite know how to tell you this," Jake chose his words with care.

"Is it about Gemma?"

"What...? No."

"Then what?"

"It's about Claudine."

"If you're going to tell me that you're dating her…" I tried to inject some humour into the awkward atmosphere that had settled over the room.

Jake stayed serious while he replied that he wasn't. "I'm just going to come straight out with it…" Still, he hesitated. "She was sleeping with someone else all the time she was with you."

"I know."

"You know?"

"Caroline told me a while ago. How did you find out, though?"

"Why didn't you tell me?"

"You never said how you found out," I countered.

"I heard a couple of blokes chatting in the men's.

Laughing about the scene in the bank the other day when the previous manager's wife was confronted by his ex-and-very-furious lover, who decided to spill the beans out of sheer spite. Well, there aren't many Claudines around, so I asked them and, over a pint or two, they were more than happy to oblige."

We sat in silence until Jake asked, "You still think about Gemma, don't you?"

"Have you taken up mind-reading?"

"No, but she was the first thing you thought about when I said there was something wrong. Come on, show me the rest of this place; just hope it is better than this mangy old sofa."

Cass and I had papered the bedroom walls the night before – three walls in a plain duck egg blue and a feature wall consisting of Habitat's finest designer range in chocolate brown.

"You up for a party Friday night?" I asked.

"Now you're talking." Jake grinned.

"Where shall I put these cans?" Keith said, lumbering

under the weight while Cass carried a solitary bottle and a broad grin.

"The bedroom's shaping up. The rest of the house still looks like it's in a time warp," Jason said, coming down the stairs as Keith stumbled past with the cans. "I'll follow him, then, shall I?"

"How's things?" I asked, checking that Cathy wasn't within earshot.

"Strained, but we're working on it. It's definitely better in front of the kids. I guess it will take time to forgive and forget."

"But you think you can get back to how you were?"

"Yeah, I'm sure, given more time. Now, let me cruise to the booze."

I laughed, shaking my head.

"Your bedroom looks inviting." Cathy sidled up to me and gave me a hug.

"Don't let Jay hear you say that." The words were out before I could stop them, and given the circumstances, they couldn't have been worse had I tried. Cathy stiffened in my arms.

"Come on, you can replenish my wine glass en route to the garden. I want to know what grand plans you have for out there."

"You should ask Cass. She seems to think this whole project is her domain, and maybe it is... Who am I to argue?"

"Have you filled Cass in?" Jake appeared with Chris at his side.

"Hi, Chris."

"Theo."

"No," I said in response to Jake's query, "and for God's sake don't say that in front of Cass today. We don't want World War III erupting."

"Too late. What are you hoping to keep from me?" Cass sidled up.

I awaited the fireworks, the explosion of her famous quick and deadly temper. Her lips became pinched, whitening around the edges, and a cold look stole across her eyes, one I'd never seen before, not even in our lifelong anger concerning our parents. This was something altogether more frightening. Cass shrugged aside the restraining hand Keith placed on her arm. Like a Jack-in-the-box awaiting discharge, she stood unnaturally taut. I feared the release.

Keith was fooled, but maybe that was because he wanted to be. I knew different. For Cass, it wasn't over. If she'd let loose and exploded, I might have expected at the most an abusive call made to Claudine in the near future. This reaction worried me; I knew Cass would exact retribution.

I sometimes wondered whether there was Sicilian blood running through her veins; fiery with a fierce sense of justice, she also believed there was a lot to be said for their ancient custom of vendetta. I shivered.

My home came to life as it filled to overflowing with people. The tired walls vibrated with the sound of the music that pumped from the house.

"Funky wallpaper, Theo. Did you choose it?" one of the lads from the football team ribbed.

"Are you still up? Thought you would've been in bed by now. Run along home and leave the big boys to it," I shot back.

"What makes you think I plan on doing anything?" Cass demanded as Keith left us to talk.

"I know you too well."

"Oh, come on, you can't let her get away with it, Theo. She cheated on you for years and then blamed you for the death of her baby, which she aborted."

"She's not worth it. She's sick in the head, and one day she'll get her comeuppance, but not from us. Do you know she also told me her mum was dead, and it was her inheritance that paid for her sleek flat? Turns out Mummy is still alive but dirt-poor."

"She's evil. Even more reason to do something about her."

"We've both wasted enough time on her, and now I think there's something to be said for holding our heads high and walking away."

"Dignity at all costs?"

"Something like that."

"How can you have dignity when you let her get away with it?" Her dark brows furrowed.

"What do you want me to do? Hit her? Is that what you want?" When Cass shook her head, I continued to drive my point home, "I can walk away with the dignity of the righteous or… oh God, that sounded pompous, didn't it?"

Cass threw back her head and laughed. I joined in.

"But seriously, I refuse to stoop to her level, and I don't want you to, either. No, I'm serious, Cass. You have to promise me."

After a groan, she mumbled a half-hearted, insincere promise. She used to mumble the words and leave out the "p" so she was actually saying "romise". She could then claim it didn't count and would go ahead and do whatever she'd originally planned.

"A real one, on my life."

She scowled at my being able to remember her ruse and said, loud and clear, as she used to as a child, "I promise not to do anything to Claudine. I promise on Theo's life." And as juvenile as it sounded, having its roots firmly in childhood, I knew she'd be bound by it.

Chapter 13

Gemma

I pulled up outside Lucy and Jen's Regency house and sat for a moment, thinking about the last time I'd seen the girls in Crete. We'd spoken a number of times since, over the phone, and e-mails had flown between us, but actually seeing them was different. The blinds twitched, and moments later, the front door flew open. Both women appeared and hurtled down the steps to drag me from the car, hugging me to death. I was pulled into a three-way hug.

"Gemma," Lucy and Jen shrieked.

"You guys haven't changed." I laughed.

The flat was decorated in cool shades of magnolia with the odd splash of colour. The furniture was modern, and the whole effect was minimalist.

"Come on into the kitchen. We've got a bottle already open."

The kitchen held all the state-of-the-art equipment any self-respecting modern kitchen should have. Chrome units and appliances were framed by a deep red backdrop. The room was a good size. A breakfast bar and chic glass table graced the floor space.

Jen half-filled a goldfish-bowl-sized glass with red wine and handed it to me, giving me an excited squeeze at the same time.

"Are you trying to get me drunk?"

"If memory serves, it'll take more than this glass to create an adverse reaction." Jen grinned.

Locals and holidaymakers converged with ease as Brighton's heart pounded to a beat of its own. You could be anyone doing anything and still fit the rhythm of Brighton. Those who refused to conform to society's idea of what they should be came here to explore their originality; artists sought and found inspiration. It was into the very heart of this scene that we headed. Bars pumped out music and restaurants enticed people in. Brighton was the place you met people, somewhere to see and be seen. Anyone could leave their mark there, although not in indelible ink. Fads and scenes came and went, and yet the vibe stayed the same.

"I can see why you live here."

"Not sure I could live anywhere else, or at least not until I'm old, grey and ready for a retirement village." Jen laughed.

"Mm, not sure the other residents could cope with us," Lucy said between mouthfuls of Thai.

"I can picture the two of you knocking back gallons of wine when you're old and grey."

"I expect we will be," Lucy replied, popping the last prawn into her mouth.

It surprised me that not once during the night did we discuss Theo. I wasn't going to bring him up, but I had assumed that Lucy and Jen would want to dissect it fully. Even when I showed them the wedding photos, they positively drooled over Jake, and I informed them he was Theo's friend. I crawled into bed in the early hours of the morning, groggy and tired.

"Good morning." My chipper voice surprised me almost as much as the absence of a hangover.

"Morning, Gemma," Lucy and Jen replied with warm smiles but muted voices.

"Everything all right?"

"No," Lucy replied. "We've had a minor emergency. We hate having to do this to you, but we're going to have to abandon you for part of the day. Why don't you head down to the beach?"

I wondered what had happened but didn't like to pry.

"We'll tell you later, but for now we can't say anything," Lucy said with a reassuring smile.

"I'll go and top up my tan."

"This is a lovely time of the day to walk along the

front. In fact, we often stop across from the Odeon and watch the world go by," Jen recommended.

"There's a particularly nice view from there," Lucy added.

As soon as I left the house, I heard Jen pick up the phone. I'd have to curb my curiosity until later, when we'd discuss it over a bottle or two. The sun warmed my skin as I walked along the front. I stopped outside the Odeon but couldn't work out why that stretch of the front was any more spectacular than the rest. *It must be a personal thing that has some significance for them.* I nearly walked on but instead wandered over to the railings to look out to sea.

The sun reflected off the water while the waves washed to shore, lapping at the stones in a playful tease. I breathed in the sea air, grinning. It was good to be here, soaking up the sun. *Maybe I should book a holiday.* I thought, subconsciously, I'd avoided it because of what happened last year. But standing there now, with the clean salt smell brushing the air around me, it was time to consider my options. I watched as a speedboat skimmed the water's surface, leaving a trail of white foam in its wake.

After a while, I became aware of another presence alongside me. A familiar smell wafted on the air, making me freeze in shock. *It can't be. There must be thousands of people who wear that aftershave.* My heart thudded in my chest. *Why do I need to be reminded of him now?* The easiest thing would be to glance across to confirm it couldn't be Theo and to steel myself for the inevitable disappointment. I peeked sideways, trying to catch him within the radius of my peripheral vision. Bile rose in my throat and I became light-headed. I tried to control my increased breathing. What I hadn't been prepared for was that it might actually be him.

My fingers tightened on the chipped aqua rails, knuckles whitening. I felt like I was in the centre of a vortex that had picked me up, spun me until I was dizzy, and then flung me down.

Can this be another coincidence? The suspicious side of my nature couldn't help but smell the distinctive aroma of conspiracy. *Had Jen and Lucy planned this? How?* My time was running out before he spotted me. If I moved discreetly away, I could go back to how things were. A sharp intake of breath told me otherwise. I tried to pretend I hadn't seen him. Training my eyes on the horizon, I saw nothing but a light haze. *Don't let me cry,* I entreated.

"Gemma." The word sounded like it was torn from him.

I steeled myself, turning once more to face a pair of eyes that haunted my dreams. The force of my emotions was stronger than I'd expected. A lump formed in my throat, threatening to choke me. I turned away. *I can't deal with this.* Hunching back over the rails, I blinked back tears.

His arm encircling my waist caused me to gasp. He stood behind me now, with both arms wrapped around me, pulling me close, his head buried into the curve of my neck. A surge of energy pulsated through me. Words weren't needed, but I knew the time would come when we would have to talk. *Would we be able to work things out?*

"It'll be okay," he whispered into my ear. "Everything'll be fine now."

"Will it?" I yearned to believe him.

Slowly, with gaining confidence, I turned in his arms and faced him. His arms still enfolded me. I looked questioningly into his eyes, the fusion that had taken place so long ago when green eyes met blue once more ignited. Tentatively, I raised my hand and traced along his cheekbone. Grasping his face with tender hands, I brought his lips to mine for a bittersweet moment. Feeling more sure of myself, I buried my face into his chest and relaxed in his embrace. Tears, full of emotion, tumbled onto his shirt front. We smiled at each other while his loving fingers wiped away my tears.

"I'm sorry," he murmured.

"I know. Me too."

"You weren't to blame."

"We both were."

"There's so much to tell you, I don't know where to start."

He told me about Claudine and her treatment of him. Although it didn't make what we did right, it no longer seemed so wrong. If she hadn't manipulated him, we'd have had all this time together without the painful experiences that had clouded our lives for the last year. We talked about the past and we contemplated our future because neither of us had any doubts now.

We made excited plans and barely noticed how far we'd walked. At some point, we must have turned back and headed in the direction we'd come from. Amusement followed on the heels of amazement at the scene that confronted us: our respective friends sitting outside a bar, drinking a toast to our union, which they'd engineered.

Theo

"Remind me why you wanted me to go to Brighton with you next weekend."

Jake frowned at me. "I told you the other night."

"Ergh yeah. After half a dozen pints, which were then followed by half a dozen more, so excuse me if my memory is somewhat vague on the details."

"So what was it you wanted to know?"

"Are you being deliberately obtuse?"

"Have you swallowed a dictionary, Theo?" Jake teased. "It's no big deal. Don't come if you don't want to..." A pregnant pause followed. "It's personal stuff, and I wanted a mate with me."

I wondered what he meant, but confirmed that I'd go with him and left it at that.

"I need to go see someone," Jake said.

The one thing he'd said to me was to be on the beach or the front waiting for him, near the Odeon so that he could find me. He walked away like a man on a mission. *Is it something to do with his parents?* I took a deep breath, inhaling the sea air, and strolled along the front, passing the Odeon. *He can ring. I'm not hanging out in this spot all day.* The tranquillity of the shabby chic air radiating along the front suited my craving for calm. Stopping by the rails, I gazed pensively out to sea. I pictured myself on those waters on a forty-foot cruiser, the boat rising and falling on the majestic crests, the spume left in my trail white against the green-blue murky depths. It was possible to believe anything in a place like this.

I became aware of someone next to me; a strange prickle encompassed my body. The long curtain of blond hair and those long gorgeous legs that had once held me imprisoned identified the owner. From the stiff way she was staring out to sea, I knew she'd already seen me and was struggling with what to do next.

"Gemma." My voice was shaky, a bit of a pre-puberty squeak.

She didn't turn, didn't respond. *She doesn't want to know; I've hurt her too much.* I knew she was the woman I was meant to spend the rest of my life with. *Go get her.* I wasn't quite sure what I was going to do until I'd done it. I gathered her into my arms and wasn't going to let her go again.

We left nothing out as we walked along the front, even the uncomfortable stuff that others may have buried deep. Her response to the Claudine situation was in keeping with Cass'. I had a sudden longing to introduce the two most important women in my life.

My frame trembled with suppressed anger when she told me about her close encounter with the attacker. At that moment, my anger for Claudine resurfaced. There was no doubt in my mind that none of it would have happened if Claudine had stayed out of my life with her poisonous lies.

We found a larger crowd of well-wishers than we'd

suspected, all sat together, downing beers and admiring their handiwork. It seemed no one wanted to be left out of this, as all of Gemma's friends had travelled from London, and my own side was fairly large, too, with my sister and Keith amongst the number.

PART II

FIVE YEARS LATER–2009

Chapter 14

Gemma

The waiting room was crowded, babies crying and children running amok. *Can I be? But no, I mustn't. Well, not until...*

"Gemma Perkins to room five." The voice over

the tannoy called out twice before falling silent.

Even after four years, I couldn't dispel the pride I experienced when I heard someone call me Mrs. Perkins. Theo had proposed to me two months after Brighton, one after I'd left London and moved to Devon, straight into Theo's house. I can still hear my mum's voice declaring for all to hear that it was indecent haste and I'd live to regret it. My musings were brought to an abrupt end when I stopped in front of Doctor Steiner's door and, raising a trembling hand, tapped on the wood.

"Come in," Doctor Steiner called out.

Taking a deep breath, I opened the door and entered, smiling at Maryam Steiner.

"So what can I do for you today, Gemma? Not often I see you in here. How's Theo?"

"He's great." I grinned. "I'm hoping you can confirm my pregnancy. I've done the home test."

"Congratulations. Of course we'll check, but the kits these days are very conclusive. Is Theo celebrating already? He'll make a good father." Doctor Maryam

Steiner was a personal friend of Jason's wife, Cathy, so we knew each other socially. Cathy had admitted that she'd been on the verge of attempting a match between Theo and Maryam.

The candles flickered, dipping and waving as Theo came through the door. He threw his jacket over the back of the chair. Tugging at his tie, he threw it on top of the other discarded garment.

"Hello, gorgeous." Theo planted his lips on mine. I responded with my usual ardour. "What's the special occasion?"

"Can't I treat my husband?" I laughed, throwing my arms around his neck.

"Mm, I like these treats. Carry on, madam." His hands covered my buttocks, pulling me closer. "How about we put dinner on hold?" he suggested before moving in to nibble my ear.

The doorbell rang.

"Oh, who's that now?"

"We can always ignore them." My excitement

bubbled up and transferred to Theo, who nodded like a naughty schoolboy.

The ringing became more insistent. Theo walked away with a weary shrug to open the door. I wandered back, intent on heading into the kitchen to see to the dinner while Theo saw to our unexpected visitor.

"Hiya, Jay." I smiled, despite the untimely interruption. "What's up?" Mild irritation turned to concern when I saw his red-rimmed eyes.

Jason covered his face with his hands, drawing his elbows into his chest, doubling over as though in pain. Theo and I rushed to his side.

"Jay, mate, what is it?" Theo's face crumpled with concern. He asked Jason if he'd been drinking.

"I've only had a few, to drown my sorrows."

"What sorrows, Jay?" I urged, "Come in." I took his arm, leading him into the living room.

"I'll make you a drink, and you can talk to Theo."

"Have you got beer?"

"I think you've had enough. I'll make you black coffee."

"Don't go." He grasped my hand, squeezing it. "Why'd she do it?" His voice broke as he sobbed.

"Oh, hon, what's wrong? Is it Cathy?" I held him, seeking to give comfort to this man who was normally the life and soul of the party and who was now crying in my arms.

"She's left me. It's all over. Fifteen years of marriage…"

I rubbed his back not knowing what to say, because no words could ease his pain.

"She's taken the kids to the States."

How could she just take them? They're his life. I breathed a sigh of relief when he said she'd be back in two weeks, but she expected him to have left the family home by then.

"Cheeky bitch," Theo growled.

"She needs the house for the kids," he said. "I won't get the kids; they always go to the mum… so she needs the house. What'll I do?"

Theo looked at me; I knew what he was asking, and I couldn't deny him the chance to give refuge to one of his oldest friends. I nodded and, squeezing Jason's hand, escaped to the kitchen to make the coffees.

I went to bed early, leaving the men talking. I was asleep when Theo came up so I didn't get a chance to share my news. The next morning, he spent more time in the en-suite bathroom than usual. When he came out, we both needed to leave for work. He kissed me and fled the house.

"Where's Jason?" Theo asked.

"I've only just got back myself, but he doesn't seem to be here."

"We need to talk about something."

"Oh, darling, I have something to tell you, too. I wanted to tell you last night but then Jason turned up and I really must tell you before he comes back. I'll burst if I don't tell you now."

Theo smiled and nodded.

"We're going to have another person living here..."

"We can't. Not now. Who, for heaven's sakes?" I frowned at his unusual show of ill humour.

"It won't be for another five months and..." I grinned. "He/she will have to call you Daddy."

I let the words sink in, and then bounced excitedly into Theo's arms, kissing him. It took a few seconds to realise that he'd stayed quiet and unresponsive. I pulled back.

"Well, say something."

"It's fantastic, sweetheart. Really incredible." His words lacked conviction.

"Don't sound too enthusiastic, will you? I mean don't go overboard or anything," I snapped, scared by his response.

"I'm excited, of course I am. But I'm a bloke. We don't show emotion like you women." He planted a kiss on my lips.

"Bull!"

"What?"

"Bullshit. I know you, Theo Perkins. Last year you were bounding around the house like an excited puppy because of your poxy fucking promotion." I flounced from the room in tears and was shocked when he didn't attempt to stop me or follow.

I cooked as usual, dishing up in silence. Theo and I said very little during the meal in front of Jason, who'd arrived shortly after our row. I think Theo was pleased to have Jason there to prevent further conversation. I retired to bed alone and exhausted, leaving Theo and Jason alone again. I'd dropped some none-too-subtle hints that I wanted Theo to follow me soon. He chose to ignore me, and again, I dropped off to sleep alone, but this time in tears.

I'm not sure what woke me, but I heard a single voice in hushed conversation; at first I thought it was Theo talking to Jason. Rising from the bed in need of the bathroom, I realised that Theo was on the phone. I hadn't meant to listen.

"...how can I tell her? It will destroy her. To top it all, a baby she may have to bring up as a single mum. She'll find out soon enough."

I couldn't hear what the other person said, which was frustrating. I knew what it sounded like, but I couldn't believe what the obvious implications of this conversation were telling me.

"I can't fool her for long, though. Since I've made senior partner, I don't even go to London. I never stay overnight on business. She'll smell a rat; she's not stupid. But I'd need to be away overnight, and soon it will become obvious. But the longer she's kept in the dark, the better. I hate to think how she'll take it. Yes, yes, I know, but what if telling her causes her to miscarry?"

After a brief pause, Theo added, "I know, but this time it's different."

I stumbled back to bed, burying myself under the duvet. *Theo's having an affair and he's going to leave me.* It made sense now why he didn't want this baby. A sob tore from me; fear gripped my stomach muscles, causing them to contract painfully. *How will I cope? I love him. How could he do this to me? Yesterday we seemed fine. Before Jason came, he couldn't take his hands off me... so what happened?* Clarity hit me with such force that I raced for the bathroom and vomited into the toilet.

"Gemma, honey, are you all right?" Theo sounded concerned from outside the door.

"Go away." I sobbed.

The door creaked open. Theo stooped over me and brushed back my hair tenderly, kissing the top of my head with what I once would have read as a sign of his love. I turned around, slumped on the floor, looking up at him with red-rimmed eyes.

"Get away from me, you bastard."

"Gemma, what is it? Are you still miffed with me for not jumping through hoops because we're about to have a baby?"

"Well, I understand now." My tone was hysterical. "Why would you be excited about a baby you don't want? Maybe if it was Cathy having your baby you'd react differently."

"Cathy?" His face screwed up.

"It all fits. Yesterday we were fine, till Jason came and told you he and Cathy had split up."

"Oh, well done, Einstein. Really brainy, aren't you?" he snarled. "Jason splits with his wife, and because we get on well, I'm now having an affair with her. Well, I can see your reasoning there, and all because I didn't pick you up and spin you around with excitement at our new arrival as you had planned would happen all afternoon."

"It's not like that... I heard you."

"Heard what?"

"You said I was going to be a single mum. You said you couldn't fool me for long. That it would destroy me, and you wanted to spend the night with her..." The words were torn from my lips. "You said I wasn't stupid. But I am... I am! Because I loved you and believed in you completely..." I slumped down, lifeless.

"I'm not having an affair." His words came out agonised, and his hands trembled as he took mine between his. I tried to remove them, but his grasp was too strong.

A tear dropped down on my hands. I saw his agony of indecision.

"I'm not having an affair," he repeated. "I'm... just not. You'll have to trust me."

Theo

I rubbed my back wearily. *I must be getting old.* My back seemed to be aching almost constantly at the moment. *I probably need to see a Physio; too much sex with my gorgeous wife.* I smiled as I thought about the whirlwind that overtook our lives after Brighton, and the wedding day on a white sandy beach in Australia. I still got aroused thinking about her walking toward me in that ivory satin shift dress.

Mm, a romantic night planned. I walked through to the open-plan kitchen/diner. Candles were lit, and a delicious smell emanated from the kitchen. I remembered how this room had been when I'd first bought it and how lonely I'd been until Gemma had come back into my life. The old lady had been right about me living here happily with the woman I loved. The marital bliss I'd once blindly believed in did exist, although I'd since learnt that it took hard work and dedication. Love alone wasn't enough; you needed to understand each other, to practise a certain degree of compromise on both sides and have the will to make it with that person forever. I couldn't imagine a life without Gemma. There was nothing I couldn't talk to her about. Nothing seemed impossible with her at my side.

The doorbell sounded, disturbing our embrace. Gemma's eyes raked me with unsuppressed desire as she suggested we ignore it, except the person outside wasn't taking no for an answer. I pulled the door open, frustrated at the interruption, which changed to concern on seeing Jason's distraught expression.

Gemma and I led Jason to the sofa, where he spilled his guts.

"She's left me. It's all over. Fifteen years of marriage…"

A cold shiver ran down my spine as I contemplated losing Gemma. I'd smugly assumed we could get through anything, and yet here was Jason, who'd in all probability thought the same thing. Now, after fifteen years, he was a broken man because his marriage was over. I looked at Gemma. *Is she thinking the same thing? Does the idea of losing me rip at her guts? I couldn't ease Jason's pain when I knew that if I were in his shoes nothing could ease mine.*

How dare she throw him out of his own house when she's the one ending the marriage? I used to have a great deal of respect and affection for Cathy but now I felt only anger.

"She needs the house for the kids," he said. "I won't get the kids; they always go to the mum... so she needs the house. What will I do?"

I knew he meant more in that sentence than mere speculation as to his living quarters. There was one thing I could do, though, if Gemma was all right with it; she nodded in response.

Jason talked throughout the evening. Their

problems had started all those years ago, with Jason's insecurities when Cathy returned to work. Working alongside her ex had been the beginning of the end for them. They'd worked at it, but Cathy felt he didn't trust her, and couldn't fully forgive him for doubting her. The resentment had simmered under the surface until it had risen up again. She said there was no one else, but she no longer loved Jason. She couldn't live under the same roof as him for the sake of the children. Jack was eleven now and Katie nine.

Gemma disappeared to bed so Jason and I could talk. I wished I could join her. I gave Jason a beer when Gemma had gone and took one for myself but only drank half as I had a tummy ache. I rubbed my hard, flat stomach, something I had to work harder on these days to keep, as the discomfort intensified. It was this in the end that forced me off the sofa. My desire by now dissipated by tiredness, the ache in my stomach, but also a heaviness in my balls as I headed upstairs and into the bathroom.

Standing in front of the full-length mirror, I

dropped my trousers to have a proper look at my affected privates. I cupped them in my hands, wincing at how tender they felt. *Is the right testicle slightly swollen? I swear it is. It's probably nothing. I'm probably a bit run down.* I tried to dismiss it as I climbed into bed next to Gemma. For the first time in my life, I wore my boxers to bed. For some reason, I wanted to cover myself.

My stomach was tied in knots as I sat in the surgery waiting room. *What if...? It'll be all right. It has to be. It can't happen to someone like me.* I stared at the wall as the agonising seconds ticked by, feeling like a lifetime. The loud, bombastic ticking of the clock grated on my nerves as I imagined my own body clock grinding to a halt. Hearing my name called over the tannoy, I felt an urge to run away. *I don't want to know. If I don't know then nothing can happen.*

"Theo, I don't normally see you. Doctor Steiner booked up, is she?" Doctor Goodchild said. His warm eyes sparkled and his bushy eyebrows twitched in his attempt at humour. I didn't want a woman examining me. *How could a woman understand how a man felt about his testicles?*

I endeavoured to smile out of politeness to this affable man, but it was more like a grimace.

"Sit down, sit down. Now tell me what I can do for you."

"I...I..." My eyes welled up. Swallowing hard, I tried to push aside the emotions threatening to choke me. "It's my testicles, doctor."

"Let me see, lad." His tone became business-like. "Have you felt a lump?"

"No, but they are so tender..." My words were failing me as the implications hit me again. I had naively hoped the doctor would tell me it was all very natural, to go home and not worry. From the set of his face, I knew he was taking it seriously. "They felt swollen last night and heavy, so I checked them, but it was so tender to the touch that I didn't...."

"How long have you felt like this?" he asked as he hesitated over an area with a frown.

"Have you found something?" Beads of sweat

broke out on my head.

"I'm not sure." He indicated I pull up my trousers. "I'll refer you to a specialist to investigate further."

"Did you find a lump?"

Doctor Goodchild nodded, seeking to reassure me that it didn't necessarily mean it was cancer. He went on to add that cancer was very treatable these days. I wasn't reassured.

"Have you had any other symptoms?"

"Backache and a stomach ache yesterday."

Doctor Goodchild tried to keep his expression neutral, but I could see he hadn't wanted to hear that. He asked about my family history and general health. My breathing began to get shallow. *I need to get out of here.* Words flew around me with the dizzying speed of a golden snitch in a Quidditch match; I had difficulty processing them. He was saying something about blood tests and ultrasound scans, and I couldn't think why as the blood pounded inside my head, increasing my desperate need for air. *I need to get away; this can't be happening to me.*

"I need to go." I rose from my chair.

"Theo, you'll get a call in the next few days to arrange an appointment for the tests. Try..."

I opened my mouth to reply, but no sound came out as I stumbled from the room and through the surgery, where noises intruded on my brain. Voices and faces blurred whilst the room spun, and I floundered out into the bracing air, taking deep breaths.

"It can't be as bad as all that." The supercilious, smiling face of the parking attendant made me ball my fingers into a fist. I longed to drive it into his smug face.

"Fuck off!" I snarled and shouldered past him, heading for my car. Climbing in, I slumped against the steering wheel while sobs racked my frame. *I've got cancer. I don't want to die. How can I leave Gemma? The doc said it was treatable these days.* The optimistic side of my brain interjected but was battered back by the prevalent pessimistic voice that jeered, *Oh, give over, it's a death sentence; everyone knows that.*

"Where's Jason?" I pecked Gemma on the cheeks distractedly.

The words drifted around inside my brain like a marble rolling around in an otherwise empty vacuum. I'd driven away from the doctor's with no idea where I was going but found myself back at my old family home. No one was in, which was probably good as my parents were the last people I needed to see. Heading in the direction of the stables, I had one of the staff saddle up a horse. Chalky, a docile grey mare, required little effort on my behalf. After mounting, I let her chose our route. The "C" word reverberated around my brain, but I came no nearer to understanding what was happening or why. Words and phrases that I couldn't make sense of cascaded around. I needed the comfort and the unswerving support of my wife.

"We need to talk about something."

"Oh, darling, I have something to tell you, too. I wanted to tell you last night but then Jason turned up and I really must tell you before he comes back. I'll burst if I don't tell you now."

She was probably going to tell me about a divine pair of shoes she hadn't been able to resist. I let her have something to say that wouldn't have anything to do with cancer or death but her words pole-axed me. I felt as though I were drowning. At any other time, I would have jumped with joy, sure that my wife and I would now have the family we wanted. But to bring a baby into the world when the odds were already stacked against his father's survival seemed cruel. Gemma reacted as I would have expected: full of enthusiasm and bouncing around like a Jack-in-the-box. She pulled away from me, her eyes darkening and confusion knitting her brows together.

I tried to head it off, but she was like a dog with a bone. *Why is she doing this to me right now? I need her support, and all I'm getting is emotional overload.* I resented her for giving me a hard time, and for her happiness and ability to view our future as positive when I couldn't. She flounced out of the room, expecting me to follow, to apologise. *She'll wait a long time for that.*

The thought of confiding in Gemma scared me. I

knew she'd support me but what would this knowledge do to our unborn baby? Boy or girl, I might never know. Would I watch it grow up or would it know some other man as its father? My fist clenched as I contemplated something ultimately worse, another man touching my wife.

"What is it, Theo?" Jason was watching me intently.

How was it I managed to dismiss my problems as nothing for the sake of my friend, yet I'd treated the woman I loved with a callous disregard for her feelings?

I hadn't planned on telling Jake over the phone, but the urge to confide was overwhelming. Expecting his reaction to come in the form of expressive profanities, I hadn't anticipated the long oppressive silence. "Mate, I don't know what to say."

I'd thought Jake would say something reassuringly irreverent. I was shaken when he didn't.

"How's Gemma coping with it?"

"I haven't told her. She's just told me she's pregnant."

Jake growled deep in his throat.

"I don't know what to do. My head is fried. I'm too young to die... aren't I?"

"You have to tell Gemma. Aside from anything else, you need her support. You can't do this alone. I'll do all I can but I'm pretty useless at the touchy-feely stuff. You know that."

"How can I tell her? It will destroy her. To top it all, a baby that she may now have to bring up as a single mum. She'll find out soon enough."

"So what other options do you have? Have the tests without her knowing and hold off telling her for as long as you can?"

"How can I fool her for long, though? Since I've made senior partner, I don't even go down to London. I never stay overnight on business. She'll smell a rat; she's not stupid. But I'd need to be away overnight, and well, soon it will become obvious. But the longer she's kept in the dark, the better. I hate to think how she'll take it."

"She's stronger than you give her credit for."

"Yes, yes, I know, but what if telling her causes her to miscarry?"

"You're thinking about what Claudine said that time, but she was a lying, scheming tart, and she didn't lose the baby. I'm sure babies are hardier than that. Otherwise, women would be miscarrying all over the place."

"Gemma, honey, are you all right?" I stood helpless outside the bathroom as Gemma vomited.

I felt awful about the way I'd treated her. It wasn't as though she knew what I was going through, and she was right, I would have spun her ecstatically around the room. We'd wanted a baby for so long now.

"Go away." Her muffled cry ripped through me. I couldn't leave her alone with her suffering.

I held her hair back, kissing the top of her head as my stomach plummeted at the pain I'd caused. She turned around with bloodshot eyes that had shed many a tear.

"Get away from me, you bastard."

"Gemma, what is it? Are you still miffed with me for not jumping through hoops because we're about to have a baby? I am happy, you know." *Now what did you go and say that for?*

What came out next blew me sideways. All the anger and fear spun through my brain surging up to spill over Gemma, whose opinion of me, despite over four years of marriage, was obviously low. I understood at that moment why Cathy had reacted so badly to Jason's suspicions.

Bitter recriminations flew between us until I heard the terror in her voice as she informed me that she'd heard me. It made sense now. Of course she'd suspect the worst when she'd overheard that. I watched as she crumpled against the wall, and shame replaced my previous anger.

"I'm not having an affair." I took her hand in mine. She looked up at me now with trust in her tear-stained eyes; she believed I would tell her something to allay her fears.

"I'm not having an affair," I reiterated. "I'm just not." I couldn't hurt her worse than I already had. "You'll just have to trust me," I said and walked away.

Chapter 15

Gemma

I hadn't slept a wink on the sofa, but I couldn't face sleeping in the same bed as Theo, and I left the house before he woke.

"Chris," I said when the phone picked up.

"Gemma, is everything okay? It's early."

"I need an EGM," I said.

"Have you spoken to the others?"

"Not yet. Have you got plans for this weekend?"

"We can head out tonight."

"Thanks." The EGM, Emergency Girls Meeting,

370

had always been a code between us; it meant you dropped everything you were doing for the friend in need unless you really couldn't. She arranged to pick me up after work.

"Okay, what gives?" Jackie demanded.

"I know I dragged you guys away from your weekends, but can we leave me till last? I just want to hear about you all first while I get my head around what I'm about to say."

"Well, whatever the reason, I'm glad to see you both. It's been too long," Susie asserted.

"We're all so caught up in our own lives now. I mean, who'd have thought I'd have four kids, all under the age of five?" Jackie grinned as she passed around the photos of her two sets of twins.

"How's Rory?" I asked as I fiddled with my nails.

"He's good." Jackie threw me a speculative glance.

"I'm back to work in two weeks. Only part-time, though."

"Who's going to mind them while you're working?

Let me see, Summer and Brad are four now so they're part-time nursery, right? And Dustin and Joelie nine months, quite a handful, I'd have thought."

"Mum was going to have them, but, as you say, quite a handful. She'll do a day with Sum and Brad and a day with Dust and Jo, and Susie's doing the rest of the time."

"I thought you were child-minding other kids at the moment." I turned to Susie.

"They've moved on."

"Don't you have enough coping with Bob's two kids?" I referred to the children of her second husband. The quiet wedding two years ago had been the antitheses of the lavish affair of her marriage to Ted.

"We could do with the money coming in. Two kids aren't cheap. Their mother contributes nothing. She sees them once a fortnight and will only take them out if we give her money. We've just heard from the adoption agency, and we're going to adopt a three-month-old baby."

"Congratulations." We beamed at each other.

Amanda's house was spotless. It was hard to imagine a three-year-old lived here. The relationship with her managing director had ended when she'd announced her pregnancy and refused to abort. She'd also refused to bow to the pressure he'd put on her to move out of the company.

"So how is little Amabel?" Chris asked.

"As precocious as ever. She thinks the whole world centres around her. But I do have some other exciting news..." She left a pregnant pause as we edged forward in our seats. "I've been accepted by the bank for a loan to open my own ad agency. There are a number of people at the firm who have expressed a strong desire to come with me, and I don't plan on starting small."

"So you still haven't managed to drag Jake up that aisle?" Jackie asked Chris as she opened up a new bottle of wine and poured us all a glass, although I stuck at half a glass.

"I despair of ever getting him there or having kids. But I have no complaints in any other department. He's loving and affectionate. In fact, the perfect partner in all other ways."

In all other ways except where it really matters.

My pregnancy was greeted with, "It took you long enough," and, "Welcome to the club." I told them of Theo's reaction and the subsequent telephone conversation. I rubbed my sweating hands against my jeans as I looked around at my group of friends.

"Wow, that doesn't sound good," Jackie broke the silence. "You say he promised you he wasn't having an affair but wouldn't explain himself?" I could see the cogs going around in her brain – in fact in everyone's – as we tried to untwist the truth.

"Sure sounds like an affair," Susie said reluctantly, "but Theo isn't Ted. No, I don't believe it's that."

"Mm," Amanda mused, "but if we're ruling that out, what could it be then?"

"What were his exact words?"

"How can I tell her? It will destroy her. And to top it all, a baby she may have to bring up as a single mum. She'll find out soon enough," I repeated.

"She'll find out soon enough – now what does that

mean? What the fuck is he playing at?" Jackie growled, contemplating his words.

"Who was he on the phone to?" Chris asked.

"I don't know. Why?"

"You didn't check?" Jackie's tone was incredulous.

"Was it last night? I think it was Jake. He was very strange last night after a call. He spent at least half an hour in the bathroom with the door locked. Then... well... he wasn't up for IT, which is very unusual. In fact, I've never known him not to be in the mood."

We all pondered the new evidence. Theo being unfaithful wouldn't produce this reaction in his overly-sexed mate.

"Ring him and ask him," Jackie demanded.

"He won't break a confidence, but maybe I'll get a clue from his tone." She picked up her phone and dialled Jake's number. We all sat in silence and listened to the one-sided conversation. "As I said, he won't tell us what is happening, but he did say it isn't an affair. He swore that to me. He said Theo had rung. Apparently, your phone is off, and the note you left told him little. He's worried about you."

"Let him worry," Jackie said. "Let him know what it feels like."

"What if...?" Susie hesitated. We all looked at her. "The single mum bit and the comment about finding out soon enough... I mean, if he's not having an affair, and it's a simple explanation, he should be able to tell you. Unless it is worse than what you're worrying about... what if... if he's found out that he's ill."

A cold shiver swept over me. *Theo ill?* I hadn't considered that. He'd think he was protecting me and the baby. *He can't be... can he?* It would explain his strange behaviour. I felt sick. *Is he ill? Had I left him in a strop while he was coping with some illness?*

"Let's not get ahead of ourselves; we don't know anything, and it's dangerous adding one and one. You could end up making three," Amanda said.

"It does add up." Jackie smiled at me with an expression that smacked of pity.

"I need to go home."

The phone rang as soon as I walked through the door. The girls had advised me against rushing straight out, reminding me I needed to heed my unborn baby. So I stayed the night and left early.

"Hello?" I answered, throwing my bag down.

"Can I speak to Theo Perkins?"

"He's not in at the moment," I lied, hoping to discover some information. "I'm his wife. I can take a message."

"I'm calling from The North Devon District Hospital. We've got an appointment for him on Monday, ten a.m. Ask him to report to the Oncology Department."

Oncology – cancer. The word bounced around in my consciousness. It was one thing talking about it last night with the girls but... cancer? People died of cancer. The survival rate was better these days... wasn't it? A rush of nausea exploded through me, causing me to rush up the stairs to the bathroom, where I emptied my stomach.

Cool fingers brushed the hair from my face. "So

you're back?" His gentle tone caressed me.

I turned to him. Pain shot through my head. I couldn't lose him. "Cancer?" I croaked the word, my throat dry and sore.

Theo's expression told me all I needed to know. I rose to my feet holding out my arms to bring him close and buried my head into his chest.

"Jake tell Chris, did he?" he asked as he pulled back, still holding me.

"No. There was a phone call for you when I got in. They can fit you in on Monday morning. Theo, tell me everything."

I listened in silence. "But you may not have cancer?"

"Maybe," he sighed, "but it doesn't seem likely."

"I just wish you'd told me. I'm sorry for being such a bitch."

"You weren't." He pulled me tighter as we sought comfort from each other.

Theo

When I woke the next morning, the bed beside me was empty. *She must be pissed off with me if she's slept on the sofa.* The front door slammed shut with a resounding crash. Glancing at the bedside clock, I wondered where she was off to at this early hour. My thoughts drifted from one thing to another, and yet they always came back to the same thing, and as if on cue, I felt the heaviness in my right testicle. I wondered whether dwelling on it so much increased the feelings, almost as though you produced the feelings psychosomatically. *How do you stop it being the focus of everything?*

"You're going to have to tell Gemma." Jake walked into my office without knocking. He'd made senior partner six months before, a year later than me.

"I told you last night, I can't."

"She's dragging Chris off to London for a pow-wow with the others. She's not gonna let it drop. She knows something's wrong."

"She heard snippets of our conversation last night and thinks I'm having an affair. In fact, she even thinks she knows who with."

Jake raised his eyebrows quizzically.

"Well, she's put two and two together and has me having an affair with Cathy."

"Why Cathy?"

"Oh, of course, you've spent the past few days schmoozing clients so I haven't filled you in. Cathy and Jason have split; he's crashing at ours."

"That makes some kind of sense, or at least in relation to female rationale. You either play along with that or you tell her the truth. At the moment, you don't need the hassle that pretending to have an affair causes. You need her support. She'd be good at it; women generally are."

The faint ringing of the phone broke through my consciousness, followed by the hurried tread on the stairs and the sound of vomiting. *I knew she couldn't stay away the whole weekend.* I padded to the bathroom, bending over her and brushing back her hair. Intense feelings of love washed over me for my beautiful wife who carried my child. In that moment, I knew I had to be strong for them.

"So you're back?" I whispered.

I shuddered at the misery written over her face.

"Hey, it's okay. It's only morning sickness. It will pass," I reassured her.

Bloodshot eyes stared at me. I watched her lips trembling as she uttered one word, the word I'd tried to keep from her. *How did she know?* The heaviness tightened around me again, causing me to wince. Her arms extended with an invitation for the comfort I craved.

Taking a deep breath, I grasped Gemma's hand and,

without a word, we walked into the hospital.

"I want my wife to stay."

"Good to know you have support." The doctor's moustache twitched, reminding me of a ferret.

"She's pregnant." *Why did you tell him that?* My nerves were taut.

Doctor Robson smiled at me, attempting to calm me. A thin film of sweat covered my brow, my chest tightened, and the urge to run was strong. Cool fingers curled around my arm, caressing. My breathing steadied, and I took the chair the doctor was indicating.

Doctor Robson took my medical history, and after what seemed like forever, he told me to "drop 'em". Well, maybe not those exact words, and for the second time in my life, another man's hands cradled my crown jewels.

"Humph." Doctor Robson rose to his feet. "I've arranged for bloods today, and you'll need to go for an ultrasound."

"So is it cancer?" Gemma asked, her voice trembling.

"Mrs. Perkins, Theo, I believe so. A blood test may help to confirm my diagnosis."

May help? He went on to explain something about markers being found in the blood, but not everyone produces these markers.

"These are called AFP (alpha-fetoprotein), BHCG (beta human chorionic gonadotrophin) and LDH (lactic dehydrogenese). Don't worry about remembering all that now," he finished with a smile as he noted my bewilderment.

No kidding. Remember them? I don't think I can repeat them. I realised he was still talking.

"What I need to do now is to arrange for an orchidectomy, with your consent, of course. I have little doubt you have a tumour, but the only way to know whether it is malignant or benign is to remove the testicle and perform a biopsy on it."

His voice droned on. I'd stopped listening as the reality of what he said filtered into my brain. *He isn't just talking about removing an unwanted tumour. He's taking one of my nuts.* I should have expected it, but it came as a shock, a kick to the solar plexus. Panic rose. I'd always thought of rugby at school as a cruel participation sport. In the sterile environs of the hospital, my mind drifted. I found myself wishing with a degree of nostalgia for those days, and even to be back on the rugby pitch. *Take it like a man,* my internal voice screamed. *How do I face my own mortality? I can't leave my wife and unborn child. Who says you're going anywhere? If you were any kind of man, you'd be fighting this thing, not whingeing like a baby.* The internal battle raged on.

"You have to tell her," Gemma exclaimed. "No, you stay there and rest. I'll get dinner tonight."

Gemma had me wrapped so tight in cotton wool since coming back from the specialist, already I knew I wouldn't be able to take much more of it.

"I'm not telling Cass, and that's the end of it."

"Give me one good reason," Gemma demanded, trying not to show her exasperation.

"If I tell her, she'll give up her dream job. She's worked too hard to have it spoilt by her brother who needs his hand held. Is that good enough for you?"

"No." Her voice was softer now. "You're not asking her to give up her career. If she does, then it's her choice, a choice based on the facts. Theo, she has a right to know. If the worst... I mean..." A thin, transparent film of liquid formed in her eyes as her subconscious forced her to face something that neither of us was ready for. "She needs to know." She hurled herself into my arms. "Honey," she whispered, "if you don't, I will."

I pulled back.

"You'd betray me?" I asked, too tired for anger.

"Only when I know what you are doing is monumentally wrong."

I hugged her, knowing how hard it had been for her to utter those words. I took comfort knowing that, with her at my side, I could conquer anything.

"Okay, darling brother, to what do we owe this unexpected invite to dine with you both?"

"Are you saying we never invite you over?" I

teased.

"Not at this short notice. So I can only deduce that you've called us here to tell us something. Now, let me see if I can guess... You're either getting a divorce..." she grinned, "Or Gemma's going to make me an auntie. Oh, she is, isn't she?" She fluttered around us in a totally un-Cass-like way. When she'd stopped hugging and kissing us, she picked up the vibe wasn't as it should be.

"Okay, what's up?"

Gemma gazed at me with an air of forlornness that tore at my heart, tears streaked down her face, and she fled the room.

"Is there something wrong with the baby?" Cass probed when I stopped her following Gemma.

I swallowed hard, not wanting to utter the words I couldn't avoid.

"I've got cancer," I blurted. "Testicular cancer. I've got to have one of my nuts removed at the end of this week. It's called an orchidectomy." I rambled, trying to fill the void their silence left.

The stricken look on Cass' frozen features pulled at my heartstrings. I tried to focus on Keith's words as he broke the silence. "It's supposed to be very treatable these days, the highest recovery statistics. Remember the article in the magazine a few months ago?"

"Fuck the magazine! Fuck stat-fucking-istics! This is my brother."

Gemma came back in, tear-stained but calmer. She walked over to Cass holding out her arms to embrace her. Cass and Keith had questions I couldn't answer, making me realise I needed to do research. I wasn't going to go through this whole process in ignorance.

"Well, I can't go now," Cass' strident voice broke through my thoughts.

"No, that's not what I want. It's why I didn't want to tell you."

"What do you mean, you didn't want to tell me? Of course I'm going to stay and see you through this. My career is not so important that I would leave the number one person in my life."

I winced. *Shit. I may be the one with testicular cancer, but she's just put Keith's nuts in a vice.*

"Gem, will you help me get something?"

"The number one person in my life?" Keith parodied, his voice shaking as Gemma and I left the room, but stayed outside.

"You know what I meant. Stop being so obtuse."

"Obtuse! Is that what you call it when your wife refuses to give up her precious career for her husband, to start a family, but will sacrifice anything for her darling brother?"

"I've made it clear I don't want a family."

"Shame you couldn't have let me know before we married."

"For God's sakes, we've been here before. Now isn't the time for you to indulge in your favourite argument. Can't you put it into perspective? My brother has cancer. I could lose him." Her voice wobbled.

"You could lose me. Our marriage isn't strong, and all you seem to do is push harder." Keith sounded like he'd reached breaking point.

Gemma and I exchanged a glance. We decided now was the time to re-enter, before things became bloody.

At that moment, Keith chose to make an irreverent comment about me, which, rather than upsetting me, I found amusing.

Cass and Gemma gasped, making me laugh; three pairs of eyes stared at me in shock.

Chapter 16

Gemma

We should've been rolling up to the hospital with unquenchable grins, like any other doting parents-to-be, but we were here instead to see whether my husband had cancer.

The room we were taken to was warm and inviting for a hospital consultation room. A small round man greeted us and introduced himself as Doctor Robson. His florid face was open and friendly. China-blue eyes sparkled with warmth, and his nose seemed to twitch, almost, as though the handlebar moustache that sat beneath were tickling him.

Theo exhibited a display of bolshie behaviour that wasn't typical of him, and then proceeded to walk the precipice of a panic attack. My heart flipped. *Shit, what do I do?* I managed a weak smile. It seemed to be enough. I'm not sure how much Theo took in, but I knew that my mind had wandered. I was brought back to reality, though, when Doctor Robson confirmed a tumour and spoke about removing his testicle. I didn't need to see Theo's face to know he was freaking.

We barely spoke on the way home. Words seemed banal, a fruitless attempt to soothe. I watched the road speeding past and wondered how we were going to get through this. *Other people do.* If I were going to support Theo whilst going through my first, maybe only, pregnancy, then I'd need help, someone to lean on. I knew the only person who could do that with any conviction was Cass, whose feelings for him were as strong as mine, albeit in a different way.

"You have to tell her." I tried to keep the exasperation

out of my voice. "No, you rest there and I'll do dinner tonight." I cringed as the words were uttered, but I couldn't take them back. I knew he wouldn't like it; he'd never been like the rest of the male species that called the slightest sniffle full-blown flu. It's the mothers who are to blame. That was probably why Theo was different; you couldn't accuse Margaret of being maternal. Hell, what hope did we have as parents with the example we'd been set between us? *Will we be parents or will I have to play both roles?* A shiver travelled down my spine.

"I'm not telling Cass, and that's the end of it."

"Give me one good reason."

He went into the predictable spiel about not wanting to spoil Cass' career. The saying 'Hell hath no fury like a woman scorned' wouldn't even come close to describing the scene if my sister-in-law was kept in the dark. At first I'd felt intimidated by their relationship, but it didn't take me long to realise they were just especially close siblings. Neither Richard nor Margaret had played an active role in their lives, so Cass and Theo had adopted parental-type responsibilities toward each other. He gave in eventually, after a long and tearful embrace, mostly on my side, but I couldn't swear that Theo hadn't shed a tear, too. It was one of the things I loved about him; he was secure enough in his masculinity that he could show his feminine side.

Cass turned up with a bottle of burgundy and a beautiful bouquet of lilac roses. I couldn't help noticing how youthful she looked. Her jet-black hair didn't show a trace of grey. In all the time I'd known her, the only concessions to femininity she made were the slash of red across her lips and the manicured nails with French polish, squared, not rounded. I wondered whether that was a statement – no soft edges. Keith, on the other hand, was distracted and ill at ease. Maybe they'd had another one of their infamous rows. Keith's slanted hazel eyes were lifeless and his over-tall body slightly stooped. His hirsute face and shoulder-length hair gave him an unkempt appearance.

Comparing him with Theo, Keith fell short as a

man, but then no one came close to Theo. If I hadn't met Theo, I could've fancied Jason, not that I'd ever admit it to Theo.

"Okay, darling brother, to what do we owe this unexpected invite to dine with you both?" Cass said in that overly dramatic way she had when speaking to Theo. *They must have had an interesting childhood together.*

The usual banter passed between them until Cass guessed the news we'd forgotten about. It hadn't occurred to us to tell her tonight so her exclamations of joy were more than I could handle. I fled the room in an emotional state. *Is this how you support your husband when things get hard?* I had to get a hell of a lot stronger.

Cass threw a complete hissy fit. The anger directed at her husband was a palpable thing. I knew I couldn't hide out any longer.

Keith appeared tired and deflated, Theo exhausted and Cass stricken. Her lovely face seemed to have aged ten years in the last few minutes. *I'll need to be strong for her, as well.* I went to her and held out my arms. Her robust frame felt frail. This damned curse was going to bring out many facets of our personalities that had hitherto been undiscovered.

"So what happens now?" Keith asked, trying to bring a practical aspect to the funereal atmosphere that hung shroud-like over the room.

"I have to have blood tests, and they need to remove my testicle." Theo faltered over the word.

Keith blanched in sympathy and with, I'm sure, no small amount of relief that it wasn't him. It's as though they feared the removal would somehow emasculate them. *How would you feel if it was your breast?* I felt the urge to cry again. *How am I going to cope?*

"And then it'll be gone?" Cass asked, hope threading her words.

Theo admitted that he knew very little more than what he'd already relayed.

"Well, I can't go now." I cringed at her words.

She'd have been better off slapping Keith. Even such a placid, easy-going person had a breaking point, and Cass had slammed this home to her husband. Theo rather tactfully removed us from the room.

Theo and I stopped outside the room. We listened as the accusations flew between husband and wife. Theo wore a grim expression. I wondered where his sympathies lay; I hadn't quite made my mind up. On the one hand, Cass was over-powering but she'd just found out her brother had cancer, and her husband had chosen the wrong time to air his dissatisfaction. When we went back into the living room, Keith further queered his pitch.

"If your precious brother wasn't so pedantically moral, I'd have suspected there was more between the two of you than is healthy for siblings." Keith's vile words caused me to gasp, which was echoed by Cass, who looked like she was going to fly at him with flailing fists. We were both struck dumb as Theo laughed out loud.

"Oh, for fuck's sakes, people, lighten up. I've got cancer; I'm not made of bone china. I won't break because Keith's pissed. I don't blame him. I wouldn't want to be on the wrong side of you, Cass. I want to be treated as normal; it's not too hard to comprehend.

Gem, darling, I can still do my share of the chores. Cass, I don't need you to sacrifice your career, and Keith, keep on saying what you mean since you might be the only one to keep me grounded and sane. What I'm saying is, I'm still the same person – well, at least for now."

We all wore crestfallen expressions. I, of course, had been wrapping him up in cotton wool. Cass' sacrifice was one she knew he didn't want her to make, but Keith had to be feeling the most guilt when Theo was being so magnanimous after his despicable words.

Theo

Over the next few days, I told all the people who were important in my life. Everyone was really supportive.

One of the real tests of friendship is how they fare through hardships and how at such times the so-called friends are notable for their absence. Jason, who was due to move back in a day or so, offered to find a place to rent. Gemma and I insisted he was welcome, which was a relief to him as he could ill afford a huge rent until he and Cathy had sorted out their financial arrangements.

A few people surprised me; none more so than Jake, once he'd got his head around it. He trawled the internet and bookshops for information to read, staying up until all hours with enough coffee to sink a battleship. He then passed all this information onto me with the name of a website that I found immensely useful. It had been set up by a survivor of testicular cancer and had testimonials from many other survivors. He emailed links and pages of his internet research to my friends and family.

The other people who took me by surprise were my parents. Cass insisted on accompanying Gemma and I as we set out to break the news to them.

"I couldn't have you facing them without me."

"Where's Keith?"

"Oh, off sulking somewhere."

"You should take more notice of him; he's your husband," I advised, putting the car into gear and moving away from the kerb.

"He'll keep." She said no more for the duration of the journey, but I felt her tension. When we alighted from the car, I gave her a quick hug.

"I'll be okay, Cass."

She looked at me with red-rimmed eyes.

"How can you know that?" she demanded.

"I don't, but I have to believe it. I need to be strong for Gemma, our baby, and you, of course." I tried to inject some light-heartedness into the moment and was rewarded by her watery smile.

"Come on; let's go see 'The Parents'."

"So how much do you want?" Father asked when we'd settled down and Maria had placed the tea tray in front of Mother.

"What do you mean?" I asked wearily.

"Well, we don't usually have the pleasure of your company unless it's an occasion so I concluded that it must be money you're after."

Mother looked on with a decided lack of interest as she lifted the bone china teapot and poured the tea. I wondered whether her hand would shake if I told them now. She'd probably berate me for my timing in case I caused her to chip a cup; a broken cup was resigned immediately to the bin, to be replaced from the store of exact replicas in the cellar. *The doddering old coot must be senile.* I'd never taken anything in my adult life from them.

Cass and Gemma looked at me with raised eyebrows as Mother prattled on, disregarding our silence. I waited until Maria had placed the tea in front of us. Mother might pour but she wasn't going to get up from her throne to distribute the drinks. Maria closed the doors, and her feet pattered away in her Scholl's.

Mother stopped chattering and looked at us, a

close and uncomfortable scrutiny. "Are you going to enlighten us as to the reason behind this unprecedented visit?" The squeaky pitch of her voice irritated me, and I found myself wondering if she'd be bothered.

"I have cancer, testicular cancer." I squared my chin and blurted the words out.

For the first time in my life, I witnessed emotion on her hard, cold features. Her face sagged, as though she was having a stroke. Her mouth was open and slack. She lost all semblance of colour. Before me was a woman I no longer recognised, and a thought as light and wispy as a butterfly fluttered across my consciousness that maybe I never had. I turned to Father, whose face, too, seemed to have shrunk and aged. *They do care, after all.*

"What happens now?" Father asked. "Do you need…"

"Monday." There wasn't a dry eye in the room, my own included.

"Is there anything we can do, Son?" I'd waited a

lifetime to hear him say those words but before I could respond, Mother ran from the room in tears, the first time I'd seen her cry.

Father lurched to his feet and, indicating where Mother had fled, said falteringly, "I should…"

I nodded, watching him shuffle from the room. *Where is the rod that holds his back?* Stumbling over words for a man so erudite. *Have I walked into the twilight zone, a parallel universe?*

"So they do have feelings." Cass' words slashed the air, albeit without their usual bite.

"Shush." The alien sound of raised voices shocked me. "Listen."

"It's your fault." Mother's voice trembled, on the verge of hysteria.

"I cannot be blamed for our son's cancer," Father shouted back.

"It's your fault that they hate us."

"She sounds like a fishwife," Cass whispered.

Silence descended, and the door creaked open. We weren't sure what to expect. The perpetual stiff upper lip seemed to have gone; visible signs of their distress were gouged into their faces.

"We have something else to tell you," Gemma ventured, to change the strangeness that had settled around us. We were on virgin soil here. None of us knew what we should do or say, the old order annihilated; a coup flying under the banner of cancer.

"I can't handle any more news." Mother's voice held the distinct tones of abject terror.

"I'm pregnant."

Mother sat in stunned silence not knowing how to respond. After several attempts, she said, "Oh well, that is good news." Her words were so lacking in conviction that I realised what Gemma had experienced when she'd told me.

Chapter 17

Gemma

"Cancer," I whispered, but the words resonated around the room as though I'd roared them at the top of my lungs.

"Oh, Gemma, we couldn't have been more wrong." Chris sat across from me in the Mermaid Café.

"What am I to do, Chris?"

"Sweetheart, I don't know, but we're here to hold you up."

"But what if..." I couldn't finish the sentence.

"We'll deal with 'if' as and when we need to."

"Jake's been great."

"I don't think he could cope if he lost..." She left the rest unsaid, realising what she'd been about to say.

"Are you finished with these?" The waitress collected our empty cups.

"Can we have two more lattes, please? Make one of them a decaf. Thanks." Chris smiled and then answered in a measured tone, "He has such a bond with Theo, stronger than with me."

"I think Keith feels the same about Cass' relationship with Theo," I replied.

"That's one special guy you have, Gem."

"So Doc Robson said you need to shave your privates." *God, I sound like a virginal schoolgirl.* "Do you need help?"

Theo's face creased into a huge grin, and then he burst out laughing. "Yes, please." His suggestive voice left me in no doubt that I was in for a night of passion.

"Razor, wax or Immac?" I grinned.

"You know what you can do with the wax."

"I'll bet you don't fancy the Immac either. Hey, I can't believe your parents today; I thought they didn't do emotion."

"Me too."

"What do you think your mother was blaming your father for?" I asked as I shaved the last of his pubic hair.

He shook his head. Leaning toward me, he nibbled on my earlobe and continued blazing a trail down my neck. I felt the tell-tale signs of my arousal. Even after four years of marriage, it took little for him to excite me. A shiver ran down my spine as I tried to block out what was happening to him.

"Are you okay?" he asked, scrutinising me.

My response was unconvincing.

"Is it this?" He indicated his shaven groin. "Does it turn you off?" A vulnerable look crossed his face.

"No! It's not that. I just... I love you so much." Gazing into his eyes, I realised I hadn't conveyed what I meant. I grasped his face between my hands and placed kisses on his forehead, nose and lips. "I can't imagine living without you, my darling... and I know I need to be strong for you. My life has no meaning if you're not in it."

Theo, in turn, cupped my face. "I'm not going anywhere. I'll never leave you."

His voice was as charged with emotion as my own. In that moment, the spark re-ignited, and what occurred was the best sex we'd ever had, so full of love and enhanced by the unspoken fear that it may be the last time for a while.

"I love you," Theo whispered as I drifted off to sleep in his arms.

The next day dawned before either of us was ready for it. After falling asleep with the ease of the sated, I failed to sleep through and awoke in the early hours. Theo also lay awake; I sensed he didn't want a conversation, so I stayed silent. When the alarm trilled, harsh and remorseless, I turned to Theo. He appeared hollow-eyed and pale.

"I'll beat you to the shower," I tried to inject some humour into the day, not even sure if it was appropriate. *What is right or wrong in this situation?* Theo smiled wanly and said I should go first.

"Hello, Theo. How are you feeling?" Doctor Robson asked before running through the process which he called an orchidectomy. An orchid is an exotic, beautiful flower. How had the removal of a testicle been given this name?

"We'll be giving you a general anaesthetic." The words seemed to be coming to me from a distance, and all I could focus on was seeing Theo's defencelessness as he tried to digest what was happening to him.

His hand reached out and took mine as he winked. *I should be the one supporting him.*

"I'm going to be okay."

"*Yes*, you are."

Every minute felt like an hour, waiting for Theo to come out of surgery. I paced the floor. I prayed, cajoling God and promising him the earth. I threw in a few threats, too; something about never darkening his door again if he let anything happen to Theo. It wasn't much of a threat from someone who only went to church for weddings, funerals and christenings. But I was desperate, and I would have sold my soul to the devil to keep my husband. Five years isn't a long time to have shared when we'd sworn to a lifetime. I wanted to see him with a pipe and slippers, grumpy because the grandchildren were too noisy or the kids didn't visit enough.

When Theo was wheeled back on the trolley bed from his surgery, he was drowsy. The gown he wore was so clinical that I couldn't help but shudder at how frail he appeared. He tried to hide it, but his eyes told me how much pain he was in. In the way of a mother, I wanted to take that pain from him, even if it meant I had to have it. The nurse attempted to adjust his position to make him more comfortable, but his face contorted in agony.

"I'll get you some more pain relief, Theo," the nurse said, her eyes soft and warm, a striking contrast to the crisply starched uniform she wore.

Theo lay pale and unsmiling; he merely nodded in response. I wanted to say something to him but yet again words failed me. I was learning a sense of inadequacy about myself that I hadn't previously known existed.

Theo

"So how does it feel? Or are you sick of that particular question?" Jake asked, throwing himself down on my bed.

It was refreshing having him here, being as real as ever. Everyone else avoided eye contact or sat gingerly on the bed as though anything could hurt me more than the surgeon's knife.

"You're the only one who's asked."

No one else knew what to say as they shuffled about until Gemma ushered them away saying that I needed my sleep. I didn't; I needed rest. I think it was a good excuse to help them escape. Even Gemma feared saying the wrong thing and so avoided asking me how I felt.

"Do you really want to know?" I asked, trying, albeit with little success, to hide my anger.

"Only if you want to tell it, mate."

"The hospital was stark and sterile." I stopped for a moment. "Maybe I expected something more comforting. The doctors and nurses were great, but I couldn't help wondering whether they ran a book on the patient, and if so what odds they gave me. They fitted one of those prosthetics, but it's not mine – it doesn't feel right. And I can't help thinking, why me? What have I done that is so wrong to deserve this? Self-pitying, isn't it?"

"Yes, it is."

I barked out a harsh laugh – nothing like a dose of Jake.

"But I won't hold it against you, because if I were where you are now, I'd be wallowing in it like a pig in shit." This time my laugh pulled at the stitches, causing me to wince.

"Are you okay?" Jake's tone changed to concern.

"It hurts when I laugh. I didn't know that. I haven't laughed since."

My mind wandered back to when I'd come around in the recovery room, groggy and as yet unaware. I'd known what I was going in for but part of me didn't believe it would happen. Then the anaesthetic wore off, and my brain functioned again, followed by the mind-numbingly painful truth. It was gone, and in its place I had a foreign body that was no part of me... and yet now it was part of me. It couldn't replace what was there before, and with that realisation I felt like half a man. I tried to tell myself to look at the bigger picture, but at that time I couldn't see past my emasculation. Jake sat and listened as angry words and wretched self-pity spewed out. He didn't make any banal observations about how brave I was or how I'd get through it. He just sat and listened, and somehow, at the end of it, I did experience some relief at having been able to unburden myself.

"Gemma said your parents picked you up from the hospital."

"Yeah, they've been quite good about all this."

"They're your parents; they should be good. Unfortunately, we both know that what parents are and what they should be are two different things; a good reason why I've avoided that particular trap."

"My sentiments exactly," Cass said, sticking her head around the door. "Safe to come in, is it? Or are you two too busy playing with each other's..." She left the rest unsaid, realising what she was about to say. Her eyes darkened with anger at herself.

"Oh, for fuck's sakes, if you're going to pussyfoot around me, too, you can just leave."

"And if you're going to bite my head off, then I might just do that."

"We'll be all right." They laughed, but I just smiled. I didn't want to rip my stitches.

"Gemma's done in," Cass said to me after Jake had left.

"She's done in? I'm the one with cancer. I'm the one who has just lost half of my manhood."

"For someone who doesn't want anyone pussyfooting around him, you're putting on a bloody good show. And I'm sorry, but you're not the only one affected by this. Do you forget your wife is pregnant? She's having to deal with hormones, see her husband through cancer and try to stay strong for everyone. She also gets bollocked by her ungrateful wretch of a hubby for not acting in the way he wants her to. Well, now, isn't she just the bad wife?" Cass' scorn was hurtful but mainly because I knew I deserved it. "She's just feeling her way through this in the dark as we all are." Her voice softened. "We'll get through this together."

I stared at the décor in my room thinking back to when Cass and I had chosen it. *It's time for a change. Gemma and I can redecorate when I got through this.* Laying there prone for two days gave me a lot of time for quiet contemplation, even with a regular stream of visitors. I had a feeling that Gemma was carefully monitoring the timings for visits and how long everyone stayed so that I wouldn't get too exhausted. It's surprising how tired you get doing nothing. Cass had been right to berate me about my attitude toward my wife, but I hadn't found the right words to say to her.

Chapter 18

Gemma

It didn't seem to matter what I said, it was wrong. I tried not to mind. Truly, I did. It wasn't that I resented Theo's attitude, I just couldn't find the right words. The inadequacy I felt in childhood reared its ugly head again. I knew it must have been me when I overheard snippets of conversations he had with Jake and Cass. *Why can they make him laugh, and all I seem to do is make him angry?*

Jason gave us space so I barely knew he was there, but he appeared at the times when I needed someone the most. He, too, struggled to talk to Theo, so it was a relief to be able to offload to someone who knew what I was feeling. I think our problem was we were always so careful not to offend Theo that inevitably we seemed to do just that.

Jason could be found in the kitchen when I was cooking or washing up. It was great having someone to help. I thought wistfully of the times Theo and I had shared the chores, and I couldn't help wondering whether we would again. I don't mean that I was dwelling on Theo's mortality; on the contrary. I was worried about the schism that was opening up between us, which I had no idea how to bridge.

I need to fix this. I placed the basket of washing down, in the middle of the kitchen floor, and headed upstairs, praying once again, this time for the right words to say to my husband.

"Theo, I'm sorry."

"What do you have to be sorry about?" Theo's response was guarded.

"For not being the supportive wife you deserve," I finished, feeling lame.

"Gem, darling, you've been great. I've been such an arse. I've been taking it all out on you."

"You have every right to be upset. You're going through hell, and I've said all the wrong things."

"You're going through hell, too, and I'm not sure there is a right thing to say. I think I needed a whipping boy, and I'm sorry to say, you were it."

We were back where we belonged.

It was two and a half agonising weeks after the orchidectomy when Theo was called back for the results of the biopsy to determine whether the cancer was benign or malignant. The tension in the days following our heart-to-heart intensified as Theo was sent for more rounds of tests: bloods to determine whether his markers had gone down after the orchidectomy, an MRI, chest x-ray, and CT scan, which was the primary tool in showing whether the cancer had spread out of the testicle. The results were due, and I couldn't disguise my fear.

I smiled, thinking back to the day of his MRI. We'd been informed he could bring some music to listen to in the chamber, which got very noisy. *Theo asked me to choose a CD for him. My hand hovered over the CD collection. I reached for one of his favourite jazz CDs but pulled out a Robbie Williams CD instead.*

"You minx," he gasped.

"I didn't want your music to have bad associations."

Theo kissed me long and hard, causing me to yearn for more.

"You do realise you won't be able to play Robbie Williams ever again while I'm around," he whispered as our lips parted. "Bet you didn't think of that."

"I'll keep him as my secret guilty pleasure for when my husband's not around." I giggled as he tickled me.

His tone changed. "Thank you."

I knew I'd done the right thing.

"You okay?" I asked, knowing it was a stupid question but unable to formulate a better one.

"No. You?"

"Ditto. Actually, I feel sick."

"Baby or worry?"

"Don't know. Maybe both."

"Theo, how are you feeling?" the doctor asked before glancing back down at his notes. Part of me wanted to freeze this moment in time. If we stopped here, we wouldn't hear anything bad, but we'd also never know if the news was positive.

"You tell me, doc." Theo's voice sounded calm.

The doctor coughed and murmured an "Ahem," before continuing, "We've had the results back from the biopsy and all the other tests we ran..."

Come on.

"The tests prove conclusively that it is malignant; the HCG and AFP levels have increased, the cancer has spread out of the testes... Chemotherapy..." I could hear words resonating in my ears, then plummet to the pit of my stomach.

"Bring it on." His words were alien, his tone a challenge. "I'm going to fight this bastard, and I'll beat it." He looked at me again, with triumph tattooed firmly in the air around him.

Theo

That morning, when I woke up from the fragmented night's sleep, I knew the cancer was still there, enveloping me. I also knew that self-pity wouldn't make it go away. Gemma thought I was in denial. She thought I hadn't fully comprehended the doctor's words. I didn't need a doctor to tell me what already was; merely to confirm what I already knew. Like a woman who went to the doctor for confirmation of her pregnancy after doing a home test.

When I'd first been told I had cancer, I'd began to feel it within; a destructive force, a woodlouse devouring its way through an antique table, spilt red wine spreading across a crisp, white linen tablecloth.

This thing, this word, 'cancer', was eating away at me, spreading through my body, and I could feel its presence. I don't mean a specific, quantifiable feeling such as an ache or pain. It was more elusive, could so easily be missed, but I knew it was there.

For a few days after the orchidectomy, I wasn't sure. The pain, the discomfort of the surgery had left me uncertain. Then one day I woke up, and I knew it was still there, almost like an old friend who'd betrayed me. I was so used to the feeling that it was familiar, and familiarity can be comforting. Then I remembered what it had done to me, what it was still doing, and a great mushrooming cloud of hatred welled up inside.

So I knew, before the doctor with the round glasses, black pinhole eyes, rotund nose and thick fleshy lips imparted the news. I'd decided I would be strong and fight it the moment I'd heard Robbie Williams' voice coming from the round chamber of the MRI scanner and knew Gemma had done that for me. I would do this for her and our baby. I watched her face drain of all colour and feared she'd faint.

Is This Love?

I listened as the doctor talked about chemotherapy; radiotherapy wasn't an option with Teratoma, my form of cancer. Teratoma, terra...toma. I played with the word in my mind, words so like any other more common ones. Terracotta... red earth, terra firma... solid ground. Was there a reference somewhere to earth/ground? And if it referred to earth, then how did that relate to my cancer? My cancer – I'd already claimed ownership of it. Or had it claimed ownership of me?

The doctor told me about TNM staging and number staging, which were relevant to testicular cancer. Yet again, my mind drifted to irrelevant quarters as I contemplated numbers. As an accountant, numbers were my field of expertise, but these figures represented something that lay outside of my realm of knowledge. I made a mental note to talk it through with Jake, who seemed to have understood all the complexities that my brain was struggling to comprehend. T2, N2, M0 or stage three. The doctor explained it all to me. It had spread to the lymph nodes, and the markers were high, but the finer details eluded my wandering mind.

"Have you got any questions you'd like to ask? Anything you don't understand?"

How about all of it? I said nothing as I didn't think I could take in any more information at this stage. I memorised the numbers and their accompanying letters. Never before had innocuous letters and digits been so imbued with doom.

"Tumour, Node, Metastasis," Jake said. "T2: The Tumour has grown into the lymph nodes. N2: at least one lymph node is between two and five cm wide, M0: it hasn't spread to any other organs."

It was as though Jake thought that by swatting up on the subject, he could do his bit to save my life, when really, his hands were as tied as mine. I glimpsed a side of Jake again that I'd struggled to make other people see. Chris had been with him for over six years, and I was sure he was faithful, but his reputation had been well earned, so it would probably take another six years before others changed their opinion of him.

"If you do that when the oncologist is talking to you, no wonder you're not getting it." Jake's exasperation was palpable.

"Do what?" I was perplexed.

"Tune out, daydream, fantasise about Jordan for all I know."

A rumble of laughter rolled up and out of me.

"And the funny bit is where?"

"Oh, come on, Jake, it's my cancer. I can laugh when I want."

"It's not just your cancer. It's mine and Gemma's, it's Cass' and everyone else's who cares about you, so please get your head out of the clouds and get serious about this. We can laugh when you've kicked its butt all the way back to where it came from."

Jake was right. I needed to understand this enemy of mine if I was going to fight it.

Chapter 19

Gemma

Hospitals played a big part in our life over the next couple of months. My twenty-week scan was the highlight, a ray of sunshine peeping out through the thick curtain of clouds. The day of the scan was set for the day before Theo's first chemotherapy treatment. We went to the hospital and blocked out all thoughts about the next time we'd be back.

"I don't have any records of your previous scan," the sonographer said.

"This is the first one. We found out late."

"The referral says you found out at sixteen weeks."
I felt her reproach.

"Yes, but we also found out my husband had cancer."

"I'm sorry." Her smile held warmth and pity in equal measure.

"Boy or girl?" Theo asked the sonographer as she rolled the scanner over the cold gel on my stomach.

She looked at me, an unspoken question between two women. *Do I want to know?* Then I saw the expression on Theo's face; he needed to know. I nodded. The sonographer gave a little chuckle, the knowledge of our baby's gender her delicious secret. Suddenly, I wanted to know. The pale, gaunt face with twinkling eyes beamed at us. "A boy and a girl." She thrust her knowledge at me like someone who has a Christmas present that they're excited for you to open.

"How can that be?" I heard her chuckle and Theo's laugh as his brain comprehended before mine that we were having twins.

"We'll have a mini-me each." Theo's eyes warmed

in a way that I hadn't seen since the C-word had entered our lives.

"Let's go and celebrate."

"Shouldn't you go home and rest? Tomorrow's going to be a long day."

"Tomorrow all the madness starts, and we don't know how it'll end, so let's have today to celebrate the twins."

I didn't need telling twice. "What did you have in mind?"

"I don't know. Maybe we could go out for dinner? Take in a movie or a walk by the river? In fact, why not all three?"

It started with a vengeance. Theo spent the next five days wired up to a drip, with so many drugs and fluids going through him that it made my head spin. My morning sickness reared its ugly head on the second day of his treatment. There was something about the smell in his ward that I reacted to, and I found myself reaching for the recycled grey sick bowl with more regularity than the patients in Theo's ward.

At first, I tried to make it to the bathroom. Thomas, one of the patients, told me to use the sick bowls as that was what they were there for; he even joked that they were the lucky ones as Chemo came with anti-emetics.

Aside from Theo and Thomas, there were two other men in the room. Joe was on his second cycle. His wife breezed in for half an hour a day, on a cloud of Chanel No. 5, looking immaculate. Christopher's tearful wife came in daily with tales of their five children. Thomas' wife and I were the ones who stayed as long as we could. The guys referred to me as the volcano.

Camaraderie developed straight away; the guys were in for three to five days, dependent on their regimen. They would then be replaced by the next patients, like a chemo conveyor belt. It was almost as though the room itself held a magic that sought to bind the patients so that as soon as a new one was admitted, it pulled him in and made him one of the gang. And I guess that's what they were: The 'Cancer Gang'.

"He will be all right, won't he?" Theo's mother, Margaret, asked me during one of her now regular visits; the vulnerability she'd shown when Theo had informed her about his cancer hadn't left but the standoffish behaviour had.

A steady stream of visitors invaded the house, all eager to see that Theo would be okay. I couldn't say that any of them went away with the reassurance they craved. His green eyes dulled inside his white-as-snow face.

Theo

My day started with a needle being stuck in my arm; of course, technically, it didn't. I was at home, in bed with my wife. I watched as her eyelids fluttered open, struck anew by the piercing blue eyes that sought mine straight away as they had every morning in our five years together. Her long blond hair fanned on the pillow. Reaching out, I touched the silky softness of it, knowing that I wouldn't wake up next to her for the next four mornings. It was a poignant moment.

A smile touched the corner of my lips as I thought about the perfection of yesterday; suddenly, being a father was a real prospect. I had to be around to witness it. I wanted to teach my children to play football, to go to the park and push them on swings, and whatever else a father does.

The way I saw my day starting, though, was with that needle, drawing out my blood to send it to the laboratory for tests before my regimen commenced. This was followed by them collecting stem cells to be replaced after treatment, and a run-through of what to expect.

"This is the room that you'll be in for the next five days," the nurse informed me cheerfully as though she'd given me the key to a suite at the Ritz.

My first impression was of the soulless quality of the room and the three patients already ensconced in their places. One man lay back on the bed, and the other two sat on large padded upright armchairs.

"Welcome."

"Hey."

"Come on in."

The three voices welcomed me in unison.

It didn't take me long to work out that this room wasn't soulless. It might not have been the Ritz, but it contained a character of its own. My fellow 'inmates' were Joe, Thomas and Christopher. Joe sat on the bed, on his second cycle of treatment, pale, gaunt, every inch the advertisement of what to look forward to from chemotherapy. Thomas, a rugged redhead with ruddy cheeks, and Christopher, whose skin was the shade of ebony and whose smile stretched across his face, were both on day two of their first course of chemo. A bond grew between us. Gemma said that the room contained magic. I came to believe she could be right.

The nurse said it may be a little uncomfortable when they insert the cannula into my vein, but I can't say I really noticed it. The thing I came to dread was the continuous drip of the drugs, sliding like a snake beneath my skin. On the first day, it was Etoposide and Cisplatin, drip, drip, drip, crawling, writhing through my system, mingling with my blood, flowing through me. I was also given anti-emetics to combat or lessen the vomiting.

Days two, three, four and five: the same combination of drugs, with the addition of Bleomycin on day two. The routines of the days were the same, a tedium only broken by the other patients and the visitors. I don't think I'd ever realised how long twenty-four hours could be. Part of me thought I should appreciate every moment since time was precious, but that didn't account for having a needle in your arm and a steady stream of poison flowing through your veins. The only other sound that filtered through was the beep when the drip bag needed changing.

"Have you seen that website... what's the name again?" Joe pondered for a moment. I could almost see the cogs going around in his head. "The one set up by testicular cancer survivors? It's on the tip of my tongue. *Check 'em, boys,* that's it."

"Yeah, my mate Jake told me about it," I answered, conscious of a metallic taste in my mouth.

"Has he had it, too?" Christopher was looking sick. I could see he needed distracting.

"No. It's his way of feeling useful – to find out everything."

"It's difficult to take it all in." Christopher leaned forward but then looked like he regretted it, as he returned to his original position.

"I have to know everything," said Joe. "The only way I could feel like I'm doing something. I hate feeling that I have no control. I haven't stopped reading since I found out."

"It doesn't seem to sink in for me," I admitted. "Small bites work better than huge chunks. I seem to drift off into a dream world after a couple of minutes."

Chapter 20

Gemma

The next few months were intense, with Theo's treatments, the side effects and my own feeling of nausea that refused to go away. The first five days of his first cycle were relatively uneventful. I kept watching him for side effects, but other than a funny taste in his mouth, he seemed relatively unaffected. The anti-emetics helped, but after arriving home he was so tired he could do little more than lie in bed. He was lethargic and didn't want to eat.

"But you must eat," I cajoled.

"I don't want to." His voice was flat.

"You need to keep your strength up; you need to fight this." I could hear the nagging quality in my voice but was powerless to stop it.

"Leave me alone."

His family and friends rallied around, someone turning up daily. He lay there with a blank expression which I'd come to dread. The eyes that had struck such a chord all those years ago lacked any sign of life.

"We need to do something to help him." Jason was a great help. Without his support, I don't think I'd have made it this far. When everyone went home, when the silence was more than I could bear, he was the one I confided in, the one who held me while I sobbed, who wiped my tears with his rough hands.

"What can we do? No one seems to get through to him. It's like he's given up already."

"You need some time off." Jason handed me two plates of pasta carbonara he'd cooked while he carried the garlic bread and drinks to the table.

"Time off!" I exclaimed. *Has he gone mad?* "How will that help? Who'll look after Theo?"

"I will. I'm serious. Gemma, you're exhausted, and you've now got the twins to think about. You need some time away from Theo. Meet up with your coven of friends to have a bitch at our expense. It might help you to clear your mind and work out how to rally Mr. T upstairs."

I laughed at the new nickname for Theo.

"So how are things?" Jackie asked.

"Not good, but please let's talk about you guys; I need to focus on anything other than cancer."

I was grateful to Jason for bullying me to meet with the girls. Chris and I had driven to London, although only Susie lived there now. Jackie had relocated with her family to a sleepy village in Lincolnshire, and Amanda now lived in Berlin – both very recent developments.

"I'm so glad you could make it, Amanda. You have so far to come nowadays."

"A call for help has to be heeded by us all." She smiled. Amanda showed no signs of ageing in any way, no little lines to give away the fact that she was nearer to forty than thirty.

"Who would believe the changes in the last couple of months?" Chris said.

"I would never have pictured you settling into village life, Jackie."

"And Amanda dropping everything for a high-powered career in Berlin," Susie added. "Only me left here now."

"Would you move? I could see you in a sleepy village with a garden to tend," I said.

We took it in turns to cuddle five-month-old Lily.

"I could, too," Susie laughed, "but I'm not sure I will ever have the confidence to up-sticks and leave everything that's familiar. You know, meeting new people, new job, etc…"

"Move to Devon and you will have two ready-made friends," I coaxed. "I'm sure Lily would love to grow up in the country. She could become best friends with my two when they arrive."

"Come on, Jackie. You've been a bit silent as to

your sudden move to Lincolnshire," Susie deftly shifted the focus away from herself.

"Rory was headhunted by an international company who are setting up a base in Lincoln. They want him to spearhead it. We've been thinking for a while that we'd like the children to grow up in a nice community, somewhere a bit more innocent, if you will, so this was the perfect opportunity. Although we could do with the house selling now; this renting lark is not much fun."

"Have you got any interested parties?" Amanda asked.

"A couple. Let's hope one of them buys. So, over to you, Amanda. What made you give up the chance to be your own boss?"

"Sorry, we haven't finished with you yet... not by a long way." Amanda laughed.

Theo

Going home was hard. At the hospital, the camaraderie amongst the other cancer patients and the feeling that I wasn't alone kept me sane. The nausea started with a vengeance at home, alongside the horrible metallic taste that I couldn't shift. Gemma was great. She hit all the right notes but couldn't know how I felt, like I couldn't imagine what she felt during her pregnancy in the way another pregnant woman could. Listening to someone and understanding were two different things.

I could feel my withdrawal happening but couldn't do anything to stop it. I guess it would be termed by a psychiatrist as depression; another label, cancer and depression. Could you get the former and not the latter? If so, why did I seem to be so bad at coping with what was happening to me?

I was aware that the only person on my radar at this moment was me. An unedifying truth when your wife was having the equivalent of a hormonal H bomb exploding in her body and facing the possibility she may have to bring up her unborn twins alone. So yes, I knew how things were for Gemma but all I could focus on was how they were for me.

People paraded in and out of my bedroom, a veritable circus performance all aimed at cheering up the cancer patient. Even if they told me it had been a mistake and I didn't have cancer, it wouldn't have put a smile on my face, as it would have meant I'd lost a testicle for nothing; forever half a man, and for what? If someone offered to wave a magic wand to pull me out of this depressive state, I would've refused. Being able to wallow so indulgently in my woes was the nearest I got to pleasure. It was almost cathartic.

I could hear the remnants of whispered conversations between Gemma and Jason. This should have engendered the jealous streak in me, but I found even that took too much energy, and I had none to spare. The only thing I could be grateful for was that the snake crawling under my skin had stopped, but only until I went in for the next part of this first cycle.

"Chris is nagging me again to marry her," Jake was trying to distract me.

"Sounds like a good idea," I said, hoping that now he hadn't got the response he wanted, he'd leave.

I should've known better; he was an awkward bugger to the last. It wasn't Jake though who snapped me out of my inertia, it was good old dependable Jason, who'd sent Gemma off to see her friends and offered to babysit the patient.

"She's in London. Won't be back till tomorrow," Jason answered when I asked where Gemma was.

"Why didn't she tell me?" I demanded, finally outraged about something.

"How do you know she didn't?" Jason's demeanour had changed; he was becoming defensive about my wife.

"What the fuck? What's that supposed to mean? Of course I'd know if my wife had told me she was going away," I exploded, all my pent-up emotions breaking through the mist like a volcanic eruption.

"Have you taken any notice of her or how she's feeling since you came out of hospital?" He raised his voice when I tried to protest. "This from a man who wanted people to treat him as normal – to say it as it is. Do you even know that she was getting pains earlier this week and was sent for an emergency scan?" He stopped as he realised what he'd said.

Why was he her confidant now? Why was my friend siding with my wife? He's supposed to be in my corner.

"You're in love with my wife, aren't you?" I said it experimentally, trying it out for size. I waited for him to deny it, but he stayed silent.

"I'll move out as soon as I can find a place to stay." His words only confirmed his guilt.

"Move out now."

"Of course," he said. "I'll ring Cass and ask her to come over."

"And will you tell her that you're in love with my wife?" I hissed.

"You're wrong, you know. I just think she's getting the rough end of the deal here, too."

"Did you hear what I said?"

"We're all a bit in love with your wife at the moment so why should Jason be any different? What? Do you have any idea how amazing she is? She's holding down a full-time job, caring for you, pregnant with twins and doing all the household chores whilst facing the idea that she might lose her husband, who is shutting down on her completely. Want me to go on, brother dearest?" The sarcasm negated the possibility of there being an endearment somewhere.

"Jason said she had to go to the hospital for a scan as she was experiencing pains. When was that?"

"The day you went into hospital for a one-day top-up of Bleomycin she headed off for her scan."

"I was pissed off with her because she'd gone off and then got back late and I had to wait."

"I know."

"Why didn't she tell me?"

"She said you had enough to contend with. I know what you're dealing with, I can't pretend to understand how it feels, but your wife is at breaking point. The doctor said that unless something gives, she risks miscarrying one or both of the babies."

It's ironic really, but since I'd known Gemma, the cause of her most heartfelt pain had always come from me. How could you love the very bones of a person and yet cause them so much grief?

"Will you tell Jay not to go?"

"It's too late; he's packed his stuff and arranged to stay with Toby until he finds a place."

I'm such a jerk! First my wife, and then one of my oldest friends.

"But Gemma needs him. She relies on him." I was aware of how incongruous that sounded.

"We'll all need to help more. Jason knows that he has to get away from Gemma before he *does* develop feelings for her."

I digested this silently; there was nothing more I could say. Left unspoken was the idea that she might develop feelings for him if I kept pushing her away. Nausea rose up, and this time it had nothing to do with the chemo.

Chapter 21

Gemma

Chaos ensued in my absence. Cass, Theo and Jason were tight-lipped about what had happened, which resulted in Jason moving out of ours and into Toby's. Theo's depression seemed to have lifted.

"Theo, are you ready to go?"

"Day sixteen. I get to take more Bleomycin. Yippee," he joked.

"You don't have to put on an act with me, honey," I reminded him, taking his hand.

"I need to protect you," he asserted. "You have too much on your plate as it is."

"I don't need you to protect me. Just don't shut me out."

He nodded. "Ditto."

I looked at him, a question performing a salsa routine in my eyes.

"Day nine?" he countered.

"How… Who?"

"It doesn't matter," he said, leaning forward, covering my lips with his.

I clung to him as a tremor swept through me. The metallic taste Theo kept telling me about sat on my tongue; fear shot through me. *What if the poison passed into my system and onto my babies?*

Day nine, Theo had gone for his Bleomycin and I'd gone for an emergency scan. Severe cramps had started the night before, pain so excruciating that I feared I was miscarrying. I made an appointment with my GP first thing and slipped out under the pretence of going to the supermarket. He'd advised me to go straight from his surgery to the hospital for a scan. I didn't tell him I would wait until my husband was settled with a needle in his arm being pumped through with drugs.

Theo had been listless that day. He'd followed me like a sheep into Cass' car. I wanted to tell him, to share my fear, not to be alone with this, but he wasn't in any state for me to tell him anything. More than anything, I feared he wouldn't react, that it wouldn't break through his apathy. As though he didn't care… and I couldn't have borne that.

I was glad to have my husband back again, even if it didn't last. His emotions were like riding a roller-coaster blindfolded so that you didn't know what was coming, but there were bound to be some scary bits.

"Theo. The last dose in this cycle. How have you been?" the nurse asked.

"I felt very tired and nauseous."

"Depression," I added.

"Oh, I'm over that now. An unhealthy dose of self-pity."

The nurse and I exchanged a look, which he intercepted.

449

"You don't think I'm better than I was a few days ago?"

"Of course you are, darling, but it's not as simple as that. We must be prepared for it to show itself again, that's all."

"Your wife's right. We do need to monitor that. We can always prescribe some anti-depressants short term."

"Yeah, because what I really need is some more drugs being pumped around my body."

Theo pottered around the house doing little jobs that needed doing and managed to go into work for a few days. Other than being a bit feverish, he seemed to have escaped any other side effects, and his spirits soared. I wondered how much of that was for my benefit. When the lights went out at night, did his mind roam into other territories, as mine did?

"Theo." I gasped, amazement etched over my face.

He rushed over to me, every inch the concerned father, as my hands clutched my stomach.

Taking his hand, I placed it over my stomach, where one of our twins was making him/herself known. For the first time since Theo's treatment had started, I read on his face pure, unadulterated joy. When the kicking stopped, he pulled me into an embrace that at any other time would have ended with us racing upstairs to the bedroom.

"We can't," he said, laying his hands reverently again on my stomach. "Let's go for a walk."

"We need to do this more often." Theo's grin tugged at my heartstrings.

"Walk?"

"No, just normal stuff."

The warm spring air brushed my skin as we strolled along, hand in hand, like any other married couple. We left suburbia, encountering only the odd rural property nestled in the landscape.

"Can you see us out here?" I asked Theo.

"Not sure we're ready for that. Maybe when we need somewhere for the twins to run around."

"Why don't we stop at that little pub and get a juice?"

"Gay bar," Theo responded.

"How do you know?" I teased.

"Oh, everyone knows."

As we approached, the door opened and out walked Stephen, whom we hadn't seen in years. His expression froze in horror. He looked around for an escape route but knew there was nothing he could do but greet us. Stephen had decided on a change of career about three years before. I couldn't remember what it was. He'd pretty much cut off all contact with everyone.

"Gemma, Theo." He was at a loss for words. "So you're still..." His embarrassment was palpable as he realised what he was about to say. He obviously knew about Theo's cancer.

"Alive?" Theo finished.

In that moment, I hated him for intruding on our oasis, for bursting our bubble. Acting out of character, I replied, "And you're still not out of the closet?"

His face turned puce. He spluttered helplessly, like a fish dangling from a fishing line. Theo's expression was amusement and disapproval in equal measure.

"We've always known," Theo reassured.

"Sorry," I mumbled, contrite now that I'd outed a guy who wasn't ready to out himself.

"Please don't tell anyone," he begged.

We stayed quiet but his expression changed as he processed Theo's words. "Who knows?"

"Everyone," I said gently, trying not to hurt him this time.

"So you were all laughing at me behind my back?"

"No one was laughing," Theo assured him. "Why don't we have a barbeque next Sunday and invite the whole gang over? You can come on your own or bring someone, if you want."

The sun rose early in the sky on Sunday morning. The last few days had been magical as we settled into our old way of doing things together. Theo was starting to believe again that life did, indeed, hold so much for us.

Over the past few days we'd rung friends, inviting them to ours for the barbeque, which surprised a number of people.

"Are you sure he's well enough?" Chris asked.

"It's exactly what he needs, some normalcy. We've had the most fantastic few days."

"Shall we come early to help? Jake and Theo can down a few beers as they fire up the barbie."

"Yeah. Not sure that Theo should be drinking while he's having chemo."

"I can probably have one or two," Theo said, walking past.

"Why don't we ring the cancer nurse for advice?" I said as I put the phone back into its cradle.

"They'll only advise me not to."

"So maybe you shouldn't. It's no big deal, is it? I won't be drinking either."

"I just thought a beer with the boys…"

"Well, why don't you speak to one of the lads? Some of them are on their second or third cycle so they're bound to know."

"That's a good idea. Maybe we should invite a few of them."

"It's turning into a wild party." I laughed.

Chris and I headed into the kitchen to prepare salads and have a proper catch-up.

"So who's coming today?" Chris asked as the lads went to dig the barbeque out of the shed.

"Toby and family, Jason and kids… We did invite Cathy, but she declined. Cass and Keith, although I hope they don't argue again. Theo has asked a couple of lads who were in chemo with him… Not sure who'll show, though. Depends on how they're feeling. Tom is coming with Janice, and we've invited Stephen... oh God, I didn't tell you."

"What?"

"We bumped into Stephen last weekend coming out of that gay bar in that little village – oh what's the name of it? You know, the one about two miles out, where they had that major road incident earlier in the year."

"I know where you mean. Is there a gay bar there?"

"So Theo told me."

We both laughed.

"Has he come out, then?"

"No, but I did it for him – long story." I told her what happened. "Needless to say, I retaliated with have you still not come out of the closet?"

"Gemma!" Chris screeched.

"What's up?" Jake and Theo popped their heads in through the door.

"Gemma outed Stephen." Chris gasped.

"Is he gay, then?" he asked in that contrary way that was typical Jake.

Three pairs of raised eyebrows turned on him

"Always knew there was something queer about him."

"Don't say that to him," Theo said.

"You haven't invited him here, have you?"

Theo nodded.

"As long as he doesn't try groping my arse." Jake's outrageous remarks were more for effect.

"Sure he'll be able to resist you, Jake." I laughed.

"Nobody else can."

"I've managed."

"Mm, but I bet you want me."

There was nothing more we could say. Jake was determined to get the last remark in, and he was stubborn enough to keep it going all day.

Theo

I rang Jason to apologise for my reprehensible behaviour.

"You're one of my oldest friends, and I'll be there for you no matter what, but Gemma's been great. She loves you so much she's tying herself in knots to please you. She's so scared of losing you and is so exhausted all the time..." He trailed off.

"I know, and I'll make it up to her," I answered. A disquieting thought lingered – that I'd been right about his feelings.

My next blast of Bleomycin left me shivering uncontrollably, but luckily this was short-lived. When Gemma told the nurse about the depression, I felt like the real words spoken were, 'He was a monster'. I wouldn't have blamed her at all, but paranoia is such an unattractive trait, and I'd already displayed enough of them.

During my first cycle, I headed into the office on the days when I felt almost human. All the client-based meetings had been divvied out between the other senior partners, and although he didn't tell me himself, I knew that Jake had taken the lion's share of my work. I'd been treated very fairly and was given three months paid leave, to be reviewed at the end of that time. I had no way of knowing how long the treatment and my recovery would last. I figured if I headed into the office to lessen the slack taken up by my colleagues I would have some brownie points in the bag.

Is This Love?

The most amazing experience happened when I felt one of my babies kicking; it gave me hope beyond belief. I was going to be a father, a fact I'd only acknowledged on a superficial level until that moment. Fighting up to the surface was that paternal instinct that made a man capable of doing anything for his children: slaying mythological dragons and walking over hot coals. I'd teach my son to play football. Hell, my daughter, too. I would hug them when they fell over and grazed their knees, read bedtime stories to them. My children wouldn't be raised by nannies, they would not lack for parental love or guidance.

I wished for them the closeness that Cass and I shared but not because of disinterested parents. I suppose every father experiences that wonder when he feels his baby kick for the first time, but without the dread of never meeting that child, knowing them, or walking his daughter down the aisle, even if that seemed like a lifetime away. So that moment was extra special because it was a milestone that I'd participated in and it gave me hope I'd be around for many more.

I pulled Gemma close, my thoughts straying to the night we'd met, when I'd tugged her into my arms, caveman-style, hoping to impress her. Like that night, my primal urges were quashed.

"Walk?" I suggested.

The lush green fields replaced the suburban jungle where we lived. Gemma asked me if I could see us living here. I could, but a picture of her here alone with the twins flashed into my mind, so I said not yet.

We walked on in companionable silence until stumbling across Stephen coming out of a gay bar. I had to swallow the inevitable chuckle, the *Oh, my God, we were all right; you are gay*, and instead offered a more traditional greeting. I smiled when he made his insensitive remark, but the unintentional barb hit home. I wasn't sure whether to laugh or berate Gemma when she shot back a poison-headed arrow.

I felt sorry for him while he floundered, knowing he'd been caught but desperately hoping he'd get away unscathed. Gemma apologised. She regretted her words, but it was a little like wishing you'd kept your hair long after the hairdresser had chopped it all off.

"Please don't tell anyone," he pleaded.

I was reminded of the sycophant who'd idolised Jake. He'd wanted to be like Jake. I realised he saw being gay as a sign of weakness and pitied him.

"You're better off not having any alcohol," Jake advised.

"I just want a beer with the boys. I'm not talking about a session." I could hear the petulance in my tone.

"It's just a beer, mate. Not worth the risk it might do to your treatment."

Gemma had said almost the same, but she was known to worry whereas Jake lived more by the who-gives-a-fuck, rules-are-made-to-be-broken train of thought. I knew how seriously he was treating my cancer. Gemma would be pleased with his advice.

According to the girls, the usual amount of male testosterone went into lighting the barbeque. Stephen, who was meant to be the unofficial guest of honour, didn't show, but he did get an airing when Jake and I walked past the kitchen and heard Gemma telling Chris about outing him.

"Is he gay, then?" Jake asked, his voice deadpan. I don't think any of us really believed Jake hadn't known, but in true Jake fashion, he had to be contrary.

Toby and family turned up soon after with Jason, followed by Cass and Keith. The latter looked less than happy to be here, and I couldn't help but think their marriage wouldn't survive much longer. Cass, as predicted, had shelved her new job so she could metaphorically hold my hand.

"Where shall I put these?" The football lads trooped in weighed down with crates of beer.

"Hey, guys, good to see you. Take them through to the kitchen and put them in the fridge. There are some cold ones outside already, in the cooler."

Joe and Thomas arrived with their wives, but Christopher was doing it tough and couldn't face leaving the house. We raised a glass of orange juice to him, with the exception of Joe's wife, Samantha, who floated in on a cloud of perfume demanding

Champagne but settling for a Pinot Grigio when Gemma informed her we didn't have any. Cass, who'd been standing next to me, began to prickle. Gemma laid a restraining hand on her arm and whispered something that deflated Cass instantly.

"Uncle Theo." Katie was standing next to my elbow. At nine years of age, she was as beautiful as ever. She was the deep one in the family, displaying a slight reserve, but somehow she always managed to cut to the heart of the situation. "Are you dying?"

A collective gasp went around the little gathering like a Mexican Wave at a football match. Jack, now eleven, hit her hard on the arm. Her tears were immediate.

"Why would you say that?" he demanded, outraged, and then to me, "Sorry, Uncle Theo. She's such a baby."

"You shouldn't hit your sister, Jack. She's only worried about me, aren't you, sweetheart?" I bent down to her.

Her blue eyes were dewy, tear droplets clinging

precariously to her lashes. She sniffed without a trace of self-consciousness.

"I didn't mean to upset you, Uncle Theo. My best friend at school said her uncle died of cancer, and when I heard Dad talking on the phone about your cancer, I thought you might be dying."

I took her in my arms and nestled her there, a tear falling down my own cheeks as I explained that although some people died of cancer, not everyone did. She seemed satisfied with my answer. I couldn't help but hope I got to see my own daughter at this precocious age. It took a while and a lot of prompting to get the party spirit back again, as Katie had only voiced the underlying fear of everyone there that day. Cass and Jake threw themselves into making the day memorable and erasing the fears that Katie had highlighted.

"You've got some good mates here," Joe said as we stood chatting with Thomas, trying not to mention the elephant in the garden for all three of us.

"Yeah, they're not a bad bunch on the whole."

"Mine won't acknowledge I have cancer." The elephant trod the lawn.

"How can they not?" Thomas asked. "Mine aren't exactly tripping over themselves to be supportive, but they acknowledge it."

"My mate, Jake – ignore your first impression of him; actually, it's probably right – but he's done more research than I have, and I go to him for anything I can't understand."

"Talking 'bout me again?" Jake walked up behind us. I did the introductions and left him and Joe talking cancer, one expert to another.

"His wife is a piece of work," Thomas said in a quiet voice.

"I guess everyone copes with things differently."

"You're right." Can we leave the subject behind?"
"Sounds good to me."

"What are you two gassing about?" Toby towered over us.

"Football!" we said in unison, and then laughed.

"Why's that funny?" Toby's perplexed expression made us laugh louder.

"You had to be there."

Chapter 22

Gemma

The most memorable day I had during the period following the revelation of Theo having cancer was the barbeque. The most beautiful was seeing the twins on the scan, but the barbeque was the day when everything seemed normal, when we were just Theo and Gemma holding a barbeque with some friends. The only thing to mar it was Katie asking Theo if he was dying. Theo always had a soft spot for her, and I marvelled at the ease with which he answered her question and chastened her brother for hitting her without sounding too authoritarian. Very occasionally, the topic of conversation would hover over the inevitable, but on the whole we talked inanities.

"So why did you move out?" I asked Jason when we were alone.

"It was time I moved on. Hey, you'd had enough of me getting under your feet."

"You never did that. Did you and Theo have words?"

"No." His tone lacked conviction, but I knew I'd get nothing more. "Another OJ?" Jason asked.

"I'm all OJ'd out." I laughed. "I'll push the boat out and have some water."

"How's he really doing?" Toby and Lisa asked me as I joined them watching the twins, now ten, running full-pelt around our little garden after Jack, a year older. Katie sat, elegant and restrained, watching Theo and her dad chatting. She'd barely left Theo's side since asking him if he was going to die. I turned my attention back to Toby and Lisa.

"So-so at the moment. Not sure how long that will last. Think he had words with Jay but neither will tell me what it's about, although they seem fine again at the moment. I don't suppose you happen to know, Tobe?"

I caught a look passing between them, a silent warning to say nothing.

"So how is the pregnancy going?" Lisa smiled.

"You mean, other than having two sets of arms and legs kick-boxing me?" I laughed.

"Oh yes, I remember that well. I can't get over how small you are." She sighed.

"Are you serious? I'm huge."

"Not for twenty-three weeks with twins."

Another glance passed between Toby and Lisa, followed by a slight nod from Toby.

"I'm pregnant; six weeks."

I gasped with pleasure and wrapped Lisa in a hug, congratulating her.

"Don't tell anyone yet."

Toby, now bored of pregnancy talk, left us alone.

"You're so lucky. At sixteen weeks with the boys I was the size of a... not quite a house... maybe a caravan." I joined her laughter.

As I wandered away, I couldn't help but contemplate the baby they'd lost a few years before, when Lisa had been six months pregnant. I wondered whether Lisa would be able to relax in this pregnancy at all. By six months, you were over the fearsome first trimester and about to enter the third and final stage. The thought occurred to me that I hadn't quite reached that stage yet myself.

I spent the best part of the next hour talking to a drunk, disgruntled Keith. I pitied Cass being married to this man who'd turned into a complete pain over the years because of his jealousy of Cass' relationship with Theo.

"She loves him more than she loves me," he said. "You must feel it, too. It's not natural."

"They spent their childhood with disinterested parents, caring for and relying on each other. There's nothing unnatural about that." I struggled to stay patient.

Chris, reading the situation, came over and told me I was needed in the kitchen. "I didn't want to see blood drawn. You looked like you were about to commit murder."

I laughed. "I might have."

"What was he saying this time?"

"Oh, you know, the usual. Theo and Cass' relationship is unnatural, blah blah..."

"Who said that?" I was interrupted by the icy tone of my formidable sister-in-law. I hadn't heard her sidle up. I should've been more circumspect.

"It doesn't matter," I tried to divert her.

"Keith." She spat his name out of her mouth as though it were dirt.

I lay a restraining hand on hers, and for once it was my voice that contained the steel. "Don't say anything here – you're not spoiling Theo's day with your marital issues."

I felt the battle of wills, and then the reality of my words sunk in and she nodded.

"Come on, Cass, let's sink a few beers." I didn't know that Jake had been standing there, too.

With Theo's next bout of chemotherapy, the shakes came back. Maybe the anti-emetics were doing something for him, but waves of nausea hit him with the force of a hurricane. The effort it took for him simply to lie in the hospital bed was immense. To do anything more, even to sit up, was impossible. My humungous belly precluded any thoughts of me staying for long periods; the discomfort was too much. I tried, but Theo insisted, "One of us has to go through this, the other doesn't."

When I protested, he took my hand. "You're going to be going through it soon enough with childbirth." That thought hadn't crossed my mind yet.

So I visited daily, like the other wives, and left after an hour. It was also getting increasingly hard to do the long drives on top of going to work. I thought back to the day, three years before, when I'd opened my own salon with my supportive husband by my side.

The twins moved restlessly every day now, and we joked that they were probably hyperactive.

"No, they'll be sedentary white-collar workers, like

their dad," I teased.

"Hey, I keep myself fit and active." The irony of that statement wasn't lost on either of us.

"You will be again," I asserted.

I awoke in a deep sweat. The sound of the IV drip beeping haunted me. I stared across the empty expanse of our king-sized bed and longed for Theo's presence there; alone, it was overwhelmingly large. I turned the bedside lamp on, looking with bleary eyes at my watch. Four o'clock. The twins kicked a steady beat.

"Hey, you two," I whispered, stroking my tummy. "Daddy's not here today to say hi, but he loves you. We both do." Tears gushed as my pent-up emotions, bottled for so long, spilled forth. Finally, spent and exhausted, I slept, no longer plagued by dreams.

Theo

It started straight away – the dread, that is, the fear of that snake scouring viciously beneath my skin. This time I felt so nauseous that, for stretches, I almost craved the release death would bring. Then Gemma would come in, her soulful eyes raking mine, begging me to be okay, silently pleading for me not to drift into the land of the un-living. She would have been horrified if she could read my thoughts. There was a time when she'd been able to, and I hers, but cancer had taught me to mask my thoughts, and this was a skill I was learning to do well.

The camaraderie was still there with the other patients, even though they weren't the same men I'd met before. Having them around saved my sanity more than once. I did notice, this time, that although they smiled, the expressions in their eyes were a mixture of hope and fear. Did I have that look, too?

The IV drip bleeped when the bag ran dry and the last drops had been drained, leaving the two sides of the plastic bags clinging desperately together. The nurse came along with a cheery smile on her face, assessing me, pulling on her extra-strength latex gloves. The bag with my name and hospital ID number on it also had the words 'Hazardous Materials' emblazoned across it. The nurse protected herself from the poison that dripped through my veins, killing the cancer cells – but it didn't just kill cancer cells, it killed healthy ones, too. It was like a tsunami taking out everything in its path: bone marrow, muscle, teeth, linings of the throat and stomach. I didn't know how much more of this I could take. I tried to be a man about it, but there was something about cancer and chemotherapy that stripped you bare and left only the raw human form.

Jake came to see me. I saw his eyes wet as he looked at me with a mixture of pity and affection. For once, he was silent. His wisecracks were absent. It was probably one of the few times in all the years I'd known him that he was at a loss for words. To give him his due, though, he didn't slink away as the other visitors who came to see my roomies did.

"I haven't got a fucking clue, have I?" he finally broke the silence.

"No. I appreciate you trying, though."

"I've been such a patronising bastard."

"You? Never."

The nurse beamed on seeing me smiling.

"You must be good for him. You're welcome anytime."

"Sweetheart, I'll come whenever you want me to." He winked, back on safe ground again.

The nurse's milky complexion grew red. I'm sure she'd encountered flirting before but maybe not from someone with Jake's appeal and force of personality. My laugh, this time, erupted right from my stomach, which in turn caused me to wince in pain. The nurse became all professional again, asking me if I was all right.

"I feel nauseous the whole time."

"I have your tablets here. If it's not enough, I can talk to the doctor about increasing the dose."

"Walking pharmacy, me. I positively rattle."

"Without the walking part." Jake was pleased to have some material to work with. "So you're coming home in a few days?" Jake asked.

"Tomorrow."

"Tomorrow's Thursday. You're in till Saturday."

My brows furrowed as my brain spun. I couldn't quite grasp my thoughts but felt uncomfortable and self-conscious.

"The days blur into each other here," I tried to joke it off. Jake and the nurse laughed, but the sound was hollow and it failed to reach their eyes.

They exchanged a fleeting glance before the nurse bustled away with the excuse that she had other patients to see, but rather than heading in the direction of my roomies, she went out the double doors.

"Keeping her to yourself, Theo?" Stuart called out.

"She can't get enough of him, mate," Jake covered,

which caused a ripple of laughter.

"They'll bar you from here if you keep making everyone laugh."

We pretended I hadn't completely lost track of what was happening. It's funny, really. People lose track of time regularly and it's joked about as senior, blonde moments or pregnancy brain, but when you had cancer and were undergoing chemo, it was a side effect to be monitored, discussed and dissected. And so it went on, a seemingly endless cycle of tedium, pain and discomfort; a bad hangover crossed with severe jet lag that wouldn't let up.

Not everyone who has chemo loses their hair but I noticed it, in the shower, at home. The water cascading over me was refreshing. I wished it could wash the poison out of me as effectively as it took away the hospital smell. Lifting my arms, I let it flow over me. I tipped my head back, luxuriating in the feel of it. Brushing the hair off my forehead, I felt some come away. I stared at it, frantically washing it off. I couldn't stop my hand from straying back to my head. More clumps followed the first, until the plughole was blocked with hair.

"You okay in there?" Gemma called out. On getting no response, she entered the bathroom. "Long time since I joined you in the shower," she joked. Taking in the scene, she changed her expression and, for a moment, I read the horror on her face I knew to be on my own.

She rallied quickly, "Always fancied skinheads. Hey, does that make you a bona-fide Chelsea fan now?"

"No, I need to tattoo your name on my arm first," I re-joined, not daring to let this affect me.

"The kids' names, too, on your back or wrists."

I stepped from the shower into the towel she held out. "What are we going to call them?"

"Who?"

"The twins."

So we distracted each other for the next few hours throwing names at each other, from the sublime to the ridiculous. We went to bed no closer to naming our twins, but we managed to distract each other for the time being.

Chapter 23

Gemma

Theo losing his hair was a huge thing; it was that badge you had, the one that made you a fully paid-up member of the 'I've-got-cancer' club. It was also about the reactions it engendered when people saw him, so to combat that, I rang a few people and, like a Chinese-whispers chain, said *"Theo's lost his hair. Pass it on."* Our lives were being lived on the edge. I struggled to get around, the size of a hippopotamus now. In Theo's better moments, we would laugh about it.

"I'm fat."

"You're beautiful."

"I'm fat."

"Mmm, you're pregnant."

"Still fat, though."

"Yeah."

I threw a pillow at him and rolled out of bed, no longer able to bounce out. *If I get any bigger, I'll require a hoist.*

I continued to work but had promoted one of the girls to temporary manager. I felt this temporary role would run into a long-term position in reality. Some days, I enjoyed going to work just to escape the situation at home. For those short hours, I had time to think about nothing but business and could pretend I was any other expectant mother coming near to the time when she would take her maternity leave. Other than the bouts of sickness during Theo's first course of chemo, I'd been blessed with an easy pregnancy.

I was now so exhausted that it was all I could do not to go to bed at seven p.m. Maybe I would have if it weren't for the endless chores. Since Jason had left, all the household chores fell to me. Theo did his best, but the effects of the chemo were hitting him harder. He had good days and bad days, but he looked like a dying man as the chemo ravaged him, and something as minor as a cold pole-axed him. I knew that whatever I was feeling, he was suffering more, so I didn't complain but I could feel the strain that carrying twins, the hormonal changes, caring for Theo, attempting to run a household and working part-time was wreaking on me.

I sat in my office, staring at the figures that jumped all over the page, making no sense at all. Tears built up in the corners of my eyes, sliding down my cheeks. All the pent-up emotions exploded out of me as loud, uncontrollable sobs racked my frame.

"What's wrong?" Cass' voice called a cease-fire to my loud display.

"I don't know how much more I can take." I poured it all out and ended up feeling self-indulgent.

"We haven't helped you much, have we?"

"You have. You've all been great, sitting with

Theo."

"We could do more: picking up the shopping, cooking dinner or cleaning."

"It's not your responsibility."

"You're carrying my niece and nephew and caring for my brother."

"I shouldn't have said anything."

"You didn't have much choice."

"Please don't think I don't love him." It became important that she knew I wasn't tiring of Theo or giving up on him because things were hard.

"Of course you love him, but it doesn't make caring for him easy. Your hormones are all over the place, and you're carrying two babies whilst working, fearing you may lose the love of your life and still being a domestic goddess. You have every right to feel the way you do. I'm surprised it has taken you this long to snap."

"Don't be so kind to me; it'll make me worse."

"Can the boss take time out to go for lunch with her sis-in-law?"

"As long as we don't talk about me anymore."

"That just leaves me, then." She grinned.

"You and Keith?" I quizzed.

"Argh. Maybe we'll stay clear of that topic of conversation, too."

In true Cass-style, she rallied everyone to pitch in and help me around the house. She even talked me into internet shopping for my groceries. At first, I felt I was failing in my duties as a wife, woman and mother-to-be. Support came from an unexpected source when my parents and sister came to stay for a week, an event I'd been dreading.

"Sit down, Gemma. I'll get dinner."

I looked askance at Kelly, her peroxide blonde hair harsh against her pale skin. When had my sister ever offered me anything? "I can cook for my own family."

"Of course you can, no one's disputing that, but you're heavily pregnant, exhausted, and that's what we're here for."

"Did someone tell you I can't cope? Is that why

you're here?" My voice sounded shrill even to my own ears.

"Always so capable, aren't you? Can't you give me a chance to do something good?"

I looked at my sister and saw love. *Has it always been there?*

"What do you mean?"

"I just want to prove to you and Mum I can do things, too." Her words had a ring of unhappiness.

"Why do you need to prove anything? We all know you're Mum's favourite."

"Have you ever stopped to wonder why?" Kelly didn't give me a chance to answer, continuing in a dull tone, "Mum felt sorry for me. I was never going to be the good-looking, intelligent, confident one. I'd never amount to much, so she overcompensated by seeming to love me more."

I stopped in my tracks as I recognised the pain Kelly had hidden.

"I'd love it if you'd cook the dinner."

She smiled uncertainly. We were never going to be

huggy sisters, but this was the closest we'd been, and at that moment I decided to open up my innermost feelings to her.

"I've never been confident. I'm in a constant turmoil of self-doubt; I just hide it well."

Theo

Once so light and nimble, Gemma's tread was heavy on the stairs, our twins slowing her down. She was still beautiful, even with her rounded belly and severely swollen ankles. Today was my first full day at home after my third cycle of chemotherapy, and I could honestly say that meeting Tyson in the ring would have been less punishing. I didn't need a mirror to see how awful I looked.

"Are you up to something light to eat?"

I shook my head, wishing I hadn't moved as another wave of nausea crested.

"You should have something, sweetheart, even if it's just to keep your strength up."

"Just some toast, maybe," I said to please her more than for any desire for food.

Her blond curtain of hair fanned around me while she bent over the bed, placing her lips on mine. We looked at each other with such burning love that neither time, cancer, a double pregnancy nor anything else could dull. *Only death.* The thought slipped unwanted into my brain, as though a portent of what was to come. I pushed it aside with every fibre of my being. *I dare not tread those paths again.*

It was now a waiting game to see whether the chemo had worked. Tests would follow, charting the progress of my markers. Would they have gone down? Had the chemo eradicated the cancerous cells? Would it have receded or, the ultimate hope, removed all traces of cancer from my body? The lymphadenectomy was still looming, a safeguard as the cancer had spread to my lymph nodes. So this seemingly endless game continued. I'd spent the last few months thinking about the end being when the chemo finished, and now I'd reached it, the goal post had moved.

The last bout of chemo floored me; Tyson delivered the knockout punch. I'd thought the nausea I'd experienced was bad, shocked by the endlessness of it. What shook me to the core on my second day home was the belly-wrenching vomiting that had me spewing forth with the force of an erupting volcano. I could feel the veins popping out in my head at the sheer effort. I couldn't imagine anyone vomiting like this and living to tell the tale.

I'd had my fair share of sickness bugs, hugged the great white elephant after too many beers with the lads, but this was quite unlike anything I'd previously experienced. After one round, I lay on the floor in a heap, unable to physically move myself, while Gemma stood there, silent tears running down her cheeks, unable to help. She couldn't even prop me up as, at thirty weeks, her belly was so swollen she could barely move. Gemma shuffled away from me in distress and came back a little while later with Jake, Toby and Jason, who carried me back to bed.

I'd thought my emasculation was when I'd had a testicle removed, but now I realised having your friends lift your limp and useless body off the bathroom floor and place you in bed while your wife sobbed was the real indignity. I wondered how she could look at me. I wasn't the man she'd met, fallen in love with and married. I was reduced to a shell.

"One of us will stay here with you at all times," Toby said.

"Mate, you're needed at home, with a new baby on the way," Jason argued.

"We'll take it in turns. I've got some holiday entitlement left, and we're quiet at the moment. Lisa understands; we don't know how long this will last. Anyway, when I'm not at the house, Lisa will have you there."

I watched them talking and making plans about me as though I wasn't there. Try as I might to protest, I didn't have enough strength to speak, so I lay limp and inadequate.

Gemma brought me a bowl to be sick in as I couldn't make my legs work enough to take me to the bathroom. Every few hours that day, I would be assisted to sit up, held by one or another of my friends, while Gemma held the bowl for me. I kept retching long after there was nothing left in my body, and there hadn't been much to start with. Each time Gemma walked off with the bowl, I knew she was escaping so she could cry; her eyes were scarlet-rimmed and her unblemished skin blotchy and red.

A call of nature with a mate standing next to you is not so unusual for a bloke, but that mate doesn't normally have his arms around you, holding you up. If someone were to ask me for the four key words to sum up cancer, I would have to say: pain, fear, waiting and degradation. I've read of people who've said cancer wrought life-changing situations for them in a positive way. I can only hope one day to be one of them but, at that moment, I couldn't comprehend feeling that anything positive would ever come of it.

"I've spoken to Phoebe, and she's advised me to increase the dose of anti-emetics. Jake is heading down to the hospital to pick up a prescription."

I wasn't thrilled to know they were increasing the amount of drugs going into my system but I knew I couldn't last long if I had a few more bouts like this.

Over the next few days, the vomiting abated but I was still too weak to stand unaided; true to their word, my friends took shifts at staying with me and walking me to the bathroom and back. I can honestly say that, if the grim reaper had knocked on my door that week, I'd have opened it wide.

Gradually, my strength grew and I was able to eat small amounts and walk short distances unaided. With the rallying of friends and family, I made it to the hospital for my bloods and scans. It was decided that I should wait until my strength was up before they operated to remove the lymph nodes that the Teratoma had spread to.

And so the waiting began again. The tests would

determine whether the cancer had left me. Unlike all those months ago, when I'd felt its presence, I could no longer claim to know what I felt. Chemo had killed off a lot of my healthy cells, but would it have eradicated the affected ones?

At last, the waiting was over. Gemma and I sat in the doctor's office while Jake and Cass sat outside, expectant and scared. I didn't want to ask the question I both longed for and dreaded the answer to in equal measure. Gemma's small hand was cold and clammy in mine while we waited for the verdict.

"I've got the results, Theo." The doctor paused, took off his round glasses, wiped them with a microfiber cloth and then placed them back on.

I could feel my heart pounding in my chest as I waited for his words, which would signify my life, or a possible death sentence.

Chapter 24

Gemma

Theo's chemo continued, and I finally admitted I couldn't go to work any longer. The stresses and strains were taking their toll. Just coping with home life was as much as I could handle.

In one of the rare moments we both had, Susie and I managed to chat.

"I went to my first ante-natal the other night. Theo couldn't make it so Cass came with me. The other couples kept staring at us; I swear they thought we were a couple."

"Did you get talking to anyone?"

"No. Afterwards, we were sitting around. They were mainly chatting amongst themselves, you know the thing, tittering like schoolgirls. This one woman stared at me with a smug look on her face saying, *'So what are you doing to combat stretch marks?' 'Nothing.'* I replied, making them laugh. *'Oh, I don't know how you can be so careless. Don't you care what you'll look like afterwards? It's my number-one priority.'* And out of nowhere, this pent-up anger burst out, surprisingly before Cass could say anything. *'My number-one priority is that my husband's chemotherapy works and my twins have a father.'* Cass and I got up and walked out the door just as the guilty silence was broken by murmurs of, *'Oh that poor girl.'*"

"I wish I'd been there to see their expressions."

Susie filled me in on the news from the girls. She couldn't contain the pure, unadulterated pleasure of being a mother. Reality intruded as I heard Theo making a dash for the bathroom.

"Sus, I have to go. Theo's being sick."

I replaced the phone in its cradle and plodded up the stairs, where I found my husband knelt over the toilet, throwing up with a force that was off the Richter scale. I stood there feeling useless. If it was one of the girls, I'd have held their hair back, but I couldn't even do that for Theo. Each time I thought the bout was over, he would start again. His face was ashen, his eyes bloodshot, and the veins were pressed tightly to his skin, almost protruding. I couldn't stop the tears from coursing down my cheeks. I felt a sharp, poignant pain inside my chest, watching my husband suffering again. Would this never end?

He slumped to the floor. His eyes sought mine, and I read his fear and pain as he wordlessly begged me for help. I longed to gather him into my arms, to hold him to me, to take his suffering away and guide him back to bed.

I dialled Jason first. The phone rang and rang, my heart pounding in my ears. *Please pick up*, I begged. With trembling hands, I cancelled the call and dialled Jake's mobile. He picked up on the third ring.

"Theo?"

"Jake," I sobbed, "please help. Theo's really sick

and can't get up off the bathroom floor."

"Stay where you are. I'm on my way."

I was startled by the sound of the telephone ringing.

"Hello," I sobbed.

"Gem? What's wrong?" Jason asked.

"Theo's sick... He can't... get off the floor... Jake's on his way... I called him when I couldn't reach you."

"I'm coming, too."

Jake and Jason, with Toby in tow, all turned up together at the door.

"What happened?" Jake asked as I closed the door. I gave them a brief explanation while I followed them up the stairs. Toby and Jake lifted Theo off the floor and carried him to his bed, laying him down with care.

I called Phoebe, the nurse who was overseeing his care needs. "I know it can be scary, Gemma, but you must take it easy for your babies' sake."

"I know, Phoebe."

"We can increase the anti-emetics again. If I get a doctor to write a prescription, is there someone who can pick it up?"

"Yes, I'll ask Jake to go. You'll probably recognise him."

"Is that the lady killer?"

"You do know him, then." I smiled. Trust Jake to have made such an impression.

Throughout that day, Theo continued to be sick, but the extra dose of anti-emetics worked eventually, and that night he slept soundly, exhausted by the day's events. The twins were active that night, pummelling my stomach, and my back ached all over. I longed for the release that sleep brought, but I lay awake staring at the red digital display that flashed each new number.

I must have fallen asleep, because I woke to the smell of bacon cooking. Theo's body lay inert, tiny snores escaping his open mouth. I said a silent prayer that he would sleep longer, as that was when he escaped the hell.

My exhausted brain struggled to assimilate who was downstairs in my kitchen, cooking. I trundled down to the kitchen, where I discovered Jake in his trunks with an apron on – one I'd been bought as a

Christmas present by my mother but had never used. The sight of Jake in it with only underwear underneath made me roar. I could only be grateful that he had chosen to wear the trunks, as I wouldn't have put it past him to have gone commando.

Jake spun around with a grin on his face and a utensil in each hand.

"Morning, sleepy."

"Morning, Jake."

"Sleep well?"

"No. Next question."

"Theo?"

"Still asleep, thankfully. Has been spark out all night."

"Do you think he's finished being sick?" Jake asked as he turned back to the frying pan.

"I hope so."

"What'll you have? I've done the works here."

"Just toast and a cup of tea."

"Aren't you supposed to be eating for two or three now?"

"That doesn't mean three times the amount, and not sure doc meant fry-ups, but thanks."

"Maybe when Theo's awake?"

"He won't touch it. You'll have to eat the lot."

"There's enough food here to feed an army."

"I noticed. Didn't think we had much in the house."

"You didn't. I popped down to the supermarket and stocked the shelves."

"I was going to shop online yesterday but, well... let me know what I owe you."

"Don't be silly." He inserted a couple of slices of bread into the toaster.

Touched by his kindness, I kissed him gently on the cheeks. He turned to me in surprise, and I read the fear in his eyes that I knew to be in mine.

"He will be all right, won't he?"

I hugged him. For a few minutes, we clung together, desperate for comfort. I wished I could give him a definitive answer. I enjoyed having the company around the house, someone to help, to talk to, to share the worry.

Toby came in just after Jake had finished clearing away the breakfast things and helped himself to a plate of food that Jake had left. Jake and I grinned to see Toby polish it off.

"Wife not cook for you this morning, mate?" Jake queried.

"Porridge. She doesn't let me have cooked breakfasts during the week. Cholesterol."

"We won't tell her, then." Jake laughed.

"How is he?"

"He settled down mid-afternoon and has been asleep since about eight o'clock," I answered.

"I'll go look in on him now," Jake said, "and then I need to head straight off. Got an important meeting this morning that I can't reschedule."

"Well, I've taken the day off, and then Jason will be around tonight to take over."

In all this horror and despair, I couldn't help but marvel at these three friends of Theo's who disrupted their own lives in order to help us with ours.

The day we'd been waiting for finally arrived. Both Jake and Cass insisted they accompany us to the hospital for the results.

Doctor Robson looked up from reading Theo's notes as we walked in the door. We sat down opposite him, with the vast expanse of his desk to separate us. His desk was kidney-shaped, with the computer on the adjacent angle of where we sat, some files, a pen and a cup with the dregs of a hot drink.

Beads of perspiration broke out on my brow. Theo reached out and took my hand as we sat there as nervous as two naughty children in front of the headmaster. I expelled my breath, unaware that I had been holding it, as Doctor Robson said, "I've got the results, Theo." In the pregnant pause as he removed his glasses, I held my breath. "The cancer has gone. The chemo worked."

Stunned silence. My heart pounded inside my chest. A smile cracked with infinite slowness across my face until I was beaming. I looked at Theo. He still had to have the lymphadenectomy, and would need regular monitoring, but he had, for now, beaten cancer. We'd beaten cancer.

The End

Glossary Greek to English

Kalimera	Good Morning
Ti Kaneis	How are you? (Modern usage)
Parakalo	You're welcome
Exi	Six
Efharisto	Thank you

About the Author

Self-published author bursting with enthusiasm and ideas that can't be contained in my head so spill out onto paper. I predominantly write romance but I am playing with other genres.

I have enjoyed reading and writing from a tender age, and I realised recently that the magic of childhood that we lose as an adult can be found again if we open our eyes to the beauty all around us. I find inspiration in so many different situations and have approximately thirty something WIPs. Is This Love? Is the first book I ever wrote and it took about thirteen years. I put it aside while I published three novelettes and a novel before I felt ready to revisit this book which means so much to me.

Is This Love?

Thank you for reading Is This Love? If you enjoyed this book, please consider dropping by Amazon or Goodreads to leave me a review.

Also if you would like to connect with me you can do so by visiting my website, signing up for my monthly newsletters which will give you access to except from all future books by me, sneak preview of my covers and entry into a prize draw to win an e-copy by the author of the month. (For as long as this is applicable)

If you loved Is This Love? You may be pleased to know that there is a sequel which will follow shortly. Watch out for Illicit Love.

Website: https://gibbsdream.wordpress.com/

Facebook: http://on.fb.me/1Iu9LuY

Twitter: https://twitter.com/gibbsdream

More by this Author

A Boy from the Streets (Novel)

Two babies abandoned at birth—one grows up in a life of privilege, the other in poverty.

On the 12th of September, 1981, twin boys are born in a Brasilian hospital and left to their fate as orphans. Jose is adopted by a couple who takes him to England, but the other isn't so lucky. Pedro ends up on the streets of Rio, left to fend for himself in a harsh and unforgiving world.

Love and betrayal.

Twelve years later Jose's family returns to Brasil, where he learns the truth about his adoption and his twin. Thinking his adoptive parents no longer want him, he runs away to find his brother. What follows will shake Jose to the core and shape the rest of his life—if he can survive.

Murder.

Jose isn't the only one whose life will change. Pedro is offered an opportunity beyond any of his wildest dreams, but to keep it will mean the betrayal of someone he loves. This proves to be a far greater challenge than he anticipated when the orphan finds himself suddenly surrounded by family who, unfortunately, don't all have good intentions.

Hopes and dreams.

A Boy from the Streets will tug at your heart-strings and have you rooting for the little guy as you follow the twists and turns this multi-continental tale takes.

As Dreams are Made on (Novelette)

Newly wed Matty Taylor is plagued by visions that force her to seek out a Gypsy at a local fair. Dragged violently into a frightening dream world, she is soon rescued by the mysterious Thomas Trevelyan and taken to his secluded house in the woods.

Will her husband, Donald, suspend his disbelief and wake her from her nightmare?

Can Thomas win her heart and keep her from the lure of her real life and the love of her husband?

Is This Love?

A Lifetime or a Season (Novelette)

Athena finds herself in the wet and windy South Coast of England as she tries to forget the enigmatic man who ignited her dreams.

Roberto seems determined to hold her at arm's length but can't seem to set her free once and for all.

Having lived in the shadows of her self-centred mother, Athena struggles to find her true identity.

A Lifetime or a Season is a journey of personal discovery for Athena as she takes an independent step into the unknown in order to achieve a life-long dream.

Will she find the love that she is searching for with Roberto or will the sacrifice be too much?

The Storm Creature (Novelette)

At eighteen, Lucy had everything going for her: a supportive family, a rapt audience, and her dream of becoming a published author about to be realised. A single moment in time on a dark, rainy road changes things forever.

That was then, but this is now. Lucy has suffered through eight years of haunting visions and thoughts with every raging storm thanks to a tempestuous storm creature who torments her. What does the baleful creature want with Lucy? Will the troubled woman ever be able to let go of the past and forgive herself?

Or will she sacrifice everything she holds dear?

Recommended Indie Author

Chris Turnbull

Chris has always been a keen reader and writer, he loves the feeling of being drawn into a good book and the escapism into another world after a long day at work. In 2013, after finishing his first full story Chris decided he wanted to get it professionally edited in the hope to print it out for himself. After very little persuasion Chris finally released time travel story The Vintage Coat on Amazon and had a successful book launch in Leeds. With the publishing bug now set, Chris is enjoying writing more than ever and has plenty of projects up his sleeve.

Check out one of Chris' books:

Jonathan was supposed to be getting married today, but instead he is in Paris; and what's worse he is now over 120 years in the past.

Transported back by an old amusement carousel, Jonathan finds his life turned upside down as he finds himself stuck in 1889.

Desperate to return home, he goes in search of the carousel. Although his wish to return is high, he soon learns that his reasons to stay could be just as compelling.

Website: https://www.chris-turnbullauthor.com
Amazon Link: http://amzn.to/2g24S9w

23533439R00285

Printed in Great Britain
by Amazon